Kat Fight

a Novel

Dina Silver

Happy Birthday Brooke! Enjoy! the fight ♡

Copyright 2013 © Dina Silver
All rights reserved.

ISBN-10: 1470173271
ISBN-13: 9781470173272

This is a work of fiction. Names, characters, places and incidents are either the product of the author's imagination or are used fictitiously. Any resemblance to actual persons, living or dead, events, or locales is entirely coincidental.

No part of this book may be reproduced or transmitted in any form or by any means, electronic or mechanical, including photocopying, recording, or by any information storage and retrieval system, without permission in writing from the author. For more information visit: dinasilver.com

To my husband

Prologue

I've always wanted to get married. Not simply because I enjoyed fairy tales and layers of tulle at a young age - and I did - but because I truly wanted a husband and family of my own. My parents divorced when I was nine years old, leaving me desperate for my own chance at getting it right. A chance to meet my soul mate, fall in love, and stay committed. A chance to do things my way. A chance for a normal family with no screaming, no cowering children and no more loneliness.

And while I've held onto that dream like a child holds onto a ratty, drool-stained blanket, I've never really obsessed about the particulars that are typically important to a bride. Things such as the gown, the flowers, and the color scheme never entered into my imagination. So on my actual wedding day, I was a little surprised to realize how meticulously every detail had been attended to.

There I was, all dressed in white with a soft veil loosely brushing against the skin on my face, feeling blissful and resplendent. I wore a strapless satin sheath and in my hands was a bouquet of dark red roses. I started walking slowly toward my groom standing curiously far away from me at the end of the aisle. So far away, in fact, that I was having a difficult time focusing on his face. The more I walked the farther he seemed. I paused at one point to observe the people standing on either side of me on that gloriously sunny day and marveled at them smiling in my direction. It was finally my day. My chance.

Feeling much more secure, I closed my eyes for a second before continuing. When I opened them, I was lying on the lobby floor of my apartment building, trying to remember what made me lose consciousness.

CHAPTER ONE:
Marc My Words

I burst off the elevator like a racehorse out of its gate and ran to my desk before Brooke realizes I've taken a two-hour lunch. I managed to get most of the groceries home before rushing back to the office, but I had to make one last stop on the way back to get Marc's favorite salad dressing. Since the only things I've learned how to cook in my twenty-six years are baked potatoes, potato skins, spaghetti with jarred sauce and tuna salad - my kitchen is not equipped to make much else - so I knew when I planned this steak dinner for Marc that I would have a ton of shopping to do. I'm sweating as I dump the salad dressing in my desk drawer and then grab my phone and scramble to the conference room for a creative meeting. Adam stops me before I enter the empty room five minutes late.

"Where is everyone?" I ask him.

"Dave canceled the meeting," he says, delicately placing an Altoid on his tongue. "Which you would have known if you hadn't fled the building earlier. You ran out of here like I did when I had that phantom farter in my Bikram yoga class."

"I'm making dinner for Marc tonight, and work has been so crazy that I haven't had any time to go to the grocery."

He looks me up and down as if he doesn't recognize me. "You're making dinner for Marc?"

I nod.

"You'd have better success climbing Mount Everest in those dated wedges you're wearing," he says and points at my feet.

"Thank you." I smirk. "But I'm honestly not in the mood for you at the moment. I love you, and I will see you later."

"Ta-ta," Adam calls after me.

I finish my work by six-o'clock, and after one last stop to grab Marc's favorite beer, I'm back at my apartment ready to make dinner. I live alone in Lincoln Park, a city neighborhood just a couple miles north of the Gold Coast area, where my job and the offices of Lambert & Miller Advertising are located. A brief commute is a must for someone like me who has trouble being on time. My apartment is a microscopic habitat that isn't referred to as a studio only because there is a cupboard-like kitchenette with doors that separate it from the main room. Besides that, it's four hundred square feet of home-sweet-home. The unit is located in a century-old Chicago high-rise that's two blocks from Lake Michigan; however, my apartment is on the opposite side of the building and overlooks the much less serene Clark Street. This is nice because if I ever happen to sleep through my alarm, I can usually count on the #22 bus to grind its brakes outside my window and wake me up with that clatter instead. I try not to complain too much because at eight hundred bucks a month, the price is right, and I've suffered through enough roommates to appreciate any abode as long as I'm the only one living in it. Simple pleasures like my own leftovers in the fridge, my own socks on the floor, and my own long, brown hairy mess in the shower drain.

I asked Marc to come over at eight o'clock, so now I have roughly one hour to pan-sear two steaks, make two baked potatoes (my specialty), rinse and toss the salad, bake the Pillsbury crescent rolls and soften the filling for the cannolis, Marc's favorite dessert.

Things between Marc and I have been strained lately. He's been so busy with work, that we haven't spent any time alone together over the past few weeks. I'm hoping this dinner will not only give us time to reconnect, but also give Marc a renewed sense of appreciation for what we have. When he moved to Chicago for work last year, everyone assumed we'd get engaged soon after. Including me.

I initially fell for Marc in college, and I fell hard. He definitely brought out the best and the worst in me. I'd never fought with any boyfriends before Marc, so the few times I would find myself screaming at him about something, I was really surprised at my behavior because I hate arguing. I hate listening to people argue and I hate being in the middle of an argument. But after years of listening to my parents rip each other apart, I figured those were the struggles you had to endure for unconditional love. That to have someone care about you like that, you had to suffer a little bit too. "Some things are worth the fight, Kat," my mom would tell me after one of her fights with my dad. Then they divorced.

But despite my arguments with Marc, there was always a lot of love between us. In fact, there were times when I thought no one else in the world would ever be capable of loving me as much as he did, even my own parents. If my parents truly cared about me, they never would have broken our family apart. They never would have made my sister and I choose whose house we wanted to go to for Thanksgiving - or who we'd rather have sitting in the bleachers during our ice skating show - or who we'd rather celebrate our birthday's with. Choices that made my stomach turn. Choices that made me soak my floral bedspread with tears. Then Marc came into my life and repaired my heart; he loved me unconditionally at one time and I was wise enough to appreciate it.

My cat Curtis is shout-meowing at me, so I tear open a can of tuna and dump it in his bowl. At about five minutes to eight I decide to pour myself a glass of wine and heat up the cast-iron pan. I double check the recipe book, which confirms to heat the pan slowly, that way, by the time Marc gets here he can have a beer while I finish up the meal. Small, non-threatening billows of smoke begin to rise from the empty pan at about ten past eight, so I lower the flame. At eight fifteen I send Marc a quick text, also non-threatening, asking what time he thinks he'll be here. At eight-thirty I turn the flame off and call him at the office. There is no answer. I call back five minutes later in case he was in the bathroom or something. Still no answer. At nine o'clock, I put everything back in the fridge, send another text and microwave myself a baked potato. At nine thirty I get a text from

Marc saying that he's in a meeting, and that's when I begin to lose my shit.

"Can you believe him!?" I scream aloud, although Curtis and I are alone in the apartment. And despite the volume, he sleeps through my outburst.

My stomach churns into a tightly wound mess as soon as I realize that, once again, Marc has simply brushed me off like an annoying fly buzzing in his ear. As I bravely prepare to call him for the third time in twenty minutes, I wonder which of his canned excuses he might use this time: "Someone is in my office" or "I've got another call," were likely candidates, but I am determined nonetheless. I take a deep breath; I pick up the phone and dial his number *again*. I can feel the blood racing through my veins as the line rings and goes straight to voice mail.

"Unbelievable!"

My throat clenches as I pace the dusty hardwood floor of my tiny apartment before sitting on the couch. Then I take a sip of wine and deep breath, and then snatch the phone from the table in front of me. Tears of frustration begin to blur my vision, but I remain undeterred and repeatedly dial his number until I hear his voice on the other end.

"Marc Nolan," he says curtly, as if it were one word.

"Where are you?" I blurt out.

"I'm at work, you just called me here," he says.

I straighten my spine. "We need to talk," I respond swiftly, shocked to hear both his voice and the apathy in it.

"Kat, I have someone in my office and I can't talk now."

I wasn't surprised by his response, and in that moment the memory of countless other unreturned phone calls and texts come pouring down like a hailstorm. Like the time when my car died in front of Costco and I had to transport a trunk load of unbagged household crap into a taxi because Marc refused to answer his phone during the Bears game. And the time when I cooked lunch for him one Sunday and he never showed up. I sat and watched cheddar cheese congeal on two tuna melts because his phone was on vibrate. But I always forgive him because I love him. That's what I do, and that's what he expects from me. Why shouldn't he?

"Then I'll be brief," I bravely interject, hoping he won't hang up before I get everything out that I want to say. A fire has erupted inside of me as I stare at my empty kitchen. "I want you to leave me alone. I'm sick of your bullshit, Marc, so lose my number and don't ever call me again," I say as my hands begin to shake along with my lower intestine. Not exactly the confidence-laden monologue that I jotted down on the spiral notebook in front of me, but as the words exit my mouth, a wave of contentment washes over me.

There is a short pause and some muffled noise surrounding his phone receiver before he speaks again. Maybe he actually does have someone in his office. If I hadn't lost my pride the thirteenth time I'd hit redial, I might be somewhat embarrassed.

"*My* bullshit?" he shouts and whispers simultaneously. "You call me at work fifty times in the past five minutes to tell me this? It's nearly ten o'clock. I'm trying to get out of here and I said I would call you back." He makes no mention of our dinner plans.

"All you ever tell me lately is that you'll call me back," I enlighten him. "And that's assuming I can even get you on the phone in the first place. You've been brushing me off and ignoring me for weeks now and I'm done." I swallow, but the lump in my throat doesn't budge.

My tactics for getting his attention have never been all that original, but they have proven effective in the past. After four years together, I know how to manipulate him to get what I want. And what I want now is for him to stop taking me for granted. I'm not one to publicly toot my own horn, but privately I think I'm a decent catch. I enjoy a good sporting event, I'm not a nag, I get asked out at the gym on occasion, and I don't have a habit of throwing ultimatums around - until now. Because at this moment I swear that things between Marc and I will either go back to the way they were when we first started dating, or I will be forced to end our relationship. Right now.

Marc and I met during our senior year of college when we were both carefree and happily living off Ramen noodles and cans of tuna. We'd had the same Mass Communications class and became friendly over the course of a semester. After about six flirtatious communications of our own, he'd asked me to go to a fraternity barn dance, which, not surprisingly, included a roll in the hay and a suede flask filled with peach schnapps. At the time he was one of the funniest, most energetic people I'd ever met and we were inseparable for the remainder of our final year. He was always there for me, always doing sweet things like bringing me lunch or surprising me outside of my classes to walk me home. But those are distant memories, and lately he's made me feel more like a burden than a girlfriend.

"You're done?" he questions me with a snicker in his voice that only increases the pace at which my blood is speeding through my body.

"Yes," I answer as calmly as I can so that he won't accuse me of being irrational. "I'm sick of waiting around every night wondering if you're going to text me or come over, or break our plans, or do nothing at all." I wait patiently for him to respond and realize it's taking longer than normal. His usual reaction is to appease me in the moment and then convey his annoyance later in the evening, a move which always puts me on the defensive and turns whatever was initially his fault into a situation where I'm apologizing to him. Another ten seconds pass.

"Fine," he says.

"Fine?"

"Fine, Kat, I don't have time for this. You're done, I'm done. I won't bother you anymore and you won't bother me anymore," he says, leaving a deafening silence in his wake. "I have to go, so goodbye."

"Goodbye, Marc," I say and punch the talk button on my phone.

Did he really just say "fine?" Did the conversation seriously just end with him saying *fine* and *goodbye*? I stare, frozen and confused, at the ceiling hoping for some sort of clarity to come shining through the recessed lighting. Why didn't he try and appease me? The coffee table in front of me is as good a place as any to put the phone down, but instead I hurl it all of six feet across the room and watch it bounce off the faux metal base of my Target floor lamp. Curtis lifts his tiny head from his front paw and glares at me.

"What?" I snap at him and then lunge for my wine.

I had a few preconceived notions about how the conversation would pan out, but what just happened wasn't one of them. There was something different in his voice this time. Something indifferent, actually.

I flip through a magazine and wait for the phone to ring, but it doesn't. At eleven thirty I tuck myself into bed and he still hasn't called. As I drift off to sleep, I'm a little surprised by the absence of more tears. I can hardly remember a time when Marc and I had had an argument that didn't conclude with my signature waterworks. It is liberating to lie my head down without the angst I typically endure. However, when my pea-sized bladder wakes me up in the middle of the night, I immediately check my phone for a text from him. There is none. I'm sure he'll contact me in the morning. He doesn't.

Today is Saturday, which will consist mostly of me lying in bed, watching TV, replaying my conversation with Marc over in my head a good forty-five times, checking my cell phone, and eating pizza-flavored Combos.

When the sun comes up Sunday morning, I crawl out of bed and sit on the floor in front of the mirror behind my closet door. My complexion is smooth, and my hazel eyes look especially green in the natural light. Curtis saunters in as soon as he realizes I'm awake and rubs against my hip. I grab my hair and fold it underneath itself to imagine what it might look like four to five inches shorter, then quickly release my grip. Just because one thing in my life has changed doesn't mean everything else has to. As I sit staring at myself with Curtis now aggressively shoving his nose into the small of my back, my muscles become limp, like the air being let out of a balloon. Two nights before I'd been full of life, but once Marc called my bluff, he left me drained. Curtis climbs into my lap and I burst into tears.

After ten self-indulgent minutes on the floor I walk to the kitchen, give Curtis a can of Fancy Feast, and decide to call Julie. If anyone can help get my confidence back to the elevated state where it should be, it's her. Julie Duncan and I have been friends since grade school. She has a long mane of strawberry blond curls, a fiery personality almost as big as her ego, and a voice that any ringmaster would envy. She's like a motorcycle gang: you always know when she's arrived, and she can command a room like no one else I've ever met. She's funny, loud, abrasive, and a little scary, to be honest. People either love her or hate her.

"I did it," I say almost as quickly as she answers her phone.

"If you went and got the Brazilian…" she begins to reprimand me.

"I broke up with Marc." The words are equally empowering and difficult to say.

"And?"

"And nothing, it's over," I say to her and to myself. "We ended things Friday night and I haven't heard from him."

"It's only been two days," she chides me.

"I realize that, but he normally would've called by now," I tell her.

"Are you okay?" she asks and coughs away her hoarse morning voice.

"I'm conflicted I guess. I set out to make a statement, and I got what I asked for," I conclude and begin to make some coffee. "I was really only looking to ruffle his feathers, but he didn't seem interested in arguing."

"I thought you were making dinner for him?" she questions me.

"He blew me off."

Julie sighs. "He's unbelievable."

My friends have tolerated the good, the sad, and the ugly when it comes to my relationship with Marc, and they're more than used to our routine. They always predict that we'll be back together sooner than later, and they're usually right.

Julie yawns. "He's going to call you and come crawling back, he always does."

I grab a mug from the cabinet, shaking my head as if she can see me. "I think it's different this time," I say. "It feels different, and even though it's only been two days, this is the longest he's gone without a text or anything."

"He probably wants to make you call him."

"He knows I won't," I say flatly and retrieve the amaretto-flavored Coffee-Mate from my fridge.

"Then call him if you want to," she suggests.

"He completely blew me off! "I even bought a bone-in filet for him and borrowed a cast iron pan from Adam. I won't be calling him," I declare and then wipe up the coffee that spills out the sides of the glass coffee carafe every morning without fail.

"Okaaaaay, are you upset?" she asks, trying to feel me out. "You've been frustrated for some time now, Kat."

"I'm sort of numb. I thought he'd at least put up an argument or make some effort to defend his selfish behavior, but he didn't." I pause to relive my conversation with him. "It was so quick Julie. He didn't even hesitate."

"Maybe he's been unhappy too?"

"What does he have to be unhappy about?" I screech. "It's not like the Anheuser-Busch factory is under quarantine."

"I have no idea, but if you've been miserable, and he hasn't done anything about it, then perhaps he's been wanting a break too."

"Well, then why hasn't he said anything?" I ask and hop up onto my kitchen counter where I sit and sip my coffee, legs dangling.

"How should I know?"

I sigh. "Don't roll your eyes at me — because I can't see them anyway - but do you think it's me? Do you think it's something I've done?" Cue my insecurity.

"No."

I shake my head. "That's it? 'No.' I'm going to need more than that."

Julie releases an annoyed, breathy noise into the phone. "No, I don't think you've done anything wrong. You've been supportive of him in every way, you go above and beyond to make him happy, and he's been a complete ass for no apparent reason."

"Maybe I shouldn't have been so harsh, you know, so absolute?" I wonder.

"Don't let this shatter you, Kat. I know you hate to be alone, but just go and do something nice for yourself today. Are you cocktailing yet?" she asks in all seriousness.

"I'm thinking about it."

"Kat," she refocuses, "I have a hard time believing this breakup will be different than any of the others, but *if* in fact it's over between you and Marc, maybe it's for the best." She pauses for effect before continuing. "Enough with his crap. You've been hoping for years that he is going to materialize into this prince charming who'll appreciate you and reciprocate your kindness at the altar one day, but I honestly don't think his ego will ever let that happen. You deserve better and everyone knows it. Maybe even you are beginning to realize it."

"Yeah, maybe, I don't know. Thanks, Julie," I say. "Who knew you could be so sensitive at this hour?"

"Well, you know I limit myself to one compliment a week, so that's going to have to hold you," she adds. "But knowing Marc, I'm sure he'll call. And knowing you - you'll run right back to him."

But he doesn't call, and I don't have the chance to prove her right or wrong. I appreciate Julie's advice, but I know deep down that it's over between Marc and me. And it's not due to infidelity or long-distance or anything I can put down on paper. It's just over. And regardless of what anyone says, I am stunned by his indifference. After years of convincing myself that marriage was in the cards for us, there's a significant amount of fear now that my safety net has been removed. I hang up the phone with Julie and spend the next two hours crying it out with Curtis in my lap.

CHAPTER TWO:
Blind Luck

Today is July 1st, and exactly three weeks have passed since I told Marc to lose my number and never call me again. Prior to that, our relationship had been four years of emotional highs and lows, a never-ending roller coaster ride that began in college and followed me into my adult life. But despite everything, I thought Marc was the one. I loved him, I wanted to marry him, and I'd imagined our future together.

Being without him has given me time to reflect on the decision I made to end our relationship. A decision that was curiously and painfully undisputed by Marc. Some days I feel like a child who chose to misbehave in order to get her parents' attention, without fully understanding there would be negative consequences to her actions. And other days I feel giddy for taking a stand, and for proving to myself that I can thrive on my own. I haven't seen him or heard from him since the day we broke up.

That's all about to change, though, because our friends Rob and Emma are getting married at the end of the month, and Marc and I will both be at the wedding. As the date gets closer, it's all I can think about, and I'm not sure I'm emotionally prepared to bump into him at a wedding of all places. I've snubbed him a thousand times before, but those were very calculated events. I'd known how to push his buttons and hold his attention back then. He'd love it when I played hard to get. He thrived on it. But after four years, when I wasn't so hard to get anymore, that's when he really started to pull away.

With Rob and Emma's wedding upon us, I'm looking forward to seeing him, and my hope is that this break has made him appreciate what we had. It's been hard to understand why he hasn't reached out to me. And if he considers for one second about bringing a date to this wedding, I will not hesitate to throw blue cheese olives in her hair.

So I guess time has not completely healed my wounds but it certainly has numbed the pain. And although the frequency at which I check my phone for a message from Marc hasn't lessened much either, emotionally I'm making progress. Of course, the minute I begin to accept my status as a singleton, my friends start pestering me to meet someone new. However, while I'm actually stronger and more optimistic lately, I can't say that meeting someone new is my first priority. I enjoy going out with my friends, but since I've been with Marc for so many years, I've never had to put much effort into dating; unlike Julie, who's constantly on the prowl and never without a male companion…or two.

Tonight she and I have gathered her at her apartment to drink wine, watch reality TV, and discuss my options.

"I'm setting you up with someone," she declares while pouring me a glass of cabernet.

Julie knows that I've never liked being set up on dates, but she always tries, regardless. Even when Marc and I were together she would try and get me interested in the friends of whichever guy she was dating at the time.

"Lovely, a blind date," I cheer, unenthused, and fold my legs under my butt.

"He has his sight," she snaps, annoyed at my lack of appreciation.

I smirk.

"Come on, Kat, get over yourself. It'll be fun. We'll double with you."

"Who will double with me?" I look at her curiously.

"Me and The Chef," she says and pours a glass for herself.

I can't help but laugh. "Who on earth is *The Chef?*" I ask, eager for her answer.

She sets the bottle down on the coffee table in front of us. "My new guy, the one from Trader Joe's," she clarifies and plops down on the floor next to me.

"He works at Trader Joe's?"

"No, you piece of shit, I stalked him at Trader Joe's; he works in advertising like you," she adds with a tone that indicates I should be intrigued. I'm not.

"What agency is he with?" I peer at her over the rim of my glass before taking a sip.

"I don't know, who cares, but he says he has a guy from his office to fix you up with."

I place my glass on her table and cross my arms. "You and some cook I've never met have a guy for me?"

"Yes…and it's *Chef*. He's apparently a self-taught gourmet cook, even makes his own pizza dough from scratch," she proudly informs me.

"Does he know you call him that?"

"Of course not."

"I don't know, Julie," I waver.

"There's nothing to know, he promised me his friend is good-looking." She takes a sip of her wine and stretches her legs out in front of her.

"Oh, please, they always think their crotch-itching co-workers are worthy."

"I told him you were super cute and had been off the market for a while, and that he had to *promise* me a good-looking guy or he was in trouble," she tells me and leans back against the base of her couch.

"What exactly did you say about me? And yes, I'm fishing for compliments."

"I said you were petite, okay, short…had long brown hair… and that you work in advertising too," Julie says and reaches for the remote.

"There's a reason you're not in sales." I shake my head. "Fine, I'll go."

The fact that he works at one of the local agencies isn't exactly the bonus Julie thinks it is. Advertising is a pretty incestuous industry, and I have always scoffed at those who date amongst themselves.

"Good, because it's all set for next Saturday."

"Next Saturday, already?"

"Yes, why all the gasping? You and I will grab a drink somewhere first and then we'll meet them for dinner. No big thing." She shrugs.

No big thing to her because she's a dating pro. But I'm not as familiar with blind dates or picking up men out in the wild. It's not that I resist blind dates for the typical reasons that people resist them; it's just that it's been a few years since I've had the opportunity to welcome them into my world, and my comfort level is nowhere near Julie's.

A few of my other friends have enjoyed lucrative set-ups before, and one or two of them have even become engaged after surfing the web for love. I imagine Julie will make Internet dating my next move if I fail to impress anyone in person. But she's right—I need to stop hoping for something that may never happen, and take a chance on finding someone new. I decide to embrace my newfound optimism and set my 20/20 sights on a blind date.

"Sounds like a plan," I agree and Julie extends her arm as though a handshake means there's no backing out.

Julie called me twice a day during the week to plan our agenda for Saturday, and now that the day is actually here, I can honestly say that I'm not dreading the evening entirely. My nerves, however, are not quite on the same page as my mind. I woke up this morning with an uneasiness I haven't felt in years. That first date anticipation, a combination of fear and excitement - often confused with fear and loathing - but I've chosen to be at least partially optimistic this evening. And even though I'm clever enough to keep my expectations in check, that doesn't stop me from wanting to make a good impression. My frustration kicks in as I survey my closet and realize my floor is littered with rejected outfits and accessories. There is an overwhelming theme amongst the wire hangers, and that is: solid colors. Lots of black, lots of navy, and almost nothing with a pattern can be found for miles. My choices are frighteningly limited, so I decide on a navy top, dark jeans, and a beaded necklace. Once the outfit is laid out on my bed, I hit the shower. It's been a long time since I've prettied myself up for anyone, because honestly, ordering pizza and watching a ball game with Marc and his roommate was hardly a cause for clean hair. I dry myself off, blow out my curls with a roll brush, and have to fight off the urge to throw it all up into a ponytail. Hair down is a first-date must, regardless of how many times I will run my fingers through it during the course of the evening.

Clothes and sparkly imitation baubles. Check.
Hair. Check.
Perfume. Check.
Emergency cab fare. Check.
Nerves…getting there.

Julie and I have decided to hit P.J. Clarke's for starter cocktails and then meet our dates at Gibson's Steakhouse afterward. If nothing else, I am content to get a good meal out of the evening.

When we arrive at P.J.'s around eight o'clock it's predictably overcrowded. Luckily Julie knows the bartender and he has saved us two stools behind the bar, which he hands over as soon as we see him. P.J. Clarke's is a hot spot known mostly for attracting single, khaki-wearing working stiffs - and for having cute bartenders. It's a Chicago landmark of sorts, a real old-school type of place. There is an expansive oak bar against the wall with a long brass footrest around it and wood-paneled walls surrounding the entire place. An enormous antique mirror hangs directly behind the bar, and shelves of assorted spirits flank both sides. It has been around forever and people still clamor to get in.

As soon as we sit down, a trio of guys starts checking us out. They appear to be younger than we are, possibly still in college, and I immediately zero-in on the one wearing a baseball cap. For some ungodly reason, I am a sucker for any remotely cute guy wearing a backward baseball cap. Not something I'm proud of, yet not something I can seem to resist either. Julie has just disturbed the three of them by shoving them out of the way with her hip in order to make room for our stools. Her rude intrusion leaves me obligated to apologize for her. Lord knows the thought to do so would never cross her mind.

"Can we buy you a drink?" I make eye contact with my favorite of the three and ask.

Julie raises a hand and comments before they can answer. "That's a great idea," she butts in with her signature pub-crawl charm. "We'll buy the three of you one drink to share."

I smile sheepishly at them and ignore her. "Seriously?" I ask again.

"We're good, thanks. As long as you two are comfortable, that's all that matters," Backward Baseball Cap replies.

Julie pats him on the shoulder. "Funny, now I like you. You can stay," she declares.

"Are you sure? It seems like you have some clout around here, and we wouldn't want it to take any longer than it already does to get a drink," he says gesturing to the bar.

"Well, young one, thank you for knowing your place," Julie jokes with him.

He extends his right hand. "I'm Scott, and this is Trent and Jacob."

"Nice to meet you fellas. You can call me Julie." She nods and takes a sip of her drink before shaking his hand.

"Hi, I'm Kat," I add with a mini-wave and adjust the purse strap on my shoulder.

"So, I guess 'come here often' seems like an inappropriate question?" Jacob asks.

"Trust me, it's nothing I brag about," Julie says with a smile. "But if it scores my lazy ass a seat at the bar then I'll suffer through the reputation."

"What do you brag about?" Jacob smiles back at her.

She lifts a brow and grins, but gives no answer.

"So, cutie, what are you up to tonight?" Scott asks me. Instantly reminding me of how much I loathe the word "cutie." Just because I top out at a measly five feet two inches does not automatically make me cute. My whole life people have referred to me as cute. Never sexy, never stunning, never statuesque (obviously), always cute. I smile at him, knowing he means it as a compliment. At least he didn't say "kiddo."

Julie interjects. "I'm setting little 'cutie' here up on a blind date in about twenty minutes."

The three of them nod at my misfortune. "Nice," Scott says. "Who's the lucky guy?"

I blush.

"Like you might know him?" Julie replies.

"Just trying to make conversation so maybe you two will stay here instead," he explains.

Personally I like Scott's idea at this point. It isn't often that we encounter three charming guys within the first ten minutes of being anywhere, let alone P.J.'s on a Saturday night. I give Julie a pleading look that indicates I approve of his suggestion. Maybe we should just stay camped out on our backless swivel stools and get to know Scott and his cap a little better. What did I owe this other advertising guy anyway? I decide my new plan is to convince Julie to stay.

"Nice try, we're leaving in five minutes," she snaps at me and puts a hand in my face.

Plan thwarted.

"Sorry, boys, if there's any chance of you getting laid tonight, it's not going to be with us," Julie graciously informs them, causing me to shake my head in embarrassment.

"Ouch," Jacob winces.

I roll my eyes. There goes my fantasy of getting looped and making out with B.B.C. at the bar as "Wanted Dead or Alive" plays on the jukebox.

"Nice meeting you ladies," Scott says as he and his friends grab their Bud Lights and disappear into the crowd.

Julie opens her wallet and pays for our drinks. She never lets me pay for anything. Ever since we were young, and she had to listen to me complain about how my mom would make me ask my father for the child support checks, Julie has been my sugar daddy. She comes from married, wealthy parents, who always make sure she has enough cash on her. Enough to charter a helicopter if necessary. Even now that she's an adult, her father still gives her a monthly stipend, which she and I now refer to as our child support.

"Aw, come on, they were funny," I comment. "Let's stay."

"Are you high?" Julie asks and grabs her purse. "I have two grown, employed men waiting for us, not to mention a filet covered in béarnaise with your name on it," she smartly reminds me.

I nod and take one last swig of my beer. "You're right. What was I thinking?"

She stands and salutes the bartender. "Let's get out of here before some guy walks in with a skateboard under his arm and sends you into a lust-driven frenzy."

We step outside, walk the four blocks from P.J. Clarke's to Gibson's, and marvel at the energy in the city. Street lamps are glowing like spotlights, illuminating small crowds of people as they wind their way along the sidewalks looking for a good time. Summer in Chicago is like no other. If you can make it through the brutal winters, you are handsomely rewarded with three fabulous seasons in between. The air off the lake is particularly warm tonight, and as we approach the restaurant I begin to feel a little more energized. The combination of starter cocktails and flirting has put me in a fabulous mood. Julie is in a similarly great frame of mind and we're both laughing and holding on to each other as we enter our second bar of the evening.

Much like P.J. Clarke's, this place is packed with people. The main difference being that the average age has risen by about twenty years. No college cuties here; in fact, mostly divorcees and their desperate cohorts. Julie and I are the ones that look like we should be sporting backward baseball caps now. She locates The Chef immediately, thank God, and drags me behind her through the throngs of people.

"There they are," Julie says, elbowing her way through the crowd.

"Which one is mine?" I say without moving my lips.

"The one in the sweater."

"I was hoping you weren't going to say that."

"Why? He looks adorable."

"It's July!"

She cracks up. "Would you relax? He's *hot*." She can hardly say the words with a straight face.

We approach our dates and Julie does the introductions. Thankfully, I learn that her date, The Chef, is more appropriately referred to as Ryan Sullivan.

"Hi, guys," Julie says. "Ryan, this is Kat. Kat this is…" She pauses, allowing my date to complete her sentence.

"Pete," he says for himself.

"Hi," I say with yet another mini-wave. "Nice to meet you both."

"Kat's a little upset because I just yanked her away from three frat boys at P.J.'s," Julie announces.

I look at her and shake my head. "Why?"

"Don't let us cramp your style," Pete says.

"Thank you, I have since matured," I assure him and extend my hand as a more appropriate, welcome gesture. He follows through with a firm grip, which is the first positive thing I notice.

"We thought maybe you forgot about us," Ryan says with a smile.

"Only for a second, darling." Julie taps his cheek.

We hang out in the bar area making small talk for about twenty-five minutes. It's all pretty painless actually, because Pete turns out to be quite the chatterbox. He tells me about his new apartment, his recent trip to the Bahamas, his affinity for playing poker, and his love of motorcycles. Our courting period gives me just enough time to have my fourth cocktail on an empty stomach and break down the positives and negatives of both men. First of all, Pete isn't bad for a blind date. He's blond, which isn't my first choice, but he doesn't have the typical fair features that most blonds have. He has dark brown eyes and more of an olive complexion, stands about six feet tall and seems pretty slim underneath his bulky clothes. I'm going to suggest he order the creamed spinach with a side of au gratin potatoes. The biggest hurdle is going to be his outfit. He has on a pair of black jeans - potential deal breaker - and a sweater. It's not a mock-turtle neck, hallelujah, but the man is wearing a sweater in one of the hottest months of the year. Upon closer study, it's cotton, but the jury is still out on this one regardless of the natural fibers.

More surprising is The Chef. He's taller than Pete, equally attractive, but has a much more reserved personality than I was expecting. He's unusual for Julie. She typically goes for the opinionated, artsy type. Guys with lanky figures and longer hair, who prefer smoking weed to, well, working. I remember her describing him earlier on, though, that he loved to cook and he'd wanted to have her over for dinner. Julie has a habit of rebranding her love interests based on their best quality. And it's not often that something like "cooking" is considered a skill worthy enough for one of her nicknames.

"Shall we grab our table?" Pete addresses the group.

"Sounds great," I say.

Ryan offers to pay the bar tab.

"I'll wait with you," Julie says, leaving Pete and I to walk alone to the hostess stand. He hasn't stopped talking yet, so it's really no problem for me to tag along sipping and nodding. The hostess shows us to our table as Julie and Ryan follow behind.

"I'm starving," Julie says and grabs the menu from the hostess once we all take our seats.

"Well, Julie," Pete starts to say. "You realize if you order from the right, *more expensive* side of the menu, you have to put out tonight."

Did he really just say that? I think to myself.

Ryan offers an apologetic grin for his friend's sense of humor and I notice that his eyes involuntarily squint a little each time he smiles.

"Is that so?" Julie says coyly and plays along.

I chime in. "If that means I'm condemned to a bowl of soup, you're going to have one crabby blind date on your hands, Pete."

He laughs hysterically at his own joke. "Well, since we just met you get a one-time pass on the rule," he informs me and goes for the high-five.

Oddly enough I find him amusing, and so far his personality is surpassing his choice in denim. The fact that he dares to joke around with Julie gives him extra points in my book. Ryan has yet to do much more than smile and look cute.

"Well, I'm not scared," Julie declares and folds her menu so that only the more expensive, right side is available to her. "This is a steakhouse after all."

We are all discussing our food options when Ryan finally emerges from his silent comfort zone and speaks.

"So, Julie tells me you're in advertising," he says to me.

I shift my eyes from my menu to him. "Yeah, I work at Lambert & Miller. You?"

"DDB," he answers.

"You like it there?" I ask.

"It's all right," he says with a nod and takes a sip of his beer.

"Account side or Creative?" I ask Ryan, but Pete answers instead.

"Ryno's their star copywriter and I used to work with him as an account exec," he tells me. "How 'bout you, Kat?" Pete asks.

"I'm an assistant A.E.," I say with little enthusiasm. I've been vying for a promotion for a few months now, but my job frustrations are the last thing I want to bore anyone with, so I gear up for a topic change.

Julie turns to Pete. "So you're not at DDB anymore? I thought you two worked together?" She looks at them for clarification.

"We used to. I left to start my own gig about a month ago," Pete tells her.

"Good for you," I perk up with interest. "What do you do?"

I notice him glance at Ryan and then at the table; and then they both uncomfortably chuckle to themselves.

"I review porn," Pete says.

Julie looks at him, and I look at Julie. "Please continue," she says, wide-eyed.

"I have a website where I write reviews on pornographic movies, magazines, web pages, etc.," he says, slightly embarrassed...but not entirely.

"What's it called?" Julie asks, as I can barely do more than sit idle with amazement at what she's gotten me into. Food is going to end up being my only love interest this evening.

"Skankipedia.com," he says with schoolboy enthusiasm.

"Ha!" I cannot contain my outburst. I lose it and so does Julie. She does a spit-take that would do the Three Stooges proud. I glance at Ryan and notice he's having a grand old time watching this unfold.

Pete looks at me. "Ryan didn't mention that beforehand, I'm guessing?" he asks.

I shake my head trying to recover. Of course the black jeans make perfect sense now.

"I'm sorry," I say as I dab a tear from my eye. Julie obviously could have cared less what this guy was like when she pimped me out to her "Chef." More importantly, I should never have trusted her. I know better. One time when we were in high school she was dating a guy from the local Catholic boys' school, and I agreed to be set up with his friend for a winter formal. His friend showed up at my house with a rosary for me to wear to the dance, and refused to touch me even during slow songs. When I told him I wasn't comfortable wearing the rosary the entire evening he said he understood, and that he would pray for me. Since then I have done my best to avoid Julie's set-ups.

"Let's just say it pays more than advertising," Ryan chimes in with the save.

"I'll have to check it out," I comment, feigning interest.

"I'll get you a free password," Pete offers.

"Awesome," I respond and nod.

We finish our meal around ten thirty and decide to check out The Hangge Uppe, a local club that plays retro dance tunes and stays open until four o'clock in the morning. Never a good idea, but I've had so many drinks at this point that I'm in full hanger-on mode. The only thing I can concentrate on is putting one foot in front of the other as I hold on to Pete's elbow and literally try to envision a straight line on the pavement. I'm sure he must be smitten by now. When we reach the club, my earlier hopes of making out with someone to a Bon Jovi tune become much more realistic. We locate a small section of couches and Ryan and Pete head to the bar.

"So...he's nice, right?" Julie sits down and leans over in my direction.

"Nicer every minute," I chuckle at my stupor.

"Seriously, Ryan says he thinks you're adorable."

"He does?" I ask with sincere disbelief and scrunch my eyebrows together.

"Yes, Kat, he does. Even Ryan commented on how cute you were," she tells me. "Pete seems funny, talkative..." she begins a list of generic attributes.

I raise a hand to silence her. "Black jeans and porn? Seriously Julie, what am I supposed to do with that?"

We both can't help but laugh. "Okay, okay," she says. "You know clothing is the easiest thing to change. And a little porn never killed anyone," she mocks my misfortune.

I bury my face in my hands and think of Marc. Situations like these always make me long to be with him, but I could never admit that to Julie.

Pete and Ryan return with our drinks and sit down beside us. The dance floor is pulsating and people are jumping around like they're on pogo sticks. Pete moves in a little closer and thankfully gets back to reciting his filibuster. He reaches over and rubs my leg as he's talking and all I can think about is trying to keep my eyes open as I adjust my posture on the couch. I glance over to where Julie and Ryan are sitting and discover that Ryan is just staring back at Pete and me, all squinty and alone.

"Where's Julie?" I abruptly lean away from Pete.

"Little girls' room," Ryan says.

"What?" I exclaim. *That bitch knows it's a team sport, how could she ditch me like that?* "I'll be right back." I stand up quickly and lose my balance. My legs buckle and Pete and Ryan both react and attempt to save me from additional humiliation, but I fall flat on my ass despite their gallant efforts. I stagger to my feet, spread my arms in an effort to level my equilibrium, and then smooth out the front of my shirt.

"Whoa, are you okay?" Ryan asks, still poised to catch me.

"Oh, my God, I'm fine, thank you...sorry," I stammer, rubbing my behind.

"Do you want some help?" Pete says and offers me his arm.

I politely wave him off. "I'm fine. It really wasn't my fault. Didn't you guys feel the ground move?" I muster an attempt at joking my way out of it. "I'll be right back."

I stumble to the ladies' room only to find Julie six people deep in line. I obviously couldn't care less about offending anyone at this point, so I budge right in to where she's standing.

"Oh, helloooo," she says, amused.

"I think I need to go," I inform her.

She looks up toward the front of the line and then back at me. "Well, you're going to have to wait like the rest of us," Julie says.

"No I mean, go...go. Leave go."

"Why?"

I hiccup. "I'm afraid my dinner may reappear, and it's not going to be as appetizing the second time around."

"Good Lord, if you hurl I will kill you," she whisper-screams.

"Precisely why I need to *go*."

"Can I pee first?" she asks, shaking her head in disgust. "I'm not ready to call it a night yet; you seriously can't control yourself?"

"You don't have to leave. I'm sorry. I don't know what happened," I say and prop myself against the wall just outside the ladies' room to wait for her. As soon as she comes out we make our way back to the boys and find them both leaning back on the couch. Ryan kindly assures me the floor hasn't budged in my absence.

"Kat needs to go," Julie announces and throws her arms up.

Pete looks disappointed. "Really?"

"I'm sho sorry," I begin to slur. "I've hit my wall limit...I mean theresh a wall," I continue to ramble. "I've hit a bunch number of walls," I try to explain, waving my hands around.

He gives me a confused look, then cocks his head. A sober version of me would have been mortified, but I felt quite confident that I'd gotten my point across.

"She's going to puke if you don't get her home," Julie translates.

"Gotcha, let's get you a cab," Pete says and jumps to his feet.

"Why don't we all go?" Ryan asks and stands up.

I can sense Julie's eyes burning a hole through my skull so I decide not to look at her.

I shake my head no and gesture for them to sit down, like one does after a standing ovation. "Please stay, you guys don't have to leave on my account, I can get myself a cab," I plead with them.

"Don't be silly," Pete says.

As I give Julie and Ryan a hug goodbye, Ryan gently squeezes my hand and tells me to be careful. I then grab my purse and Pete walks me to the door.

"I feel terrible about this," I say, rubbing my forehead.

"It's no big thing, happens to the best of us," he says kindly.

Just as I'm about to make my escape, "You Give Love a Bad Name" starts to blare over the sound system, so I reach up and grab Pete by the neck to give him a kiss. We swap spit for about a minute, then say our goodbyes.

"Bye, Kat, I'll call you," he says with a smile.

I smile back and drop my filet at his feet.

CHAPTER THREE:
Second Chance at a Sober Impression

It's been two weeks since my disastrous blind date with Pete, after which Julie had been almost as embarrassed as me. And not surprisingly, he never called. The only good thing to come of it was that Julie vowed never to set me up with anyone again. She and Ryan have maintained a casual relationship, although she has yet to score a home-cooked meal out of him. And in true Julie fashion, she's also set her sights on another new guy as well...nickname pending.

Meanwhile, I've chosen to focus on work as a way of getting my mind off of Marc. Work and Adam, that is. Adam Sparks is my coworker and most favorite person in the whole world. Adam is gay, and like most gay friends he's the perfect mate. He's honest, funny, good-looking, has great clothes, and shares similar interests, such as men. Adam runs the Media Department at Lambert & Miller, and has been doing so for three years. He and I became close last year at the office Christmas party when Marc got completely wasted and bitched me out in the parking lot for talking to the bartender for too long. It made no difference to Marc that the bartender was my next-door neighbor when I was five years old. Marc stormed past me and out the front door, leaving me to excuse myself from the conversation with my old neighbor, and follow him outside where he was fuming. And drunk. Adam had been getting something from his car at the time and overheard our whole argument. I remember standing there alone as Marc stumbled into a cab and left me.

My relationship with Marc was never without public displays of drama, and this particular incident, only yards from a co-worker, was exceptionally embarrassing. Soon after Marc had all but spat on me and drove away in a cab that night, Adam sauntered over and asked why I let such a charming guy slip away. I laughed and cried, and Adam and I have been together ever since.

Adam is one of those people who, the more you get to know him, the more attractive he becomes. Not that he isn't physically attractive, but his personality gives him added potential that his looks alone could never provide. He's about five feet ten but swears to being six feet tall. He has short buzz-cut hair, a swimmer's build, and a super pearly white smile due to his obsession with Crest White Strips. And although he is hysterically funny and crude, he's a big teddy bear on the inside—a true romantic and a fiercely loyal friend. He and I share a desire to be happily married one day, and he has more than done his part in helping me get through my breakup with Marc. He's articulate and supportive when I need to be talked off a wall. He's strong when I turn to jelly. He agrees with me when I simply need to hear that I'm right. He never hesitates to tell me when I'm acting like an idiot. And he distracts me with snacks. Sometimes I think Adam understands - more than my girlfriends - how it feels to be thrust back to the first rung on the matrimonial ladder. Mostly because he has a greater appreciation for that which is essentially unattainable to him.

After working through my lunch hour I decide to leave work early, dust off my membership card, and head to the health club. My supervisor, Brooke, is out at client meetings and probably won't think to call me until well after she's gone home. I grab my bag, switch off my computer, and make a mad dash for the elevator before anyone dares approach me. Once outside, I quickly scan the parking lot to make sure Brooke isn't lurking around for some reason, and as I'm doing this my gaze lands on a familiar male figure a few yards away. I find myself startled by his presence, and he walks toward me the minute we make eye contact.

"Hey, Kat." Ryan Sullivan emerges from the shadows and greets me.

"Hey, sorry, I didn't realize it was you. What are you doing here?" I ask and stop in front of him.

"I was just interviewing with Dave, your creative director."

"Just now?" I ask. "I'm surprised Julie didn't mention anything to me."

"Yeah, well, I haven't really told anyone. Never want to count my eggs before they hatch. I guess it's not much of a secret now anyway; today was our second meeting and he just signed me as senior copywriter." He smiles. "Small world, huh?"

"Huh…yeah, I mean, wow, congratulations. That's great." I smile back at him. He's wearing a fitted brown T-shirt, faded blue jeans, and carrying a leather backpack over one shoulder. I haven't seen him since my date with Pete, and I don't recall him being so tall and attractive.

"Where are you headed? Want to give me a lift home?" he asks and points at my keys.

I reactively look down at my hand and then back up at him. "Sure, yeah, of course," I say at a snail's pace.

As we head to my car I begin to feel inexplicably self-conscious. I keep playing with my hair and am having trouble concentrating on what he's saying. The ride is relatively quiet, despite his gallant attempts at making small talk, and any trace of reciprocal witty banter is non-existent.

All I can think about is how gorgeous he is. I resort to nodding and smiling as I attempt to figure out why my palms are sweating like a nervous schoolgirl. He directs me to his address, which is thankfully nowhere near my health club, so I have a new excuse for avoiding it today.

"Thanks for the ride, Kat," he says as I pull up in front of his building.

I give a small wave because I have lost the ability to form a sentence, and watch as he exits my car. Once the door slams shut behind him he turns around and leans into the open passenger window.

"I guess I'll see you at work next week." He smiles again, causing his eyes to make that cute, crinkly look I remember.

"I'll be there," I respond and scan the interior of the car, looking for nothing in particular.

He pats the door. "Well, thanks again. I appreciate the lift. Good to see you."

In that moment we lock eyes and my jaw drops slightly as he smiles one last time before turning around and walking away. His being in my car has put me in some sort of a daze. I exhale little by little and drive off trying to determine what caused me to behave so stupidly just now. One moment I'm walking to my car debating what to eat after my workout - baked potato with bacon bits and sour cream or spaghetti with jarred sauce—and the next, I'm driving Ryan home without proper use of my vocal chords. My humiliation is growing as I retrace what just happened over and over in my mind. As I enter my apartment shaking my head I hear the phone ringing. Caller ID indicates that it's Brooke. Get it, don't get it, get it, don't get it…

"Hello?" Apparently, I've regained proper use of my speech.

"Did you email the status reports to Dave before you left?" she asks frantically.

"Yeah…I did," I respond slowly.

She senses my distraction. "You okay?"

"I'm fine." I pause. "Guess who I just drove home?"

"Please, Kat." She doesn't care.

"Do you remember me telling you about that horrid blind date last month with a friend of 'The Chef'…that guy Julie goes out with? Well, he's now our new senior copywriter," I advise.

"The guy you puked on?" she asks, and I cringe.

"Well, actually the one I didn't puke on. He just got the position; Dave hired him today." I pause. "I bumped into him as I was walking out and he asked me for a ride home."

"Which guy is our new copywriter, Kat?" she asks.

"The Che…his name is Ryan."

"Dave's pretty hard to please, so he must have a great portfolio."

"I guess."

"Why do you sound weird about it?" she wonders.

"I don't know," I respond and compose myself. "I mean, I'm fine. I'm not weird. Sorry, I was just reading an email. No worries about the status reports. I'll see you tomorrow."

I hang up the phone and think about Ryan again. My heart is racing and I can't quite articulate what has happened. I almost never read into things at this level and pace, but I can tell that this is a critical moment in my life. Something affected me in the parking lot today and I can still feel it. The aftershock is as jarring as the initial strike. People have told me a hundred times that when you fall for someone "you just know." But I have never bought into that idiotic theory, mostly because I'm not that simple and I'm very picky. How could someone as picky as me be struck that way? Besides, I've met him before and nothing paralyzed me back then.

No, something has just happened to me, and unlike our previous encounter, Ryan Sullivan has just taken my breath away.

CHAPTER FOUR:
Head Games

Two weeks have passed since I bumped into Ryan in the parking lot, drove him home, and began developing feelings for him. A realization that upon closer study carries two unfamiliar burdens: one, an office romance, and two, coveting the love interest of a friend. Needless to say, work has become increasingly harder to focus on.

Lambert & Miller is one of the top advertising agencies here in Chicago. I've had various jobs since graduating college but working in advertising has always been a dream of mine, so I've done my best to keep this job and make a good impression. My biggest struggle at work is that I'm supposed to be in the office by eight o'clock each morning, and punctuality has never been a strong point of mine. Since Brooke is never on time either, I feel justified arriving late as long as she's not in yet.

Sometime around nine fifteen this morning I catch Brooke walking off the elevators and into her office. Since I finished my creative briefs at home last night, I decide to feed my craving for Words With Friends, and I figure I have at least twenty minutes from when she enters her office before she beckons me. However, this morning all meager attempts to outwit my online nemesis are taking longer than normal, and Brooke manages to surprise me from behind before I can click over to my email screen.

"It's bad enough that you waste company time and make a mockery of my management skills, but you could at least act like you're ashamed when I catch you," she says as she approaches. "Proofread these for errors that Spell Check may have missed," she says and then drops a stack of thin files on my desk. "Lord knows you're not improving your skills with that Scrabble imposter," she barks and gestures toward my screen.

"Okay, that is shameful," I answer in my finest morning sarcasm.

Truth be told, Brooke and I have a civilized working friendship. Second truth be told, I'm the only account person who has been able to tolerate her for more than six months. For that reason alone I get away with more than I should. She hired me two years ago after we met in the bathroom of a nightclub. She had been crying over some guy when I walked in and sped past her to the nearest commode.

"Are you okay?" I had felt obligated to ask as I exited the stall, even though she clearly wasn't. There isn't much other protocol for that awkward encounter. Needless to say she opened the floodgates as women magically do.

"Do I look okay?" she asked and lifted her head slowly.

"Sorry, just thought I should ask." Her tone instantly caused my compassion to fade.

She mustered a fake smile and rubbed her temples. "I'm fine, sorry," she said, half laughing.

"Is there anything I can do to help?" I offered, once I finished washing my hands and drying them on my jeans. I only used soap because she was looking at me.

"Not unless you have a gun."

I smiled, unthreatened. "Nope, sorry."

"That's okay. I'm fine." She stood and went to fix her face in the mirror.

"Do you want me to get someone out there for you?" I asked, gesturing to the door.

She let out a complete laugh that time. "No! That won't be necessary or possible. I'm sure he's gone by now." She paused. "My boyfriend just told me that he needs some time apart, and that he still cares about me but just needs some... *time*. For what or whom, he didn't say."

"That sucks," I replied with honest empathy for her. She looked devastated and embarrassed. "Any idea why?"

She shook her head. "So, since I drank half a bottle of wine as he was telling me all this, I'm a little more emotional than usual. Welcome to the ladies' room!" she said, trying to cover her rejection with pathetic humor.

We stood there and chatted for about fifteen minutes until I invited her to join my friends and me. She declined, but we parted as friends. One of the great things about women: "confront my weary ass in the ladies room and I will trust you with all that is near and dear to my heart." The Insta-Friend!

As it turned out, Brooke was in advertising and had given me her card. I used the rookie therapy session to let her know I was looking for a job, and I've been doing my best to please her ever since. However, that encounter in the bathroom was the only time I've ever seen her let her guard down like that. She tends to be more reserved, and never seems to give me much insight into her private life. Although she does seem to get a lot of enjoyment out of mine.

She ended up marrying the guy who dumped her that night. His name is Drew and he's still a complete asshole. People who meet Brooke on her own, without Drew, think she's a powerhouse. Straightforward, hardworking and focused. People who encounter the two of them together will experience a much different Brooke. One that kowtows to Drew, one who is quieter and timid, and one who tolerates being publicly humiliated. It's obvious to everyone besides her that she deserves better. The dichotomy between who she is as a woman, boss or friend, and who she is as a wife is truly amazing.

She doesn't have a lot of girlfriends either. I remember when it came time to throw her a wedding shower, some strange woman from Drew's office named Hortencia called to see if I wanted to go in on a shower with her and two other girls Drew worked with. As Brooke's only acquaintance I felt obligated, but none of the other girls ever called me or asked for my input on anything - including what Brooke might've liked. They simply asked me for my one hundred dollar check when I arrived at the bowling alley where they'd scheduled the event.

I would say that, besides Drew, Brooke's biggest problem is that she's insecure for no apparent reason. And that insecurity is the one thing that's forever keeping her from being complete, and outwardly kind to others. In addition, Drew does little or nothing to heal those insecurities. I watched them at their wedding while they were taking pictures and Drew was berating her about how long it was taking. He clearly wanted to be at the bar with his friends, and all she wanted was to take a few photos commemorating the day with her new husband. I remember the clarity it gave me as I watched her nervously laughing and doing her best to appease him in that moment. It was sad. Her relationship with him is one of the great mysteries about her. There are the occasional times that her weaknesses show at work, too, albeit not often. But I've noticed that she rarely has a conversation with anyone without inserting a self-deprecating comment about herself somewhere. I think she feels it makes her more human. Mostly, it just makes me feel badly for her.

"Well, you'll be happy to know there's a creative meeting at ten o'clock in the conference room. Bring the client binders if you will. I'll be lugging the bags under my eyes so I won't be able to carry anything else," Brooke says with a wink.

"Creative meeting?" My eyes light up like it's Christmas morning.

"I thought that'd get your attention," she says smiling.

I had foolishly confided in Brooke that I felt a surprising new attachment to Ryan, and it was then when my mild panic attacks started at work. Not really panic attacks, more like panicking when I see him exit the elevator, panicking when he walks by my cubicle on his way to the bathroom, and mostly panicking every time I leave the building for the day hoping for another chance encounter in the parking lot.

The biggest obstacle to date, besides my unrequited affection, is that the only reason I have any association with him in the first place is because Julie's dating him. I'm not exactly sure where their relationship stands today, but it's been weighing heavily on my mind. They've been casually seeing each other, yet I've only heard her mention him a couple times over the past month. She has a way of never dating any one person exclusively so it's hard to keep up; therefore, it's important that I get an updated status of their relationship A.S.A.P. All I really know is that she's also been seeing some particularly needy guy from her improv class, whom she calls "The Momma's Boy."

Brooke interrupts my thoughts. "Well if I'd known telling you about the creative meeting would send you into some catatonic state I wouldn't have mentioned it. Just don't forget the binders please," she says and walks away.

The day is looking up! I have about twenty minutes to pee, apply lipstick, and rehearse thoughtful facial expressions in the bathroom mirror. First I grab a stick of gum, chew it rapidly and then spit it into my garbage can as I do throughout the day. I really don't like chewing gum because it's unprofessional, but mints give me a stomachache. Just as I'm testing my breath outside the ladies' room I run into Adam, my most treasured Insta-Friend.

"Smell my breath," I say as I see him approaching.

"Is that necessary? I'm two sips into my Diet Dr. Pepper, and quite frankly, I'm really enjoying it," he says.

"Creative meeting at ten o'clock!" I announce and breeze past him en route back to my cube.

He turns and follows me. "Your ass looks big in those jeans," he snickers.

Ignore.

Humoring himself further, he adds, "Your ass looks big and your breath smells." Then promptly spills Diet Dr. Pepper on his shirt. "Dammit!"

Karma.

"I have a creative meeting to prepare for, and as usual you're cramping my primping," I say and gather the binders Brooke asked me to bring.

"Just kidding, my darling, you look adorable as always, yet I'm still going to take a pass on the breath test if that's alright with you." He lifts his hand to his mouth and blows me a kiss.

As only Brooke and Adam know, Ryan Sullivan has entirely contributed to my newfound interest in creative meetings. Now that he's our senior copywriter I have guaranteed encounters with him twice a week. There's always a predictable buzz surrounding every new hire, but with Ryan, the office females are on high alert. First of all, he's quite tall; I'm guessing at least six feet two inches, with green eyes and thick brown hair. A little wavy but definitely not curly. And each day, no matter what the hour, his face is perfectly festooned with stubble. Not too little, yet not too much that it would scrape you during a make-out session. I'm guessing, of course. He's almost always in wrinkled button-down shirts loosely hanging out of his jeans, and gym shoes worn like slippers with the backs all bent down because he never quite has them on all the way. Most importantly, he seems completely oblivious to his charm. It's as if David Beckham and J. Crew had a baby. He's probably the biggest catch I've met in a long time.

Brooke and I are already seated when people start filtering into the conference room. Just as I check my Blackberry I am interrupted by his presence in my peripheral vision. I slowly, and not so discreetly, lift my head, smiling and sniffing like an eager puppy whose owner has just entered the house with a Quarter Pounder. Ryan sits down across from us and gives a small nod to Brooke and me.

"Hey, Ry," I say enthusiastically as I do almost every time I see him.

"What's up, ladies," he replies, acknowledging both of us. Always so polite. In my mind his eyes held on mine a tad longer than Brooke's, but I have no video surveillance to prove this.

Brooke has noticed the pathetic turn my behavior has taken since his arrival, and after I confided in her, she became a little concerned for me. She knows Julie was interested in him and doesn't want to see me get hurt or ruin my friendship. She's also well aware of the past dramatics between Marc and me, and thinks it's best that I work through that first. Not to mention the evils of an office romance. Again, she doesn't have much luck holding onto employees, so any work-related angst with me is really a threat to her. Nonetheless, she likes the gossip.

I haven't given much thought to what Julie will think, mostly because my relationship with Ryan is *entirely* in my head at this point. She has a healthy ego, but I can't imagine her giving her blessing to any of her friends in this situation anyway. I deem it best not to say anything to her before I know where she stands with him.

In the meantime, he's proven a wonderful distraction from Marc. After driving Ryan home that first time I've been picturing us vacationing together, French kissing each other in inappropriate settings, and even living together. Visions I have wisely kept to myself. Prior to this day, and for the past four years, I have imagined my life and my future with Marc. That is why it is completely out of character for me to be having imaginary elopements with Ryan.

Brooke interrupts my daydreaming again. "Ryan, we were just admiring your headlines on the Bellagio account."

"Yeah," I chime in and nod.

"You and Dave did a terrific job on this one," she continues.

"Yeah," I repeat.

Brooke shoots me a look of disgust then turns back to Ryan. "I'm presenting them on Friday and I know the client's going to love them."

Ryan smiles, bashful. "Thanks, Brooke, it's a fun account to work on. What'd you think, Kat?" he asks me.

"Yeah...," I start to complete my thought just as Dave, our creative director and head of the agency, walks in and silences the room, giving Brooke ample time to repeat her look of disgust and silently mock my third "yeah."

"Good morning, everyone. Let's be brief. I have another meeting at eleven and a plane to catch after that. Brooke?" he says, with his deep, throaty voice.

Dave is an intimidating kind of guy. His management skills are kind and fair, but firm. He expects no less than everyone's best effort and people work hard to get his approval. I never see him yell at anyone because he never has to. Those who disappoint him usually feel so badly about it, all he has to do is let them know he is not happy. Dave is also gay, and spoken for. Adam officially slept his way to the top and stayed there about two years ago. Adam fell hard for Dave when they first started dating, and I've had the pleasure of watching their mutual admiration for each other grow over the years.

"Well," Brooke begins. "We have the wonderful layouts for Bellagio that Ryan put on boards this morning. I'll be presenting them on Friday, and I know they'll be well received. Other than that, we have the outdoor campaign for Chase in the works and the corporate brochure for Smith Mutual that is still pending. That's pretty much all I have."

As other co-workers give their status updates, I nervously pretend to take notes. During this charade I casually lift my head to glance over at Ryan, and when I do, he's staring straight at me. His gaze catches me completely off guard and I drop my phone like a useless buffoon. As I go to retrieve it with the same grace, I knock the desk with my head on the ascent. I immediately look at Adam once I regain my composure, and he gives me an enthusiastic thumbs-up. I can't even look at Brooke. Instead I do an involuntary move like a turtle, forcing my head to sink, my shoulders to rise, and my body to lower itself slightly.

Always a glutton for punishment, I gear up for round two. I settle back in my chair and grab my phone so I can pretend to check for emails. Again I glance around the room and sneak a peek at Ryan. He's pointing to something on Dave's calendar, which gives me an opportunity to hold my glance for a few extra seconds. He's really freakishly handsome. I look down as someone is texting me. It's Adam.

Take a picture
He texts.

Take a hike.
I respond.

He's watching you.
Adam informs me.

For real?
I ask.

Yes, quit slouching.
He orders.

I'm going to look at him.
I text back and sit straight.

I'm going to pretend I care.
Adam answers then places his phone on the table.

I put my phone in my lap and lift my head. Sure enough Adam is right. There goes my breath again.

CHAPTER FIVE:
Take Inventory on Your Blessings

The rest of the day unfolds like normal. More online word games than actual work, and no more surefire encounters with Ryan. My goal this afternoon is to try and determine when he might be leaving for the night, so that we can bump into each other on our way home. I tell Adam and Brooke not to come near me at the end of the day from now on so I can exit the building alone. I'm mildly offended when they seem all too eager to oblige.

At six o'clock I turn off my monitor and get ready to leave. I'm willing to return to my desk at least twice and pretend I've left something there in case I don't see him at the elevator bank. When it's time to leave, I go to retrieve my purse from my bottom desk drawer and I feel my low-waisted jeans sinking way below sea level. Just as a small breeze hits the top of my newly exposed butt crack, I hear his voice.

"Any chance you're headed my way again?" Ryan asks.

Smack! My head hits a desk for the second time today as I try to pull my pants up and stand all in the same motion.

"Sure, no problem. But, just so you know, I am prepared to install a meter in the car in case this gets out of hand." Pants and witty banter are back on!

"I see, and here I had you pegged for the bighearted, push-over type."

"Sorry, nothing big in that arena," I say and gesture to my chest.

Once I realize I've all but asked him to stare at my boobs in an effort to be clever, I change the subject. "I know I didn't get to properly articulate myself in the creative meeting this morning, but I did love the stuff you did for Bellagio."

"Thanks, Kat," he smiles at me. "Is your head okay?"

"Yeah," I answer, rubbing it.

As we walk to my car we continue to discuss work, and I'm deliberately carrying the conversation this time—hardly allowing him to get a word in. He for sure thinks I'm on drugs now, given my mood swings.

"How's everyone been treating you around the office so far?" I ask with concern.

"So far so good. Dave has been really great, and the graphics team is amazing. They're making my job look really easy."

"Dave is a terrific guy, with an equally terrific team of people working for him."

"I see you and Adam are close buds," he says as we approach my car and climb inside.

"Yes, we are. But he guards his relationship with Dave pretty closely, so I'm afraid I don't have much scoop for you. I've been sworn to secrecy."

"I wasn't prying."

"I know, sorry; it's just that people do tend to think I have some unique insight into Dave because of my friendship with Adam, but it's quite the opposite."

"I'll keep that in mind," he says.

As I'd done two weeks ago, I pull up in front of his apartment and watch as he hops out of my car. And just as I'd been hoping, he leans back in through the open window, which I'd strategically rolled down as soon as we'd gotten in.

"Thanks again. I could get used to this." He smiles, and then pauses. "I was wondering if you'd like to go out sometime? You could drive."

I'm shocked and completely taken aback. So much so that I don't have a chance to respond before he speaks again.

"I don't know if you feel weird with Julie and all. And, well, with us working together, too," he continues. "I'm not sure what she's told you about me, if anything."

"I guess that might be a little awkward..." I start to explain but he cuts me off before I can finish my sentence.

"No worries, I understand. I'll see you tomorrow. Thanks again, Kat." He smiles and saunters away.

He didn't let me finish! I planned on explaining that while it might be a little awkward, I would absolutely love to go out sometime. But he didn't really seem to care. I mean, he has such a confidence about him; it was like either way my answer would have gotten the same reaction. A cool, relaxed squinty grin, followed by a slow pivot. I, however, want to crack my skull on the steering wheel. What just happened? I tear through my purse looking for my cell phone.

"Hello, hello," Adam answers.

"I need help," I blurt out, trying to turn the wheel with two hands and balance the phone on my shoulder.

"More than I can give, I'm afraid."

"I'm serious. I think Ryan just asked me out, and I just rejected him, all within like twenty seconds!"

"I'm going to need a little more information than that," he says, chewing.

I tell Adam the whole story and I can barely believe it myself. The streets near my building are packed with cars, and it takes me forever to drive around looking for a place to park. I finally find one four blocks away, and continue the conversation sitting in my car.

Adam takes a sip of something before he comments. "Look, Kat, if he asked you out once, he'll ask you out again. You're overlooking the most important part, which is that *he asked you out.*"

"You're right. I haven't properly appreciated that yet. But I handled the whole thing like such a jerk, and there's no guarantee he will ask me out again. Why should he? I made it perfectly clear that I'm uncomfortable with upsetting Julie or getting involved in something like that," I say. "And quite honestly, I shouldn't be getting involved with him until I know what's going on with them." I shake my head. "Now that I think about it, I can assure you he will not ask me out again."

"All that went down in under twenty seconds?" he asks in his signature deadpan voice.

I sense Adam is not in the mood to be a sounding board and he's going to stick to his convictions and tell me to just be happy that Ryan showed any interest at all. I understand that he's trying to make me calm down, but I feel like I've ruined the whole thing and I can already envision the gray cloud of obsession that is going to loom over me as I debate this over and over in my head for the next forty-eight hours.

Just then I get an incoming call from Julie. "Oh my God, it's Julie! I have to go," I say to Adam and switch over before he has a chance to say goodbye.

"Hi!" I say and exit my car.

"Don't forget we're going to the Hunt Club tomorrow to watch the Sox game at six o'clock. Any chance in hell you can be there early to grab a table?" she asks.

"I'll try, but I won't know for sure until I determine Brooke's mood after lunch."

"Okay, see what you can do," she adds. "And I invited a couple gals from my office too."

"Sounds great. Can I bring Adam?" I ask, still trying to balance the phone.

"I would expect nothing less. See you then."

I hang up with Julie and try to call Adam back but he doesn't answer his phone.

Bastard.

I decide to stalk him via text.

I know you just saw my call.
I text him.

I did.
He replies.

Call me pls!
I plead.

Busy, luv u
He says.

WTF?
I ask.

With Dave, I'll call u later
He responds.

Grrrrrr
I reply.

CHAPTER SIX:
Moment of Truth or Dare

The next day, despite my commitment to focus on work, I spend hardly any time at my desk and instead relentlessly wander the office floor hoping to run into Ryan. Sometime after my eighth lap, and a few minutes past ten o'clock, Brooke informs me that the creative team is out of the office all day on meetings so I won't get to see him today.

When I woke up this morning, I vowed to take a stand, confront Ryan, and accept his invitation. No more wishing for things to happen, only to screw them up when they do. I'm determined to let him know that I would love to go out with him. A task that is going to be much harder considering he's nowhere to be found.

Since my courage has been postponed and the day is free of any real excitement, I bury myself in work and gear up for a night out with the girls. When Adam and I arrive at the Hunt Club, Julie is already seated with our friend, Beth, and two girls from Julie's office. Unlike me, she'd been able to get here early and snag a table. The bar is packed with men, which is quite pleasing to everyone in our group, and nothing brings out the backward caps like major league baseball.

"Thank God for sports because I really don't know how else we'd meet anyone around here," Julie states as we take our seats and exchange air kisses. "So how's work, kids?" she asks.

"Busy, but good. Brooke gets to go to Vegas on Friday to present some Bellagio creative, and I'm trying to will her to take me with. Other than that, she busted me on Facebook again, so that should pretty much tell you how exciting things are."

Adam turns to me with a gleam in his eye. "Nothing else exciting at the office?" he questions knowingly, trying to start trouble.

I turn slowly to face him head-on. "Other than the possibility of watching you get your ass kicked at a sports bar? No, not much," I say loud enough to make my point and silence him.

Julie throws her arms in the air and invades our peripheral vision. "Well, way to hold out on me! I heard The Chef is working at Lambert & Miller now. I sent him an email inviting him tonight and he told me about his new gig." She pauses, looking at both Adam and me. "Hellooo, why didn't you tell me?" she wonders, waiting for an answer.

I'm a little too stunned to immediately respond, so I take a long, slow sip of my drink while I formulate an answer. Meanwhile, my head sinks down between my shoulders like a turtle again.

"You know, I actually don't see the creatives that often…and I just put it together that it was him the other day," I stammer.

Adam leans his elbow on the table.

Julie shakes her head. "I can't believe he's working at your office. How crazy is that? You have to keep me posted on what's up with him," she demands.

"Have you two been seeing each other lately?" I have to ask given this golden opportunity.

"Not as much as I'd like. He seems pretty busy and never has time to go out anymore. We've emailed a few times, but I haven't actually spoken to him in two weeks," she says and fishes through a small Coach change purse for some lipstick.

"So, you invited him tonight?" I confirm.

"Well, I know he's a huge Sox fan so I thought I'd throw an invitation his way," she says smiling. "He asked me if you'd be here tonight so I'm a little surprised he didn't mention anything."

I freeze at the thought of him asking Julie about me. "Like I said, I rarely see the creatives all that much."

Adam turns toward me with his eyebrows elevated and a huge grin on his face. He then turns away and addresses Julie. "Actually,

Dave had his entire creative team out of the office today, so Ryan probably didn't have the chance," he reassures her with a little more detail.

"Well, I didn't want a table filled with just us girls, no offense Adam, so hopefully he and his friend will show up. He said in his email that he'd try and make it," she adds and suddenly turns toward the door and jumps to her feet. "Oh, speak of the devil!"

Gulp.

Adam begins to silently clap his hands and I lower my head. Julie stands up on her tippy toes and frantically waves Ryan and his friend over to our table. Thankfully he's not dragging Porno Pete along.

"Hi, honey!" Julie welcomes him with a hug that is so over the top you'd think he was a soldier returning home from his call of duty.

She peels herself away. "Glad you could make it," she says. "Last one to arrive has to get the next round. Come on, Ry, I'll help you carry them." She grabs his shirt and pulls him toward the bar before he has a chance to sit.

Everything is happening so fast I can hardly keep up with which sweat glands need to be wiped. I didn't even have one complete minute to digest the fact that Ryan *may* be joining us before he arrived. The evening of stress-free cocktailing and girl talk just turned ugly.

Adam wafts me with the drink menu. "I think it's going great. Only he's with Julie, and you're still here with me."

I take a deep breath. "Why wouldn't he hang out with her?" I ask in an effort to console myself. "He has no reason not to, given the circumstances. Anyway, it's over and done with; I've decided to drop the whole thing and move on. Thankfully, Julie is clueless about any of it, and we can just act like nothing happened. Because it hasn't. And since no one besides you and Brooke even know I'm interested in him, there's no harm done." I adjust my posture so that my spine is nice and straight and put on my best happy face.

Adam quickly corrects me, "Well, true, sort of. No one but us... and Dave."

My spine curls. "Sorry?" I ask curiously.

"I forgive you?" he says guilty, with a smirk.

I take another breath and squeeze his arm as hard as I can. "No, I mean what the hell did you just say, you *sorry* ass?"

"Ow, your nails," Adam chuckles nervously and tries to pry me off of him. "I said 'and Dave.'"

I try to remain calm. "What do you mean "and Dave?'" I ask through gritted teeth.

"Well, I mean that I *heard* Dave knows you're crushing on Ryan."

As if my heart isn't already beating at a dangerous pace. "How did you *hear* that?!" I whisper-shout.

"I overheard myself telling him??"

My mouth is now entirely agape and I'm speechless. Ryan and Julie approach the table at that moment and Julie notices the cavernous hole where my lips once were.

"What's up?" she asks.

I look up at both of them as I remind myself that Ryan and Dave are never without the other during the course of a day. If what Adam says is true, there's no way that Ryan is oblivious to my feelings for him.

I start to answer her. "Well, I'm just shocked because Adam was telling me that he had diarrhea, for like three days last week, and had to have his mom come in from Terre Haute to help him. I just couldn't believe it."

She glances at Adam. "Sorry I asked," Julie says cringing.

Adam shrugs at her in defeat.

I turn and whisper to him, "You should've answered your phone yesterday when I needed you."

"Touché," he whispers back.

Then Adam lifts his drink to shield his mouth with it. "If it's any consolation, Dave thinks your feelings may be reciprocated, which you should have realized when Ryan asked you out. You're welcome," he says smugly.

After the chaos of the previous twenty minutes, I notice that Ryan has taken the open seat next to me, while Julie is seated across the table from him. The more Julie drinks, the more of her body she lays on the table trying to get closer to him. After about forty minutes of this, she is almost entirely horizontal and I simply can't take it anymore. I'm struggling to remain calm, and not overly theatrical, but I feel like the whole evening is spiraling downward. At least for me anyway. Everyone else seems to be enjoying themselves quite nicely, Adam in particular.

About one hour after Ryan's arrival, I start to feel a little nauseous, albeit, nothing to do with the alcohol. I'm watching Julie flirt with him, and a cold sweat comes over me as I sense I am losing control of something, or doing something I shouldn't be doing. I keep shifting my posture in my seat and staring at the ball game, which I couldn't care less about, as I grow more self-conscious and uncomfortable - although no one is even looking at me. Why have I put myself in this situation? Why have I let myself get involved with someone Julie is clearly interested in? The fact that she and Ryan are still communicating enough that she'd invite him here tonight means that I should back off. Thank God he was out of the office all day today. What if I had declared myself to him this morning as planned, only to end up where we are now? I need to escape this place, but since I've come with Adam it won't be that easy. Especially because nothing pleases him more than impending drama.

At this point, the ladies' room seems to be my best refuge, so I excuse myself to the crowd of zero people chatting with me and make my way through a skinny corridor and across a damp, beer-scented rubber floor mat. I'm not quite drunk enough to insist on leaving, or quite sober enough, either. I'm exactly where I should be - two margaritas down, high hopes shattered, and now staring at a mirror fashioned out of bulletproof foil. Not pretty. The mirror or me. I squint really hard and double-check the funhouse image of myself one last time before heading back to the table. As my pity party hits full swing, so does the tequila, and I'm ready to face the music. I convince myself that sulking will only make things worse, and I really need to put my big girl panties on and get over this one-sided love affair before someone (i.e. me) gets hurt.

As I exit the bathroom, eyes glued to the sticky floor, I nearly bump into the next person in line. The hallway is extremely narrow and as I slowly look up to apologize, I realize it's Ryan. He's leaning against the grease-stained drywall, arms crossed, shirt perfectly untucked, and he's not gesturing to get past me to use the toilet. Nor is he doing much of anything except smiling. Clearly this is not going to help the nausea.

"Hey, Kat," he says, breaking the silence.

"Fancy meeting you here," I say with immediate regret.

As if it's territorially possible, he inches closer to me before continuing. His arms remain crossed, all else remains perfect. "I know you were a little wary of the idea yesterday, but I'd really like to take you out sometime. Think you could reconsider?"

I freeze, all statuesque five-feet-two inches of me staring at his chest. "Yes," I say.

"Yes, you'll reconsider, or yes you'd like to go out sometime?"

I look up without lifting my chin, and simply roll my eyes to meet his. "Yes, I'd *definitely* like to go out sometime," I say, desperate to thank him for a second chance.

"Look," he says. "I don't want to put you in an uncomfortable situation with Julie, but I do want you to know that things are over between us. I'm not interested in her, and you're the only reason I came by here tonight. She said she was meeting you and Adam. And that's why I came. To see you."

Again he's left me speechless. Just ten seconds ago I convinced myself to move on. Abandon all thoughts of getting involved with him. Stick to hanging out with the gays, and maybe one day Marc will have a change of heart and grace me with his presence again.

"Okay, great," he continues before I have a chance to speak. His smile widens, and his eyes narrow as he puts his index finger under my chin to lift the rest of my face to meet his. "I'll find you at work tomorrow and we can pick a date." He turns slightly to walk away, and I manage to grab his wrist. He turns back around and looks down at me.

"Ryan, I just want you to know that I'm really looking forward to it."

He smiles again, and so do I.

We walk back to the table together and Julie jumps on him piggyback style. I start to wince as he tries to shake her off respectfully. His muscular build combined with his bashful nature makes almost anything he does acceptable. I sit back down and Adam gives me a curious look. Our synchronized absence did not get past him.

"Everything kosher back there?" he inquires.

"Crystal kosher clear," I say.

"Mazel tov," Adam winks at me. "We'll discuss this later," he whispers, before announcing he's going to look for the dance floor.

CHAPTER SEVEN:
Interested Parties

Almost immediately as I enter the office building, Adam appears next to me at the lobby elevators.

"Good morning," he greets me like a pushy salesperson. "I texted you no less than thirty times after I left. Don't think I didn't see him corner you in the loo last night," Adam says as we board the elevator together.

I take a sip of my bottled water, causing Adam to cross his arms and pout. "Sorry, I turned my phone off as soon as I got home, but yes, he did corner me, and it was awesome," I say. "He asked me out again, and this time I didn't muck it up. He's supposed to find me today and decide when we can get together." We pause the conversation as the doors open on our floor; then we head to my cubicle.

As I remove my coat, Adam gestures at my canary yellow blouse with a wave of his hand. "Well, you shouldn't be too hard to find. A drunken pilot would be able to spot this get-up. I look forward to every detail over recess." He then tosses a box of Altoids on my desk. "Don't leave home without 'em, beautiful."

My phone rings as I'm about to sit down and I see that it's my sister, Megan. She is three years older than me, married to a good man named Henry, and mother to my gloriously bald seven-month old nephew, Miles. She's also my biggest ally, my only sibling, and the one person in my life who truly understands how much I suffered during my parents' divorce. When my mother first told me of their separation, it went something like this:

"Where's Dad been?" I asked after he hadn't come home for two nights.

"He moved out," she said and left the room.

I turned to Megan for support when I had nowhere else to go. We helped each other get through hard times because my mother forbade us from talking about the divorce with her. My father basically pretended like nothing had happened, besides the fact that he'd moved out, found himself a girlfriend with a four-year-old son, and only spoke to Megan and me if we called him.

Over the years, Megan has become notorious for giving me the best advice, so I'm looking forward to filling her in on all that's happening with me. When it comes to my love life she usually has a clear read on things, and she was devastated when Marc and I broke up because she too assumed we were destined for marriage. She also knew how crushed I was. Sometimes she can be too judgmental and stubborn to a fault, but I've come to realize that she doesn't just "like to be right." She truly believes that her ideas are in the best interest of everyone else, which is not always the case, but at least there are good intentions at the root. When my parents divorced, Megan got angry and I got sad. She's very much a straight shooter and doesn't mince words too often. She studied journalism in college and worked as a news writer for many years before taking time off recently to have Miles. Lately she's been calling me at the office more than usual to see if I can meet her for lunch. I think she's desperately bored at home and has trouble relating to Elmo and Friends. Much like me, she always wanted to get married and start a family, but since realizing her goals, she's had a hard time adjusting to the perils of being a stay-at-home mom. She and Henry met on an assignment one day; he is a field producer at one of the local networks, and the rest is newsroom history. They've always had a great relationship, and I hardly ever see them argue, or even bicker. Henry is very low-key and very much a homebody. If he never had to leave his house he'd be perfectly happy. And if Megan would sit there with him and never leave either, he'd be even happier.

"This is Kat," I answer the phone. Brooke insists I answer every call this way at work, even though we have caller ID on all the phones.

"It's me. Can you still do lunch today?" my sister asks.

"Yes, does twelve thirty work for you?"

"Sure, how about Corner Bakery," she suggests.

"Sounds great. I'm looking forward to it."

If I hint that I have something to tell her, she will never let me get off the phone until I do, thus ruining my fun lunch conversation. I'm really excited to hear her perspective on the soap opera that has become my life, and I know she'll be eager to advise.

Unlike me, Megan is always early, so it's no surprise to see her seated and halfway through her salad when I arrive five minutes late.

"Hi, little man!" I run over to greet Miles. "He's more gorgeous every time I see him," I say to Megan. "And I'm sorry, but I hope he never grows any hair. I love the peach fuzz look." I smile and give Megan a kiss on the head. "You look exhausted."

"I have this guy to thank for that. He's waking up at five thirty a.m. these days, and secretly trying to destroy me." She yawns.

"That sucks," I say and then turn to Miles. "Why are you doing this to mommy? What's up with that little man?" He freezes and stares at me, then he smiles at our one-sided conversation.

Megan rubs her temples. "Well, I hate to start venting before you've ordered your cheddar broccoli soup," she says. "But, I'm just so annoyed with him lately. He's like a different person sometimes and I've simply had it. I'm at my wit's end."

"Miles?"

"For God's sake, Kat, not Miles...Henry."

"Oh, sorry, you hadn't..." I start to apologize but she interrupts me.

"He's become totally useless, and it's really making me nuts," she says. "It's like he's paralyzed when it comes to helping me with the baby."

"Well, aren't most guys?" I ask as I'm beginning to realize this lunch date isn't going to be as "Kat-centric" as I'd hoped.

"No, I mean, I don't know? Listen to this, last night I asked Henry if he could watch Miles so I could run to the grocery store, because it's just easier going alone. And I got three frantic calls while I was there, with the baby screaming in the background, and Henry asking what he should do, all the while being short with me on the phone. I couldn't have been gone twenty minutes! Needless to say, I dash out of the grocery store without half the things I needed, just to come home to the baby sleeping in his bouncer and Henry watching television."

"What was wrong with the baby?" I ask.

"*Nothing!* That's the point. Nothing is ever wrong with the baby; it's Henry. He literally cannot spend two minutes alone with Miles without it being some sort of event. And he never offers to either, it's always me having to ask him." She rolls her eyes.

"Well, I'd be more than happy to watch him for you."

"It's not that, Kat," she continues. "Henry should be able to handle it. Two days last week I had a sitter come take care of Miles while Henry was home because it was just easier. It was like I knew I could go do what I had to do without worrying about anything."

I adore Henry so it's hard for me to talk badly about him, but it's clear that's what she wants. A quick salad with a side of mashed Henry. Worse, I have no way of making the conversation about me at this point.

"Don't all your friends with kids have the same issues? I can't imagine Henry is the only guy incapable of mastering child rearing his first time around."

"He's not, and you're right, they're all pathetic. There's an epidemic out there." She's starting to get theatrical and I only have twenty-five minutes left. "Why should we, new moms, have to ask permission to do things for ourselves?" She looks at me like I may have an answer.

"Well, obviously things were going to change, and look what you got in return." I grab Miles's hand and he freezes and smiles at me again. I now hope he never gets teeth either.

She takes a deep breath. "I know, I'm sorry. I'm really exhausted, I guess. I just keep wondering what I could have done differently last night - or in any situation to help him adjust."

I shake my head, indicating I have no idea. Which she must realize.

She begins a sarcasm-laced rant, mocking herself. "Hey, Henry, I just need to run to the grocery for one minute. I promise to sprint down the aisles. Can you watch the baby? It'll take me longer if I take him with me. He's fed, changed, engaged, tired, and should be asleep in under thirty seconds. All you have to do is stare at him and keep him away from teetering bookshelves. Does that sound doable?" She pauses for air.

"Well, how could he say no to that?" I laugh.

She continues, unfazed by people staring at her. "It's like asking someone to care for your new puppy, 'Hey, would you mind watching my dog for me? I know it's a huge inconvenience, and you're not great with dogs, and you may have to pick up his poop. But I really have something I need to do and I can't bring the dog with me. It'd be a huge *favor*.'"

"You realize you're clouding my sunny image of life as a future Stepford wife."

"Sorry," she says with another yawn.

I don't have the heart to tell her about Ryan now. My approaching rendezvous with the office hottie is certain to send her into delayed postpartum depression. Instead, I turn and grab one of Miles's Cheerios and place it on the end of my tongue thinking he'll freeze and smile again. He bursts into tears instead.

"Any word from Marc?" Megan asks with hope in her voice. Like me, she had been eagerly awaiting our engagement, and was equally disappointed when the opposite happened.

"No," I say. I haven't thought much about him in the past couple weeks, but hearing his name leaves a pit in my stomach.

"Have you reached out to him?"

I shake my head.

"Are you planning on it?" She continues her line of questioning, looking for any trace of a reconciliation, but I have vowed not to contact Marc, and not even her tired, judgmental expression is going to make me consider doing otherwise.

"I'm not planning on calling him if that's what you're asking. And no, he hasn't made any attempt to contact me either."

"I must say I'm shocked," she says.

I reach for my Diet Coke, take a sip, and shrug my shoulders. "Well, Rob and Emma's wedding is next week, and I know I'll see him there for sure. We can't avoid each other forever."

"That should be interesting," she says and perks up a little. "I'm dying to know what happens."

"You and me both."

When I return to the office, Adam is waiting in my cubicle. He likes to hang out there when I'm not around so he can search old boyfriends on Facebook without Dave busting him.

"Where have you been?" he asks as he pecks away at my keyboard.

"Lunch with Megan," I reply and throw my bag under the desk.

"Oooh, I'd love to hear her perspective on the Scarlet Letter you'll be wearing."

"So would I actually, but she was too wound up about her own issues today," I say.

"Bitch," Adam says flatly.

I unwrap a stick of gum, chew it for a couple seconds, then spit it out into the garbage can. "Her poor husband, he has no idea. If Henry so much as takes his shoes off the wrong way today he's a goner." I lean against my desktop, watching Adam scan through various posts.

"Well, Ryan's been by here twice since you've been gone," he informs me without looking away from the screen.

"No way!" I gasp.

"Way."

"Did he leave a message?" I ask. "What did he want?"

"No idea."

"Did he say I should call him or anything?" I slap Adam's left shoulder.

"I don't fucking know. He didn't say anything to me. Just walked past here twice."

"Dammit, I hope he comes by again," I mumble angrily.

Adam moves on. "So, you know my birthday's coming up, just wondering what your plans for my gift are?"

"Something spendy," I tease.

"Excellent. And I think you should come out with me and the girls to celebrate. Dave has to be out of town and you promised to go clubbing with me this decade."

"And by girls you mean?"

"John, Rick, and Darryl."

"I'd love to," I say and check the time on my phone. "Now can I please have my desk back?"

Just then I notice Ryan and Dave exiting the conference room. I smack Adam's shoulder again and he swiftly logs out of Facebook. Dave turns to head toward his office, and Ryan heads toward my cube.

"Get up!" I yell at Adam.

"All right, freak!"

I swivel around and greet Ryan just as he stops at my desk. "Hey, Ry," I say.

"What's up guys?" he asks us.

"Adam was just leaving," I answer and gesture for Adam to exit the tiny square space that we're all standing in.

"I actually wasn't about to leave, but she clearly wants me to now that you're here." Adam taps the top of my head and walks away. I snicker to mask my humiliation.

"So, how's your day been?" Ryan asks me.

"Pretty good, I met my sister for lunch."

"Yeah, I stopped by a couple times earlier hoping to find you, but you weren't around," he confesses. His honesty surprises me. No game playing? I could get used to this.

I take a seat in my chair, allowing him to come further into my cube. "Oh, sorry about that - we went to Corner Bakery. She and my little nephew, Miles."

"Sweet, how old is he?"

"He's seven months old, and I only made him cry once today," I smile proudly and lean back into the chair.

"Oh, I bet you're a charmer," he replies.

I blush at the compliment and nervously look away, only to notice Adam standing with two other co-workers pointing at me from six cubes over. I give him my best "what the hell?" face, and turn my attention back to Ryan who's leaning against one of the wobbly cubicle walls all relaxed and irresistible.

"So," he starts. "How about that date?"

"Yes, great. What works for you?" I inquire, as my cheeks get warm.

"I was thinking I could cook dinner for you." He crosses his arms.

"That'd be awesome, I love dinner."

"Good to know." He grins and then reaches in his front pocket for his phone. "How about next weekend, are you free?"

Next weekend is Rob and Emma's wedding, where I will be reunited with Marc after months of radio silence. I have put way too much thought into this event, and literally imagined no less than fifty different scenarios regarding what it will be like the first time I see him again.

Scenario one: I walk in late - hair straightened to silky perfection - as he spots me from across the room. He immediately ends the conversation he's having with a five-foot-ten blonde and runs to embrace me.

Scenario two: Marc is four bites into his chicken kiev when I arrive two hours late - yet dressed to the nines. He drops his fork, hurries to my side, where we stand gazing into each other's eyes for a full minute before he kisses me.

Scenario three: Marc decides to bring a date to the wedding and has to leave early because someone accidentally pours hot gravy down the front of her dress.

"I have a wedding to go to on Friday night, but I'm free Saturday," I tell Ryan.

"Then Saturday it is. Any food aversions I should be aware of?" he asks.

"Just fruits, vegetables and salad." I smile and fold my hands in my lap.

"Perfect. A girl after my own taste buds." He places his phone back in his pocket and stands upright. I want to thank him. Not just for dinner, but for giving me something to look forward to.

"And there's no need to pick me up since I know where you live," I say.

"I'd be happy to arrange for a car service if you'd like," he jokes.

"Just let me know what time to be there and then expect me about fifteen minutes after that." He may as well get used to my tardiness.

"Six forty-five, then."

"Perfect."

I catch myself staring at his butt when he walks away. Not really on purpose, just sort of instinctively. He's really attractive from all sides and one can't help but notice. It's then I realize Adam and his gaggle of morons are also staring at Ryan's backside.

Come hither!
I text Adam.

I'm busy.
He responds.

I see u!
I say.

K, one sec
He replies.

Adam continues chatting with the other women and finally wraps up his chatter with one last belly-clutching guffaw before heading back to me. He's lucky he has an *in* with the boss is all I can say.

"So?" he inquires and parks himself on my desk.

"He's making dinner for me Saturday night," I announce with a high-five and a shaky spin in my desk chair.

"Oh, he's good," Adam remarks.

"What do you mean by that?" I ask.

"He'll get you toasted and back to his place without ever actually taking you out. I'm impressed."

"Well, we don't call him *The Chef* behind his back for nothing."

"You're right. *We* don't call him The Chef behind his back; Julie does," Adam corrects me with a chuckle.

He's right. Julie coined him The Chef, and I really have no reason to be throwing around her nicknames with such blithe effort. "Thanks for the reminder." I turn my attention to my email screen.

Adam can tell he's hit a nerve with me, so he presses on. "Which begs the question, when are you going to mention this to her?" He attempts to satisfy his inquiring mind.

"I figure I should see if Ryan and I are compatible first. Why freak Julie out if there's no reason to. Maybe we won't get along, or I'll offend him with my poor manners."

"Or your breath," he snickers. "I just wouldn't be so careless about it, you know how she is, that one. If Julie were to find out about this date before you tell her, you can only imagine how fast you will have to run to avoid her wrath."

I drop my head back and squint at the fluorescent lighting above me. Adam is entirely right; I've been selfish with my feelings for Ryan and there is every indication that it could blow up in my face.

"The honest truth is that I really don't know what to do. In some respects, I never really thought he would ask me out I guess."

"No need to play coy," he says. "Ryan doesn't strike me as the type of guy who'd pit two friends against each other, on purpose anyway. So maybe Julie's perception of the relationship is different than his. You should find out."

"I will," I assure him, and place my head back in a much more comfortable position. "As it turns out, this weekend is becoming quite eventful," I say. "Friday I will be reunited with Marc at Rob and Emma's wedding, and forced to lie to Julie and Beth about my plans on Saturday, which, despite the clandestine nature, I'm *very* excited about."

"Well I'm booking you for brunch on Sunday then. And that, I am very excited about."

"As you should be." I nod.

My affection for Ryan has taken a great deal of pressure off seeing Marc again, although it may not be enough of a distraction once I have to face him in person.

Just then my phone rings and Adam and I both clamor to see who it is.

"Julie!" we gasp in unison.

"Fancy that," he remarks and gestures for me to answer it with a wave of his hand.

I grab the receiver on the last ring. "Hello, this is Kat."

"Hey, it's me and I'm in the lobby. I was going to come up and see you...and coincidentally bump into Ryan, if you catch my drift," Julie informs me as I glance over at Adam.

"Well, right now is not the best time—I'm heading into a meeting in two minutes," I say and cross my fingers.

She sighs into the phone. "Damn, I guess I should have called earlier but I'm out running an errand and didn't realize I'd be near your building today."

"Shoot, yeah, now just isn't a good time," I repeat and lean my body away from Adam who's trying to shove his head next to mine in hopes of hearing the conversation firsthand.

"You sure you don't have five minutes?" She double checks.

"I wish I did."

"Bummer, all right, call me later." She signs off.

Adam crosses his arms. "What was that all about?"

I slam the phone down. "She's in the lobby and wanted to come up here to see Ryan."

"So she's gone now?" he asks me.

I grab a rubber band from the top drawer and pull my hair up into a ponytail. "Yes, and let me tell you, that was a little too close for comfort. I'm sweating."

"That's pretty," he says and squeezes my hand. "Well you may have dodged a bullet this time, but you better watch yourself, little one; it's time to come clean."

"No need to remind me." I release my lungs.

Adam stands up and peers over the top of my cubicle before leaving. But before he does, his eyes narrow as though he's trying to focus on something. "I take it back," he informs me and quickly squats down like he's in an army bunker.

"Take what back?"

"You've been shot." He continues to crouch down and hide. "She's here!"

"What?" I jump to my feet and sure enough Julie is standing in our reception area. I then swiftly join Adam on the floor.

"That was quick! What is she doing here? I said it wasn't a good time," I cry out and throw myself back against the makeshift wall.

"Not taking no for an answer, I guess," he says. "This is too good to miss, so I'm going back to my desk where I have a much better vantage point." Adam scrambles to his feet, cool as a cucumber and leaves me in his dust.

"Wait," I scream silently, but it's too late.

I wait for Carrie, our receptionist, to buzz me, thinking that when she does I will scurry up there and let Julie know that I'm just about to go into my meeting.

I reach up, grab my cell phone and a notepad from the top of my desk, and wait.

Still waiting.

Carrie is a notorious flake but this is taking much longer than usual. I slowly elevate myself off the floor and catch a glimpse of Julie and Ryan walking back to his office. Reactively I sit back down.

WTF?!?!?!?!?
I text Adam.

Game on.
He replies.

She didn't even ask for me?
I question her boldness.

Doesn't need u
He texts back.

What should I do?
I ask.

Start pulling hair.
He suggests.

Should I walk over there?
I ask.

You said you were in a mtg.
He reminds me.

I pick up the office phone and ring Adam's desk. "What is going on?" I beg him for some information considering he can see Ryan's office from where he sits.

"They're standing in his office," he tells me.

"Can you believe her?"

"What's the big deal? She wanted to see him, and it probably took her all of two seconds to realize that she's a big girl and could come up here and do what she wanted all on her own."

"Well, what if she walks back here and sees that I'm not in a meeting."

"That's not likely. She doesn't look very interested in you at the moment," he says. "Hold on, they're walking toward the front now."

"Are they coming my way?"

"I just said they're walking to the front," he snaps.

"Just tell me when she's gone."

"Looks like they're making out on Carrie's desk."

"I hate you."

"She's gone and lover boy is headed your way." Click.

I spastically stand up, hang up, and start clicking around my computer screen desperate to find something that resembles work.

"Hey." Ryan's voice comes around the corner before he does.

"Oh, hey there," I greet him looking clueless and feigning a pleasant surprise.

He points at me with a questionable look on his face. "I thought you weren't here," he ponders.

"What do you mean?" I swivel to face him.

"Did you see who was just here?" he asks and puts his hands in his pockets.

"No, who?" I'm ashamed at my ability to lie. The inflection in my voice alone could get me arrested for something.

"Julie was just here, at the office. She said she stopped by to see you, but you weren't at your desk, so she paged me," he says.

Since I lied to her first, I don't feel entirely justified in being annoyed by her lie. "Oh," I say. "That's weird, maybe I was at the printer when she walked over here."

"I didn't really know what to say to her." He looks at me like he wants some sort of an answer to that statement.

"What do you mean?" I ask.

He removes one hand from his pocket and turns his palm upwards. "I didn't know if you told her I asked you out or not."

I bite my tongue, so I don't spew out the truth - No! Of course I haven't told her. Can't you see through me to the way back of my insecure head where I store all of my baggage? Of course I haven't said anything to Julie because she's probably going to freak out on me and I will have no idea how to deal with it. I can't stand when people are angry with me. It makes me want to crawl into a hole and behave like a toddler.

After a beat, I answer him. "No, I haven't. Did you tell her?" I ask nervously.

"No." He hesitates. "Are you going to?"

"At some point, yes," I assure him.

"Do you want me to say something to her?" he offers.

"No. Nope. That's fine, I mean, no," I reiterate. "I will say something to Julie."

He nods his head with little confidence. "Okay, good, because that was a little awkward and I don't want this to cause any tension between you two."

"Of course," I answer, not wanting him to rescind his dinner invitation. "I haven't had the right opportunity yet, given that we just made plans," I say and clench my teeth.

"Yeah, of course, I just didn't know if you'd mentioned anything the other night, after the Hunt Club."

"I didn't," I tell him.

"Okay," he says and then stands there for a moment trying to make sense of everything before giving me one last nod and walking away.

CHAPTER EIGHT:
That's Gonna Leave a Marc

Rob and Emma's wedding is tonight, and because it's a Friday, I'm stuck spending the day at work rather than getting my nails done.

Much to my delight, Adam approaches my desk with a Tazo tea and a peanut butter Twix for me around three o'clock. "For you, my dear," he says and sets them on my desk.

"Why, thank you, kind sir."

"So, tonight's the big night," Adam says. "The wedding is finally upon us. I expect to be updated on the hour."

"I'm sure you'll be hearing from me plenty," I say and tear through the candy wrapper.

"I'm still free, you know," he offers. "My tux is always pressed and ready."

"Sorry, but my invitation didn't say '*Kat Porter and Guest*' otherwise you would have absolutely made the cut."

"How are you getting there?"

"Julie and Beth are picking me up at six," I manage to say through a crumbly cookie bite.

"Can I borrow your car?"

"No," I say.

"Well, obviously I'll be dying for an update, so let me know what happens the minute it's happening," Adam says.

"Will do."

I rush home from work—late as usual—get dressed, wash my face, reapply my make-up and shovel a frosted strawberry Pop-Tart into my mouth just as Julie calls me from the cab downstairs.

"I'm on my way down!" I answer the phone.

"Meter's running, Kat," she replies and hangs up.

The wedding is being held outside at the Museum of Contemporary Art just off Michigan Avenue. And despite the humidity, it's a beautiful night. As we pull up in front, the setting sun is casting a pinkish-orange hue on the museum steps making the building look especially radioactive this evening. The three of us enter through the main doors at the top of the steps and head toward the back terrace. As soon as we walk outside onto the concrete patio area, we run into Rob.

"Good evening, ladies," he says. Rob approaches the three of us dressed in a white tuxedo and black tennis shoes.

"Oh my, Robert, you look mighty handsome," I say as we hug.

Julie butts in. "Well, well, well, and they said it'd never happen."

"What's that, Julie?" he asks her.

"You in an ironed shirt, of course. Give me some love." She extends her cheek and Rob plants one on her lips instead.

"Thank goodness our friend Kat here looks so cute in a bikini, or this wedding may have never happened," Julie reminds him of the circumstances under which we all met, which additionally includes one of the most embarrassing moments of my life.

A few weeks after my college graduation, I'd flown out to Los Angeles to visit Julie for a few days. She lived in Santa Monica for a couple years after attending college at USC, with her roommate, Emma, who was also originally from Chicago. My first full day there Julie was unable to get off work, so she told me I'd have to entertain myself for a few hours. Since it was California, I told her all I really needed were directions to the beach and the latest copy of *People* in order to kill time. Her apartment was near the corner of Olympic Boulevard and Sepulveda, and she had vaguely assured me that all I had to do was take Olympic West until I hit the ocean. Didn't seem too hard, even for a displaced Midwesterner like myself.

"Should I walk?" I asked Julie.

"Nobody walks in L.A.: Emma is going to drive me to work, so you can have my car for the day."

"Okay, thanks," I said. "So, just to confirm, I take this Olympic Boulevard, all the way there? I never have to make one turn or anything?"

"Correct," Julie assured me.

"Alrighty then, I wish you could join me, but I am perfectly happy to hit the sun and sand alone."

"Have fun, and we'll meet you back here around five thirty tonight," she confirmed and disappeared out the door.

I grabbed the keys to Julie's car and headed toward the beach. I had my tote bag, towel, magazine, sunglasses, sun lotion, and water bottle and was ready for some west coast relaxation. Her directions were pretty much spot on, but the beach wasn't exactly as I had envisioned it. There were two deserted cars in the parking lot, and some rundown public restrooms that I immediately decided to avoid at all costs. Trash was blowing around the walkway like tumbleweeds, and it just didn't resemble the postcard image I had formulated in my head. Unfortunately, I didn't have much of a choice considering the only other place I knew how to get to was Julie's apartment. The local beachgoers left much to be desired as well. Transients and drifters outnumbered surfboards and bikinis by far. As I walked closer to the water I spied a lifeguard station much like ones I was programmed to associate with Baywatch, and for some reason it gave me the false sense of comfort I was looking for.

I strategically placed my towel near the lifeguard, behind his perch and a little to the left. I noticed him pacing the front of his station; and then he glanced at me for half a second. He was picture perfect as far as I could tell. Solid muscular build, evenly tanned skin, and a glistening pair of Ray-Bans. Aside from me, the beach was extremely empty with only about three other people around, two in the water and one man sitting on the sand who was noticeably overdressed in wool pants and a long-sleeved sweatshirt. I was expecting more of an upbeat hustle-bustle atmosphere, but tourists, locals, and frolicking children were pretty much non-existent on that Wednesday morning. Either way, I was happy to be there. The North Avenue beach on Lake Michigan just can't compare to the ocean.

I spread out my towel, being careful not to disturb too much sand and made a nice little spot for myself to sunbathe. I started out by testing fate and going without sunscreen for the first thirty minutes just to get a little pink on my cheeks and was almost done with my magazine when I decided to put it away and take a nap. I grabbed my sunglasses, lay down on my back, draped my T-shirt over my waist and closed my eyes. The warm early morning sun had me curled up like a kitten in no time.

The noise that woke me up was not a sound that one normally associates with the beach. It was the sound of a truck engine and it was almost on top of me when I opened my eyes. As soon as I realized there was a Beach Patrol Jeep less than three feet from my towel, I immediately sat up and looked at the two new lifeguards arresting the over-dressed homeless man who had apparently set up a spot of his own, inches from mine during my brief slumber. Neither of the two patrolmen made eye contact with me as they were putting the man into their truck, but I noticed that the cutie I had spied earlier was now staring right at me from his perch with a goofy smile on his face. My cheeks went flush as I looked around to see if anyone else had witnessed this spectacle. Embarrassed, I yanked my shirt over my head and rushed toward the Baywatch babe to ask if he knew what had happened.

"Hi," I said, waving up at him.

"Good morning," he answered, leaning over the tower rail.

"What just happened over there?" I pleaded for some information.

"Didn't you see that guy?" he asked me.

"No. I mean, not until just now. The truck woke me up."

"Well, your friend there was…pleasuring himself…next to you." His smile grew like the Cheshire cat.

My stomach sank and my face turned red without help from the sun as I briefly looked back at the commotion next to my belongings. "Are you kidding me?" I said in disbelief.

"Nope. It happens all the time. In fact I called in the troops almost as soon as you sat down. What brings you to this beach anyway?" he asked the question that I had been wondering myself.

"Well, my best and now former friend sent me here this morning. I'm in from out of town."

"Welcome to L.A." He waved a hand in the air. "I'm Rob."

"I'm Kat. Nice to meet you…sort of," I said.

"How long are you in town?" he asked.

"Just a few days," I said.

"I see. So, what do you and your clueless girlfriend have planned tonight?"

"I'm not really sure," I answered, digging my toes into the sand and wondering if he was really going to ask me out under these circumstances?

"Me and some of the other lifeguards are going to the Daily Pint later, around seven thirty. Tell your friend; I'm sure she'll know where it is," Rob said.

"Okay, that sounds great. Hopefully we'll see you there. I can't imagine she's scheduled us to meet another group of lifeguards anywhere else," I joked.

"And tell her to take better care of you next time."

"Will do."

As it turned out, Julie, Emma and myself did end up meeting Rob and his band of beach brothers out that night, and he ignored me almost instantly and set his life-saving sights on Emma. They've been together ever since.

Beth shoves Julie to the side. "Now back away from the groom for God's sake. Mazel tov, honey. We're so excited for you. Where's Emma?"

"She's in with her bridesmaids hogging the air-conditioner. I've lost three pounds of sweat since this afternoon."

"Everything is going to be amazing," I say. "Why don't you get a cool glass of something? Don't your lackeys have emergency tequila stashed away for you somewhere?"

"Please, Kat, that was so two hours ago."

"I should have known." I smile and pat him on the back.

"Okay, girls, I'll see you in there. Gotta run," he says and waves goodbye.

"Good luck, Rob, you're going to be great. You're a lucky guy!" Julie shouts after him.

Julie wipes her forehead and turns to Beth and me. "What possesses people to have an outdoor wedding in this town? It's ninety-three degrees in the Goddamned shade, my back is dripping, and I've been here all of five minutes."

"More importantly, what possessed me to straighten my hair for this thing? Look at it already," I say, and begin to pull on the ends in an attempt at keeping it from springing up around my face.

"You straightened your hair today?" Beth asks.

"Crap!" I pull harder.

Aside from the sauna that is this wedding, all I can focus on is seeing Marc. I'm scoping the place out like a radar gun waiting for him to appear. How will he act? How will I react? Will my newfound adoration for Ryan ward him off like a protective shield, guarding me from all that is sappy and familiar?

Beth and Julie were forced to listen to me predict Marc's behavior on the entire ride over here, and they were extremely supportive in their own way. Julie's pessimistic nature led her to inform me that it's for the best, and that my relationship with Marc was a study in dysfunction. Its demise has brought out the best in me, she said. Beth, on the other hand, has assured me that it's been a well-deserved and much needed break, but that weddings almost always rekindle old romances...and I should be prepared for that as well. Just as we walk back inside the museum for a shot of cool air and a cocktail, I see him enter the room at the opposite end. My halted pace signals the girls, and within seconds all three of us are staring at him.

Shit, he looks great. His hair is a little bit longer than he usually wears it, and the length nicely accents his disheveled surfer turned business mogul appeal. He's dressed in a suit but noticeably without a tie. His white dress shirt is open at the neck and he looks as comfortable as I've ever seen him. My stomach begins to turn as it always does when I get nervous, and I notice Beth and Julie looking back and forth at Marc and me, and then finally at each other.

"Showtime," Julie remarks. "No pressure, doll face."

"You're fine, you look gorgeous, and your hair is perfectly straight." Beth winks at me. "Do you want us to magically disappear or no?"

I adjust my posture so that I'm not facing him head on. "I'm not sure yet," I say using my best ventriloquism and observe Marc standing next to his friend Graham, looking over at us.

Julie pats the sweat under her arms with a cocktail napkin. "Why don't we all just go and get a drink like we'd planned?" she suggests.

"Fine, yes, that's fine," I waffle, head bobbing. "Wait, you know what, I think I should just go over and say hello. Why make this uncomfortable?" I look to my girlfriends for encouragement.

"I agree," says Beth. "Do you want us to go with you?"

"Bad idea," declares Julie, shaking her head. "You're going to ruin your night and Rob's wedding before it even starts."

Beth erupts with laughter. "Oh, my God, would you shut up and leave her alone." She slaps Julie's boob and tugs on her purse strap like a leash. "Go on, Kat, we'll be by the bar."

"Ow!" Julie screams, massaging her chest.

I watch as they walk toward the bar and leave me standing alone. I know I have to turn around, move an arm, blink, or do something but instead I stand there frozen. Then I close my eyes and beg the hamster to stop running around inside my lower abdomen. A second later someone walks up behind me and places a hand on my shoulder.

I manage the turn and come face-to-face with Marc. I look up and into his familiar eyes, and am immediately at ease.

"Hey," Marc says casually.

"Hey, Marc," I answer, as we hug.

"Nice to see you, you look good. I always liked when you wore your hair curly," he says.

Friggin' heat!

"Thank you. I was just about to walk over and say hello. Where's Graham?" I ask.

"At the bar with Beth and Julie."

I turn back toward the bar to see the three of them looking over at us. I give an obligatory wave to Graham and he gives me a nod.

"So how's everything? Work good?" I ask, and shift my body weight back and forth in my heels to keep myself from getting light-headed.

Marc puts his hands in his pockets. "Work's been going well, can't complain. How about you?"

"I guess I can't complain either. Well that's a lie…I can always muster up a good complaint, but I'll spare you just this once." I smile.

"My lucky day," he says, then removes one hand from his pocket and runs it through his hair.

The thin strap on my cocktail bag keeps slipping, so I fumble to secure it on my shoulder. "How's the family?" I ask. "Please tell your mom I say hello."

"I will, thanks. She'll be glad to hear from you."

I feel compelled to trash the niceties and say something substantial, something that will stick with him tonight, because I have no idea when we'll see each other next. Marc can be all about saving face at times, and I can tell that he's mostly concerned with looking confident and blasé at the moment. He would never want to let on that he's been remotely anxious about this encounter like I have. God, I know him so well. We continue to stand there, both of our eyes bouncing around like pinballs, not sure where to land or what to look at.

I decide to speak my mind and be honest with him. "Well, I wasn't sure if this would be weird or not, but it's truly good to see you, Marc. And things with me are going well," I say with as much sincerity as I can.

"Yeah, yeah, me too. Everything is good. It's nice to see you too, Kat," he says with confidence.

"I mean it, Marc. I'm doing well, and I'm glad to hear that things are good with you. And you look great." I couldn't resist the compliment.

"Thanks, Kat," he says, oozing self-assurance. "Well, I better find Graham. We'll catch up later, okay?"

"Okay, sure," I say as he taps me on the arm like he would a fellow colleague and walks over to the bar.

I stand there alone again, wondering if he heard anything I just said, and watch him approach my friends and exchange hugs and salutations. Desperate to look confident and blasé myself, I reach for my phone and text Adam.

Just saw Marc.
I text.

NFW! where?
He replies.

At Robs wedding u douche.
I say.

And???
He asks.

And not much.
I reply.

Why r u bothering me then?
Even via text he manages to sound annoyed.

I'm using you to look busy and important. Standing alone at the moment.
I text.

Lord! pls report back with something juicy. Get drunk and flash a boob on the dance floor or something.

He requests.

I'll do my breast. Luv u.
I text and smile.

I put my phone back in my purse as Beth and Julie finally make their way back to me with my drink. I suck down half of a dirty martini in two gulps.

"So?" Julie is the first to speak. "He looks cute."

"I didn't notice," I reply with my best party sarcasm.

"I'm kidding. He looks as vanilla as ever. What'd he say?" she asks eagerly.

I swirl my blue cheese olives around on their little red spear. "He was cool as a cucumber, and everything is terrific, blah, blah, blah."

"Of course it is," Beth adds. "You didn't really think he'd let you think otherwise?"

I take another swig of my cocktail and catch Marc and Graham walking outside toward the patio. "No, I just expected a little more depth I guess. I mean, it's been months since we've seen each other, and I tried to open up the conversation a little wider, but he wasn't having it."

"Well, I'm not surprised," says Julie.

"It's fine. My nausea has settled and the worst is over," I say. "As soon as I get another one of these drinks we can start having some fun."

"Woo hoo," Julie says smugly. "How about the second we hear the band start playing '*Celebration*,' we head for the hills?"

"Deal!" Beth and I say in unison.

I would like to spend the rest of the evening thinking about my date with Ryan tomorrow, but like a magnet, my mind and eyes keep going back to Marc. Much to my dismay, I'm longing to talk to him and spend time with him, but it's clear that he's doing everything in his power to keep his distance. He's not much of a dancer, so I periodically notice he's either at his table with his buddies or at the bar. We lock eyes a couple times by accident and exchange friendly smiles. I'm equally surprised and annoyed by how good he looks. There is still an underlying friendship between us, and regardless of our breakup I still care about him.

The first note of "Celebration" hits the airwaves at midnight. Beth, Julie and I find ourselves unexpectedly separated at that moment, but are able to reconvene at the museum's front entrance within seconds.

"Ce-le-brate good times…come on!" Julie sings and gestures toward the exit with her head.

"Should we say goodbye to anyone?" Beth asks.

"Why start being polite now?" I ask.

"True."

We gather our purses and not-so-discreetly head for the exit. I want to say goodbye to Marc, but he's at his table with a group of people near the dance floor, oozing indifference. I glance over at him a couple dozen times as we're leaving, hoping for the chance to wave or nod or something, but he never looks up. I try mental telepathy, but that doesn't work either.

Beth notices my pathetic attempts at getting his attention. "Do you want to go say goodbye to him?" she asks.

"Do you think I should?" I ask Beth, as Julie shakes her head, no.

"I do, if you want to," Beth says to me.

I look over at him one more time and that's all it takes. He's now staring back at me. Instinctively, I lift my hand and give him a quick wave goodbye. He just smiles and nods. Beth then takes my hand and leads me away.

I survived the wedding. All the trepidation surrounding this event is behind me now, and so is Marc. We'd been kind and civil and that was all I could've hoped for. Once we're officially out of the building, I'm pleasantly surprised by how relaxed I feel. Normally I'd be crying, or texting, or forcing my friends to recap the evening to death. But not this time.

The three of us grab a cab and head to the Weiner Circle for a tray of cheese fries before heading our separate ways. I debate whether or not to call Ryan when I get home. I know I probably shouldn't, but I can't stop thinking about him. Is there a snowball's chance in hell that he'll contact me tonight? It doesn't seem like his M.O. but I'm still hopeful. He knew I was going to a friend's wedding, but I hadn't mentioned that my ex would be there. It just didn't seem like relevant information prior to our first date.

As I crawl into bed I am genuinely comfortable for the first time in a long time. Seeing Marc wasn't nearly the drama-laden event I had assumed it would be, and I'm so looking forward to being alone with Ryan tomorrow night that I can barely keep from smiling. Just then the phone rings. I've been so lost in my state of euphoria that I actually let out a little gasp. Curtis leaps off the bed as I check the clock and see that it's two o'clock in the morning. My prayers are answered! I knock the phone off its base and hear it click to connect as it hits the floor.

"Hello?" I say and scramble to pick it up as I regain my balance.

"Hey, it's Marc."

I rub my eyes. "Oh," I answer.

"Did I wake you?" he asks.

"No, I, uh, sorry, no," I stutter.

"I'm downstairs."

As soon as the phone rang, I'd thought for sure it was Ryan. I'd hoped it was Ryan. I hadn't even considered the old alternative.

"You're where?" I ask, confused.

"Downstairs," he repeats. "Are you sure this isn't a bad time?"

I jump up like an obedient soldier. "It's fine. I was just falling asleep."

"Can I come up?" he asks.

"Sure." The words exit my mouth before I can make sense of them.

I buzz him up, run to the bathroom and scramble to put my contacts back in. I'm assuming he's drunk, but vanity prevents me from letting him see me in my glasses at this hour. Nothing good can come of this. I hurry to the front door as soon as I hear him knock.

"Hi, come on in," I say. He looks oddly as comfortable as he did earlier. I, on the other hand, look like a tired tramp who just spent the last hour with her face buried in a tray of cheese fries.

"Thanks," he says, and stops in the doorway.

"Do you want to come sit down?" I ask and gesture with my hand.

"Sure."

I follow him to the couch and he takes his suit coat off and sits down next to me. He stays there smiling awkwardly at me while I make some pathetic remark about my pajamas.

"To what do I owe the pleasure?" I ask.

He lets out a little laugh. "I wanted to see you."

"Not without makeup I imagine," I say and make my best pretty face, feeling much more self-deprecating at this hour. Brooke would be so proud.

"You look terrific, Kat."

Gulp.

"It was nice seeing you tonight, and as always you looked great. I'm sorry if you felt like I was avoiding you. I wasn't sure how you wanted me to act, so I thought 'polite and out of sight' would be the best method. I know how much you love weddings," he says.

I smile at him, touched by the fact that he put any thought into it at all. He certainly does know me better than anyone.

"You were fine, Marc," I say, and tug at my nightshirt. "And thank you for thinking of my feelings. To tell you the truth, I had actually been really nervous about seeing you at the wedding. I wasn't sure how things were going to be between us."

"That's just it, Kat, I'm always thinking about your feelings lately. I'm always thinking about you in general," he says and glances down before looking me in the eyes. "I've really missed you."

"Oh," I say.

"After our last conversation, I really wanted to honor what you'd asked of me. And at first it was easy. But as more time passed, it… well, it's been really hard not to call or text or anything. My goal was to wait until the wedding, and I made it." He smiles triumphantly and shrugs his shoulders slightly.

"I completely understand. It's been really hard on me too, and I had a really rough time at first."

"And now?" He looks at me with uncertainty and hope.

"And now, well, I felt good about seeing you tonight. First of all, it's always great to see you, and secondly, I just felt comfortable, like we were *good*. You know?" The combination of congealing cheese in my stomach and dry contact lenses has left me at a loss for intelligible words.

"Me too," he says.

We sit there for a minute staring at each other and occasionally averting our eyes as Curtis proves to be an intermittent distraction. On one of my downward glances he slowly reaches out and takes my hand in his. I look up at him as he does this and he leans in to kiss me. I don't pause to stop him. It wouldn't even occur to me to stop him. His move is so habitual, and even though it's been months, my instinct and desire is to kiss him back. My head leans slightly and we begin an all too familiar routine. Our lips are simultaneously enjoying the intimacy, and more than comfortable enough to invite our tongues to the reunion. His mouth is as soft as always, and he smells like home. Marc's other hand moves to the side of my face as his entire body shifts closer to mine. Reality sets in as I realize I could easily spend the rest of the night making up for lost time, or I could do the right thing and end this before it goes exactly where it always goes.

"Marc," I say, nervously pulling away.

"Yeah?" he responds, closely scanning my face and cradling my hand.

I swallow hard and brush the stray hairs from my face. "I...I just don't know if we should be doing this right now?"

"You seem okay with it," he says, grinning.

I let out an uncomfortable laugh. "Well, yes, you're a tad difficult to resist at the moment, and I'm always much stronger with lipstick on." I make a feeble attempt at lightening the mood.

"Kat," he says and looks at me with an understanding expression, although, more like he's an adult who understands that they're talking to a child. "You had your break and you made your point. I know I was being an ass before - I get it. You don't have to resist anymore." He leans in again.

Of course Marc assumes I was simply trying to prove a point with my silly little games of *Lose My Number* and *We Are Through*. I should have known that he would find a way to make this all my doing.

"Well, yes, I do, actually," I say.

He pulls back, and now a concerned, semi-defensive expression replaces his confident one. "Are you seeing someone?" he asks with narrow eyes and disbelief.

I scoot backward one butt length. "Well, I just started, sort of... we're going out tomorrow."

Why did I just say that? This is why these early morning hours are reserved for sleeping and not conversing. I nod slightly and with trepidation, remembering that Marc's ego is not something to be toyed with.

"I see," he says and pulls further away from me. Easily three butt lengths.

"It's nothing serious—it's our first date actually," I say defensively. Why can't I just shut up?

"Okay," he looks down, clearly flustered.

I slap my leg. "Sorry, I'm not even sure why I said that. I just think it's late and maybe we shouldn't be sitting here making out on my couch regardless." For some reason I feel the need to console him, not wanting him to regret what he's just done.

"Yeah, sorry, I had a few too many at the wedding, I guess, and it was good to see you, and…I shouldn't have come here like this," he says and tousles my hair as he stands up.

"Marc, please don't take any of this the wrong way. It was really great to see you, and it's been way too long. Please don't be upset you came here tonight," I plead with him, truly not wanting to ruin the progress we'd made earlier in the evening.

"Thanks, Kat, I'll catch up with you later. Have fun tomorrow." He heads for the door and leaves almost as quickly as he came.

I lock the door behind him and crawl back into bed. Only forty-five minutes earlier I had been on cloud nine, reveling in my maturity where Marc was concerned and giddy about my upcoming date with Ryan. I lay quietly with my head on the pillow and one long, slow tear rolling down the side of my face.

CHAPTER NINE:
A Hot Meal

After last night's "study in dysfunction" as Julie would say, I have even more reasons to look forward to this evening. I debated whether or not to contact Marc and reiterate that there were no hard feelings, and that he shouldn't be remorseful about what happened. But knowing him as well as I do, he must want to strangle himself for letting his guard down like that. I think it's best to leave him alone for now.

Instead, I turn my attention to this evening's plan and spend all morning trying to decide what to wear. I know I will wear my hair down. That's a given for a first date. And since I'm almost never without a ponytail at the office, I think Ryan will appreciate the change. As for my outfit, I'm trying to convey "cute but casual." I decide on a pair of jeans with a black V-neck top. Pretty much the same combination I decide on regardless of the occasion, sadly, but one that I am most comfortable with.

I also have every intention of being on time, but it's now ten minutes to seven and I'm at least a fifteen-minute drive away. I grab my purse and spritz a little Bobbi Brown Beach on the back of my neck before heading out the door.

Once in my car, I get a text from Adam.

Let me guess ur late.
He texts.

On my way.
I reply.

Jeans and black shirt?
He asks.

F U
I reply.

Luv u, be safe, and I don't mean driving
He signs off.

It's only five past seven by the time I reach Ryan's apartment, and I consider that a huge victory. I park the car about a block away and walk to his building. There's no doorman, so I head straight to the keypad on the wall, search for his name, and wait to be buzzed in.

"Hello," Ryan calls over the intercom.

"Hey, Ryan, it's Kat," I say into the speaker.

"Come on up. It's 4B."

As I enter the elevator, my excitement kicks into high gear. I've been anxiously waiting for some time alone with him, so much so that I haven't properly imagined what I'll do with it. Despite what Adam said, I think dinner at Ryan's place is a great plan. This gives us so many more talking points than just sitting in a restaurant and being constantly interrupted by the wait staff.

I wind my way through the halls until I reach 4B. He's propped the door open with one of his large shoes, so I proceed to let myself in.

"Anyone home?" I announce my arrival as I cross the threshold and close the door behind me. There is a warmth to his home that I can sense immediately upon entering.

"Back here, Kat," he calls from the kitchen.

I head back through a long hallway and am quite impressed. It's an awesome oversized loft with vaulted ceilings, exposed brick, three-quarter walls, and a window of glass block looking into the bedroom. As I approach the enormous granite island he's standing behind, I can't help but notice how glorious he looks. He's wearing jeans and a royal blue long-sleeved cotton shirt with the sleeves pushed up to his elbows. His hair is still wet from the shower and his face is clean-shaven. As I make my way toward the kitchen, Ryan immediately comes over and gives me a kiss on the cheek. The closeness of his body sends a chill down my spine as I catch a whiff of his intoxicating cologne. I think I actually closed my eyes for a second.

"Glad you could make it, and right on time," he grins.

"Thanks for having me. What's on the menu?" I ask excitedly and strum my fingers on the shiny black countertop.

He glides back around the island to rejoin the food. "Well, my favorite thing to make is pizza, so I thought we'd start with that. It has gorgonzola and caramelized onions. Are you good with that?"

"I'm very good with that," I reply.

"Then I'm doing braised short ribs and polenta. I typically do a salad or vegetable with it, but I didn't want you to think I wasn't listening to you the other day," he remarks. "So I made homemade sourdough bread as a side."

"Thank you. Healthy foods actually have the opposite effect on me."

"Please have a seat," he gestures toward the four stools at the island. "Can I get you a drink?"

"I'd love one, what are you having?"

"I'm having a Fat Tire, but I have wine too. Name your poison."

"I'd love a Fat Tire, thanks."

"A girl that hates vegetables and loves Fat Tire. Mmm. Mmm. Good," he says to himself, but loud enough for me to hear. He then proceeds to un-cap two bottles and pour them one by one into a set of tall glass tumblers.

I take a sip of the cool, frothy ale. "Did your mom teach you how to cook so well?" I inquire.

"Ah….no. My mom does not cook, never has. She's mostly known for eating out and sending food back in restaurants."

"Yikes."

He takes one of his wooden pizza peels and wipes some loose cornmeal off with a dishtowel. "Don't get me wrong; I love my mom, but she can't toast a bagel."

"Well, then she and I should get along swimmingly!" I say.

"Are you Jewish?" he asks with a smirk, and puts the pizza peel away into a narrow cabinet next to the oven.

I hadn't seen that question coming this early on. "Is my answer going to affect the portion size of my entrée?" I need to know.

"It may," he says without flinching.

"No, I'm not Jewish. Is Ryan *Sullivan*?" I interrogate him back.

"Half, my mother is Jewish, and my father is Catholic." He pauses, reaches for two white ceramic plates, and sets them in front of me. "Which means I'm great with guilt - both giving and receiving."

"Well, you should know that I love a good lox platter," I say proudly.

"That's a start."

"So, now you're going to tell me that your mom wants you to marr…*date* a nice Jewish girl?" I twist my hair and pretend like I'm only mildly interested in his answer.

He gives me a funny look and tucks the corner of a dishtowel into the front of his jeans. "She has no say, and will be happy with anyone who can bear grandchildren. No pressure, of course," he reassures me and takes a sip of his beer.

"Just happy to have you married off one day?"

"Yes, she's been talking about it since I was six years old," he says in all seriousness.

"Really? That's awesome. Since you were six?" I confirm.

He places his hands on the island and leans toward me like he's about to tell a ghost story. "She used to sit me down on my bed and say:

Okay, Ryan, let's practice. It's a Sunday afternoon, and you're married. I want you to come by and see me for dinner, but your wife doesn't want to. What are you going to do?

'*I'll come by and see you, mom.*'

That's right angel, and what are you going to say to your wife who doesn't want to come by and see me for dinner?

'We're going to my Mom's for dinner.'

Perfect. Let's practice again...

I burst into laughter. "She didn't!"

"Would somebody make that up?" He looks straight at me shaking his head.

"Oh my God, that is hysterical. She sounds hilarious."

"That's one way of looking at it," he says and begins to place two pizzas in front of me. The greasy gorgonzola is bubbling like a witch's cauldron. The scent is rich and intoxicating. Much like Ryan's cologne.

"So how did you learn to cook like this? And where can I sign up?" I ask in awe.

"I just really enjoy it. I watch a lot of Food Network and different cooking shows and just sort of picked it up. Self-taught, I guess." He rolls a pizza cutter through the cheese and delicately lifts a piece onto an appetizer plate, then hands it to me.

I inhale the sweet & pungent aroma. "Somehow I'm guessing even a 48-hour food marathon wouldn't help me create anything close to this. You must really love doing it."

"I enjoy it. Especially when I have the chance to cook for other people. I think I like watching people enjoy my food as much as I like preparing it."

I sink my teeth into the piece. Is this guy for real? Great apartment, likes to cook, talented copywriter, and fan-fucking-tastic looking. If he starts fanning me with palm fronds after the meal, I'll know it's a dream. I'll simply wake up, feed my cat, and move along. Pretty much, I'm doomed for heartbreak and should do everything in my power to gather myself off the stool and run back through the hallway, down the elevator, and into my pathetic car without turning back. He is too good to be true and I just don't have this kind of luck with men.

Not surprisingly, I don't move. Instead I sit firmly planted on my stool as he presents me with course after course, each one richer, and more delicious than the next. It is quite charming to see how proud he is of each plate and how intensely he watches my face for a reaction to every bite. I notice during the third course that he's not eating nearly as much as I am, but it's too late for me to act all demure at this point. We finish the dinner and I debate whether he'll be complimented or appalled if I unbutton my jeans.

"Did you save room for dessert?" he tempts me as he clears the dishes.

I hate the thought of insulting him, almost as much as I hate turning down dessert, but I am beyond stuffed.

"Of course I did. However, the room won't be ready for a couple hours," I say.

"I understand." He laughs a little and begins to stack plates in the sink.

I finally get my butt off the stool and almost fall over due to the added weight. "Please let me help with those," I offer.

He steps in front of me and blocks me with his chest. "Kat, don't you dare set a foot behind this island. House rules."

"Gotcha," I say and raise my hands in arrest. "I will then gladly test-drive your couch if you don't mind."

"I insist," he says. "I won't be doing dishes either, they can wait."

He grabs another beer from the fridge and joins me on the couch. He's so much larger than me that it gives me a really safe, comfortable feeling having him by my side. His sleeves are still pushed up, exposing his forearms, and I can tell by those muscles alone that he is a force to be reckoned with.

"So how do you manage to stay in such great shape with all this cooking?" I ask.

"I like to run."

"Oh, like on the lakefront?"

He leans back and stretches his legs. "Yeah, sometimes. I try to run outside whenever possible," he says and shifts his body closer to me, but I'm not sure if it's intentional or not.

"Have you ever done any races or marathons?" I ask.

"I do the Chicago Marathon every year. How about you?" he asks in all seriousness, and it pains me to burst his optimism with my answer.

"I don't even like to drive twenty-six miles if I don't have to," I confess shamefully.

Ryan laughs as a potential date activity is squashed and then says, "I'll be sure and keep that in mind."

We sit together for an hour or so, talking and trading stories about our friends and families. His eyes are glued to mine the entire time, so much so, that I can hardly recall anyone in my whole life having listened to me that intently about anything.

"Would you like another?" He gestures to my empty beer glass.

"I think I'm good. One more and my first date etiquette goes down the tubes," I warn him.

"We wouldn't want that to happen." He raises an eyebrow.

"Nooooo, it could be tragic, as you may recall from our first encounter. Nothing good comes from me over-eating *and* over-drinking," I say with embarrassment, and reference the horrible debacle that was my blind date with his friend Pete.

"Hey, it happens to the best of us, and besides, that was the first time we met so it wasn't a complete loss," he says.

"That's such a shame," I say and bury my face in my hands.

"What?" He asks and pulls my hands back.

"Having that be your first impression of me."

He shakes his head slightly. "My first impression was the minute I saw you. You and Julie walked in and hadn't noticed us yet. I was immediately captivated."

I give him my best "you've got to be kidding me" face and then succumb to the compliment. "Okay, I'll have another beer."

He tilts his head to one side and leans back further into the couch. "I'm serious; I think I fell for you the second I saw you."

I'm looking at him, waiting for him to make some additional sarcastic comment, but it doesn't come. Obviously Dave must have told him how much I like him and he's trying to take advantage of it. What are the chances that in addition to the pre-existing laundry list of good qualities he has, that he would be unabashedly honest as well?

"Did Dave say something to you?" I have to know.

"About?"

"About me."

"What about you?"

"That I was interested in you," I say, hesitantly.

"Are you?"

"Isn't it painfully obvious?" I ask.

"It's not painfully anything, and no, Dave hasn't said a word. In fact, Dave and I have yet to discuss anything unrelated to work," he says, "but I'm glad to hear you're interested in me."

Ryan inches closer and gives me the most subtle, irresistible squinty grin. I lose myself in his green eyes and my heart starts peddling. He sits up off the back of the couch and puts one arm over me so that his entire body is in front of me and I'm joyfully trapped under his chest. We still have not looked away from one another. Just then I see his eyes start to slowly scan my face, and he takes one hand and runs it through my hair. Then, looking like I might be the dessert, he starts to scan my entire body. I am breathing so hard that my upper body is noticeably pulsating.

He wraps his arm around the small of my lower back and lays me down on his couch. Then he leans on one elbow, so as not to crush me, and places his lips on mine. I empty my lungs as he starts to kiss me. And as he has done twice before, Ryan Sullivan leaves me breathless.

CHAPTER TEN:
The Back Room

It's been a week since my heavenly homemade meal with Ryan, and thanks mostly to our place of employment, we've been inseparable ever since. Three of the five days we've eaten lunch together, and the other two he was out of the office on meetings all day. Adam, however, is not very happy to have lost me as a companion and keeps texting me pictures of empty chairs, so I've vowed to make more of an effort with him starting today.

"Want to grab lunch?" I ask as I approach Adam's desk.

"Nooner canceled?" he responds smugly.

"Very funny. No, in fact, he's out at a meeting with Dave."

Adam crosses his arms in his lap. "And so she comes crawling back."

"Shall I beg?" I ask.

"No need. You can show your love and appreciation during my birthday celebration tomorrow night."

Adam is turning twenty-nine this weekend and is nowhere near ready to enter his thirties. Dave has to be out of town for work on the night of his birthday, leaving Adam to deal with that disappointment as well. I try to assure him that Dave's absence will only up the ante on the gift he'll get, and that seems to brighten his spirits. Adam has arranged to have me and three of his other friends over for cake, cocktails, and then some clubbing to celebrate his favorite day of the year. Luckily for him, his birthday falls on a Saturday night, and a large portion of Boystown will be out celebrating as well. Boystown is a city neighborhood close to the lake and near the more widely recognized Wrigleyville area. It's also known as one of the largest gay communities in the country.

For some unknown reason, I rarely party with Adam and his friends. The majority of the time I spend with him is either verbally bashing people at the office or having him tag along with me and the gals. But, I've never been to a gay club before and I'm excited about this new endeavor with Adam and his friends.

Saturday night arrives and I'm late as usual. I show up at Adam's house with the obligatory bottle of wine and a wrapped scented candle from Neiman Marcus, since he's more concerned with what's on the outside of the box than what's on the inside. Adam and Dave live together in Dave's house, which is a three-story brownstone on North Dearborn. It's an enormous home for two people and was built sometime around the Great Chicago Fire. It even has a plaque out front giving it some sort of residential landmark status. Adam and I giggle every time we walk up the steps together. Dave bought the place for a bazillion dollars about ten years ago, gutted it, and watched it triple in value. The interior is much more contemporary than the outside and kept impeccably clean and organized. They even have a drawer in the kitchen with a compartmentalized tray, solely for mints and gum.

As soon as I arrive, I'm handed a shot of tequila before I can even get through the foyer. I didn't think I was that late, but it's clear everyone else has a head start on the cocktailing. Adam gives me a huge bear hug and introduces me around. John and Darryl I've met before, but Rick and I are just meeting for the first time.

Adam places his hands on my shoulders. "Don't be mad, but we're leaving," he informs me, then turns around.

"No cake?!" I ask with disappointment as I follow him into the kitchen.

"Sorry, angel, we started around five o'clock and we're more than ready to blow this joint," he calls over his shoulder.

"I'm sorry, but didn't you tell me to come at nine o'clock?"

"I did, but...blah, blah, blah, have a canapé," he says and shoves a tray under my nose. "Darryl already called for the cab."

I stuff a mini mushroom quiche in my mouth. "I can't get mad because it's your special day, but I'll have you know that a lady expects cake when she attends a birthday party."

He looks me over. "Let me know when one shows up." He winks and goes to grab his wallet and phone.

"So, did I tell you that Ryan asked me for plans tomorrow, and says he has a big surprise for me?"

Adam stops abruptly and throws up his arms. "Why are you telling me about other people's big surprises on *my* birthday?"

"Don't be a brat. I'm dying to know what it is!" I say excitedly. "Did Dave mention anything?"

"Don't get too excited is all I'll say," he says, forcing a yawn.

"Okay fine, I won't say another word about myself today." I shake my head.

"That's ma' girl. Now let me gather the other ladies and we'll get out of here."

John and Darryl have been friends of Adam's for a few years after they all met at the health club. John has a wild personality and lives for a good party. He's only about five feet six inches tall, but his personality makes him seem much larger, and he has a loud, scratchy voice that can be heard for miles. Adam is always asking him to use his indoor voice. Darryl is a little more on the professional side. He works in visual merchandising and is always impeccably dressed and groomed. He typically makes me wish I'd chosen a different outfit, regardless of what I'm wearing.

We all squeeze into one cab and a frenzy of cell phone activity begins. Texting, calling, Facebook posting. So much so that I casually check my phone so as not to be left out. Nothing.

The guys begin debating where to go and finally Adam decides on The Manhole, located right in the heart of Boystown. The cab lets us out in front and I immediately start whining about the two-block long line.

"Don't furrow your brow, little one," John says, putting his arm around my shoulders. "I bartend here part-time. We're going to waltz right in."

"Thank God, because if I'm not getting any action later I should at least get a little V.I.P. treatment tonight," I proclaim.

"Oh, you'll get it darling."

As promised, the five of us walk straight past the line of people waiting to get in, and as soon as we enter the bar area it's as if I've walked in on someone's family reunion. Adam and his friends know everybody here. I'm getting drinks bought for me, compliments handed to me, and my cheeks are pink from all of the kissing. I feel like a princess. I'd originally thought I would get the least amount of attention in the group. We make our way around the circular bar, chatting, greeting, laughing, drinking. Conversation is a little tough given the volume of the music but we're managing. After a while Darryl looks bored and suggests we hit The Back Room.

"You up for some real fun?" he asks me.

"Like watching *Pride and Prejudice* with a bottle of Pinot?" I joke and smile at Adam. It's our favorite film. "The Keira Knightly version!" Adam and I yell in unison, then high-five each other.

Darryl pretends to gag himself then grabs my right arm and starts dragging me forward, so I grab onto Adam with my left hand. We plow our way through the bodies, or torsos as it appears from my vantage point, and arrive at the impending Back Room. Standing at the entry is a muscular bouncer, with a long dark tunnel behind him and flashing white lights in the distance. Over his head is a large sign that reads *No Shirts Allowed*. One by one everyone in my group takes their shirts off and walks ahead leaving me overdressed and alone. I pause, point to the sign and give the bouncer a pathetic shrug with my shoulders. Like, does anyone really care if my shirt is off or on? I'm actually willing to take it off, and kind of want him to make me, but he waves me past with a minor look of disgust. Liquid nerves squashed, I trudge ahead, outfit intact, trying not to be offended.

When we reach the end of the walkway, I'm in shock. The room is enormous, and was so unassuming from the other end of the tunnel. I can hardly believe it. We're now standing in the middle of at least two hundred shirtless men. All gorgeous, all sweaty, and all in spectacular physical shape. The cliché is at least partly right: not sure the best guys are all married, but they are definitely gay. Out of curiosity, I spin around to see if there are any other women, let alone any other people wearing shirts. There are not. John jumps behind the bar to get us some more shots, and if the conversation was difficult in the main room, it is nearly impossible in The Back Room. Instead of chatting in vain, I choose to take in my surroundings because I can't imagine the next time I'll get up the nerve to come back here.

As I slowly glance about the place, dumbfounded by the sea of unattainable would-be-male-models, I turn my attention to the wall and become immediately slack-jawed. There in front of me on what has to be a regulation-size movie screen, is gay porn. Now, in my lifetime, I have seen very little hetero-porn, let alone gay porn...let alone fifty feet of it. Over the thunderous music I can sense my posse laughing at my reaction, but I can't seem to look away.

Look away, look away! I try and tell myself, but instead I keep staring with my eyes narrowed and my chin dipped slightly toward my right shoulder. I'm thinking this is a little inappropriate for a nightclub, but clearly no one else seems to be bothered or even distracted by it.

Just then a man wearing leather chaps and resembling Arnold Schwarzenegger circa 1983 approaches us and asks me to dance. This sends Adam and his friends into round two of hysterics. Flattered, I graciously accept. Arnold takes my hand and we hit the dance floor, which is basically the entire room, so my friends are never far away.

After about three songs, all of which sound exactly the same, I thank my half-naked suitor with a big sweaty hug and rejoin the boys. I'm feeling pretty buzzed by this time and keep checking my phone for a text message from Ryan.

Adam notices my desperate, twitchy behavior. "I don't think you can will it to ring," he says to me.

"I'm dying to text him."

"Of course you are, you've had eight shots," he states the obvious.

"What do you think? Should I text him?" I shout.

"Do you want what I think, or what you want to hear?"

"What I want to hear!" I grin.

"You should text him. He already knows you're easy, what's the difference?" he says. I give Adam a slap and decide to go for it.

Whatcha doin?
All I could come up with.

Not waiting for you to call me.
He responds.

Thank God I texted then.
I add.

Where are you?
He asks.

The Manhole. Wanna meet us??
I giggle to myself.

I was just there last night, no thx.
He replies.

Lots of naked men, you sure?
I taunt back.

I'm good, thx.
He texts.

What are u doing?
I ask again.

You asked me that already.
Ryan responds.

Oh yeah.
I say.

Come over.
He replies.

I immediately show the phone to Adam and he rolls his eyes. I love how Ryan just demanded it of me. Like, don't even bother asking or playing some stupid back and forth game of "what do you wanna do." I am now riding a major adrenaline buzz, and dying to leave these bodacious bodies and go find my own.

"Buh-bye!" Adam says with a wave and a smile.

"Are you mad?" I ask.

"Mad? I'm jealous. Dave won't be back until Tuesday. Get your ass in a cab and call me in the morning - better yet, make that the afternoon," he tells me and gives me a squeeze.

I wave goodbye to the boys and blow kisses as I make my way out of the Back Room and into a cab. I'm feeling pretty good at this point, yet I never bothered to check myself in the mirror before leaving the bar. I can tell that the dancing has left my hair all sweaty at the roots, and that any trace of lipstick probably disappeared hours ago. I wipe under the bottom of my eyelids just in case I have black liner smeared all over.

The cab drops me off in front of Ryan's building, and I head inside to ring the buzzer. There's a mirror on the wall in the foyer that I regretfully glance at before moving on. I'm a wreck, hair, makeup, and clothes. I try not to even think about what I must smell like either - a winning combination of sweat, B.O., cologne, perfume, and triple-sec. I adjust my posture and ring the buzzer.

"Hello," Ryan says over the intercom.

"It's me, but I'm debating whether I should show my face up there or not," I yell back.

"Who is this?"

"You're very funny, but honestly, you actually may not recognize me."

"Come on up," he says as the door buzzes open.

I walk down the hallway to his apartment and see that he hasn't left his door propped open like before. Gonna make me wait for it this time. I knock on the door quietly because it's about one o'clock in the morning, and I don't want to alert his neighbors to my trampy behavior. The door opens and Ryan is standing there wearing nothing but a pair of sweatpants. I nearly fall over backward.

"You know, this look you're sporting is all the rage at the Manhole," I say, unable to take my focus off his sculpted abdomen.

"I hadn't realized that," he says, and waits about four seconds before speaking again. "Come on in."

I follow Ryan into his living area and he takes my hand and leads me to the couch.

"So, you guys had fun?" he asks as we both sit.

"We did. Adam and his friends are an adventure. I hope I didn't wake you," I say.

"You did, but I was hoping to hear from you."

"Oh good, glad to oblige."

He still has his hand on mine as we sit staring at each other for a few moments. My drunken hormones are a little over-anxious so I trash the niceties, lean toward him and go in for the kiss. Neither of us is looking for witty banter at this hour. He immediately meets my lips and we start to make-out feverishly on his couch. Before I know it, he's lying on top of me, kissing me and lightly pulling the back of my hair while moving his other hand all over my body. So many things are intoxicating me that I can hardly think straight. His skin is so smooth and warm against mine, I can't keep my hands off of him. We continue for about an hour, rubbing, kissing, head grabbing, more kissing, tongue, no tongue. He has a little more stubble than normal, given the time of day and my face is starting to feel raw. We both decide to halt things before they go too far - which I would have let them, no doubt. I appreciate that he's able to exert a little maturity and suggest we get some sleep.

Before heading to bed, I go to the bathroom, and as predicted, my face has lost a layer of skin for sure. I have a horrible reddish/pink color from all the chafing and my lips are barely even visible anymore. He comes up behind me and hugs my waist as I'm standing at the mirror gently touching my cheeks.

"Sorry about the stubble. I'll be more careful next time," he says apologetically.

"Sorry? Don't be silly, it's like a free micro-derm treatment. The gals pay top dollar for this abuse."

He smiles and hands me a University of Michigan T-shirt. "Here, I thought you might want something to wear."

"I went to Illinois, do you have anything else?" I playfully toss the shirt back to him.

"Nope," he answers, and throws it over his shoulder leaving me to go shirtless unless I decide to go fetch that one. Which I do.

"Alrighty then, U. of M. it is," I retrieve the shirt from the floor behind him. "By the way, any chance you're tired enough to spill the beans on the surprise tomorrow?" I give it a shot.

"Well, since you asked...no."

Rats.

I glance at the clock, two fifteen in the morning. It's been a long night, but I'm a little sad to see it end. He's already in his bed half asleep by the time I return to the bedroom and he immediately rotates his body and wraps his long arms around me once I crawl in next to him. His size is at least twice mine and I'm quite pleased at how nicely my smaller frame fits perfectly within his, with the top of my head tucked under his chin and his legs extended way past mine. I'm guessing he's probably had a king-sized bed since grade school. Unlike me, with my twin-sized fiasco and century-old Laura Ashley bedding.

"I'm glad you're here, Kat." He places one last kiss on the top of my head and falls right to sleep. Not bad for a second date.

CHAPTER ELEVEN:
Way Better Than First Base

Ryan's surprise for me is two tickets to the Cross Town Classic, where the Chicago White Sox play the Chicago Cubs. Having never been to a major league baseball game, I'm looking forward to bleacher seats and hot dogs, but he informs me that isn't going to be the case. Dave gave Ryan two tickets to the game for all his hard work on the Bellagio account, and he tells me that they are in a special "Scout" seat section. And by special I mean free pre-game buffet, free booze, free dessert buffet, and free snacks and cocktails throughout the entire game. Unlimited hot dogs, and beer from a keg backpack, what more could a girl ask for? Ryan also tells me that I'm actually his third choice as a recipient of this "golden" ticket, but his best friend and father are out of town.

"It's a complete tragedy that your first White Sox game is the Cross Town Classic - in the Scout Seats. If anyone finds out I let you have this, they may not let me back into U.S. Cellular Field," he says soon after we wake.

"I promise to root, root, root for the home team until my throat is sore!" I place my right hand over my heart. "And just so Dave knows how appreciative I am, I will make it my personal goal to eat and drink as much free food that is available to me. Even the peanut shells." I lick my lips just thinking of the crunchy salt.

"Okay, the team is counting on you."

"Fear not, I will personify the term fair-weathered fan better than anyone. And more importantly," I add as I attempt to run my fingers through the bird's nest atop my head. "I'm going to need to borrow a baseball hat."

Ryan rolls his eyes. "How do I know I'm going to regret this?"

We head to the game in my car because our Scout tickets also come with a V.I.P. parking pass. Traffic is horrific, but once we get close to the ballpark and start waving our fancy pass around, it's like the parting of the Red Sea. We drive past all the lots reserved for common folk, all of the season ticket holder lots, and pull up right in front of the ballpark. Had we parked closer to the field, we would have mowed down the concession stands.

"This is awesome," I say, simply giddy over our celebrity parking space and proximity to home plate.

"I've never seen anyone get this excited over a parking spot."

"Seriously, if we get no other perks than this, I'll be thrilled."

"I'll keep that in mind." He takes my hand and we enter the stadium through an iron gate reserved for Scout seat ticket holders… and perhaps royalty.

Once inside, we're ushered to a large dining room with tables everywhere, flat screens littering the walls, and a huge bar that runs the length of the space. Predictably there are signed jerseys, photographs, and loads of White Sox memorabilia scattered about the walls. A woman greets us at the hostess stand and shows us to a table. I look over at Ryan and see that he has slipped into his own state of euphoria, and a bright internal light has illuminated his green eyes.

"This is like the best day of your life, right?" I smile and pat him on his shoulder after we take our seat at the table.

"You have no idea how great these tickets are."

"Are you going to cry?" I ask, trying to tease him.

"If they win, maybe."

"Oh, I'll be cheering for sure now." I clap my hands. He seriously cannot keep from smiling. "Try and stop smiling, just see if you can," I challenge him. He lowers the corners of his mouth. "Nice try, but your cheeks are still elevated," I say.

"I imagine I'll only stop smiling if they start losing. But quite frankly, this is one of the coolest days of my life so far," he says, eyes squinty.

"Well, I know I wasn't your first choice..."

"You weren't," he reminds me, still smiling.

"I know, but if you'll let me finish—rude—I am thrilled to be here. This is really awesome, and I love seeing you all *guy smiley* like this," I comment as the waitress places two bottles of Miller Lite on the table.

Ryan takes a sip, then consoles me. "I'm just teasing you about the third choice stuff, I'm glad you're here," he says.

Just as the game is about to get underway, we head for our seats, and when we enter the stadium we are so unbelievably close to the field, I can almost reach out and grab a blade of grass.

"You look like you've never been to a ball game before," I say. "Seriously, what grade are you in?" I giggle at his boyish charm.

"Kat, you have no idea what it means to walk into U.S. Cellular Field and watch the Sox beat the Cubs." He turns to face me. "They will beat the Cubs," he repeats and then plants a quick hard kiss on my head. "I'm usually way up in the nose bleed section."

I spin around to observe the other fans soaking up this age-old rivalry. As gender would have it, I wasn't a big baseball fan growing up, and the only time I ever watched any games on TV was with Marc. Who, ironically, is a huge Cubs fan. A word that I wouldn't dare utter within five miles of Ryan unless I am looking to be scalped.

The game officially begins with the singing of the National Anthem, a moment that has brought almost all of the men in the crowd to tears. I can feel the sense of honor and importance that this game and these teams mean to everyone. The competition is palpable, and I do not envy the brave Cubs fans that have come here to support their team all decked out in red and bright blue. They stand out as much as I did in the Back Room, only no one here is going to extend them an ounce of kindness.

I point them out to Ryan. "Wouldn't want to be with them."

"Winning is the best revenge," he replies.

"Well put." I want to hold his hand but I decide to leave any P.D.A. initiative to him. Instead, I devour my first bag of free popcorn. Just then

I feel my phone vibrate. I pause for a second, wondering if cell phones are unsportsmanlike at U.S. Cellular Field. I wouldn't want to make Ryan's choice of companion look any more like a rookie than she already does. I pull it slowly from my front pocket and take a quick peek.

I need ur car.
Adam texts me.

No can do.
I say.

WTF??!!
He demands to know.

At the game!!!!!!
I reply.

What game?
He asks.

The cross town classic.
I type.

WTF?
He says.

THE WHITE SOX GAME!!
I laugh to myself.

I need your car.
He repeats.

I'm with Ryan and free beer, no can do.
I shake my head at his defiance.

You must be thrilled, black is the team color.
He texts.

Quite.
I answer.

Call me at halftime.
He signs off.

"What are you doing?" Ryan busts me on my phone.
"Uh, nothing...checking the time?" My head sinks.
"Kat, the phone stays put away, eyes on the field."
"Sir, yes, sir." I roll my eyes to myself. I mean, the place is owned by a cell phone company for God's sake.

Paul Konerko is the first to bat for the White Sox and the place goes bananas as he steps up to the plate. PAULY! PAULY! PAULY! The ballpark is vibrating with an energy like nothing I have ever experienced before, but as soon as the first pitch clears the plate and it's a strike, you can hear a pin drop. Pitch two is a strike. Pitch three is a foul. Pitch four is also fouled. Then comes pitch five, apparently exactly what he was waiting for because the guy smacks it straight down center field and right into the bleachers for a home run out of the gate. You would have thought the 35,000 plus people here tonight have just won the lottery because the eruption of sound and fury could rival the Colosseum in its heyday. In that moment, Ryan lifts me off my feet and into the air like a rag doll, then presses his lips on mine for the most vigorous, enthusiastic, sportsmanlike kiss I've ever received. Baseball is my new favorite pastime. My head is filled with infatuation, and I start to obsess less about the free snacks, and more about the man standing next to me. Whether he believes it or not, I am honored to be here with him, and I do not take lightly the gravity of these seats and what this game means to him. The fact that I'm here, sharing in this moment, brings a huge, cheesy grin to my face. I haven't felt this happy in a long time.

I feel my phone pulsating in my pocket again, so I grab it quickly to silence Adam once and for all, but see that it's Julie calling me instead. I hit ignore, and shove it back in my pocket. My pulse is racing faster than it was moments ago, and I'm doing everything in my power not to show my change in mood.

It vibrates again, this time it's a text from her.

Where r u?
She asks.

If I answer, then I will have to come up with a lie, and sit here texting lies during the game. Thus annoying Ryan, and lying to Julie. If I ignore her, I will have to come up with a lie later on. Either way I have to lie, and I think it's better that Ryan not be with me when I do. I finally shut off my phone and wave down the hot dog vendor.

CHAPTER TWELVE:
Coffee and a Stud Muffin

Monday morning there's a blueberry muffin and a note waiting for me in my cubicle when I arrive at work. Next to it is a Post-it that simply reads: *Good Morning – Ryan.* I'm marveling at the note when Adam pops his head over the wall.

He reads it over my shoulder. "And a good morning from me as well."

"Pretty cute, huh?" I say proudly and wave the note like a flag before saving it in a desk drawer.

"Whatever," he snips and sits on my desk.

"You're just jealous because there's no love pastry on your desk this morning," I say.

Adam crosses his arms. "You never called me back yesterday and I needed your car."

"I'm sorry, but my car was parked at the Field of Dreams."

Adam leans back, crushing a stack of papers behind him. "Well, Dave came home earlier than planned and I was able to get where I needed to go without your help," he says. "You can buy lunch today and make it up to me."

"I can't, I'm supposed to meet up with Megan. Now can I please have possession of my desk?"

"In a minute," he continues. "So, did you have fun going out with me and the boys on Saturday or what?"

"Honestly, I had a blast. It was way more of an ego-boost than I had imagined! I hope you had a fabulous birthday," I say and tilt my chin downward. "Aren't you going to ask me how the Sox game was?"

"What game?" he asks in all seriousness.

I slap his knee in order to extricate Adam from my desk and he plops down on my floor instead. "Goodbye!" I hint loudly. "I need to commence my work day," I say and turn my attention to the computer. "Brooke has been in an evil mood for the past week, and I think she's about had it with my office romance. If she sees you over here having a picnic, I'm a dead woman."

"I'm just hiding out so Maureen from H.R. doesn't chat with me on the way to her office. Her stale coffee breath is certain to reawaken my hangover from yesterday."

I begin checking my emails and notice one that looks scarily familiar. "Uh oh, I have an email from Marc." Adam and I exchange raised-brow expressions. "Talk about hangover."

"See, it's a good thing I'm here." Adam leaps to his feet and nearly shoves me out of the way with his shoulder. "What does it say?"

"I didn't read it yet, moron. Move!" I yell and push him away. "I'm a little scared."

"Of what? He's not standing here…you move," Adam wheels my chair out of the cubicle with me in it and proceeds to open the email. I roll my chair back to him with my heels as fast as I can.

Adam reads aloud.

Kat, I have wanted to talk to you since the night after the wedding. I know email isn't the most mature way of communicating, but it's just easier for me right now. Hope you understand. Like I mentioned, I've been thinking about you a lot lately and the past couple weeks have been no different. I wanted to know if we could get together and talk about things in person. Let me know when you can meet.

~Marc

"Such Monday morning fun we're having!" Adam exclaims.

I break into a cold sweat and slump down into my chair. "Wow, I wasn't expecting that today," I shake my head.

"What night is he talking about, the wedding?" he asks me.

"Yes and no," I confess. "He came over to my apartment that night after the wedding a few weeks ago."

Adam begs for more information. "And?"

"And, he kissed me. Then I stopped him and he left with his tail between his legs," I say, scrolling back to the top of his email.

"Why am I just hearing about this?"

"I don't know. It was the night before my first date with Ryan, and I was just trying not to think about Marc I guess - or you for that matter."

"Rude."

I swivel around to face Adam. "So now what? I have to see him," I say, looking for answers in Adam's expression.

"No you don't. You've moved on."

I nervously twist the ends of my ponytail with my fingers. The mere sight of Marc's name on an email makes me uneasy. "Well, I can't really just send that back in a reply. That's a little cold don't you think?" I ask.

Adam puts his hands on my shoulders and looks down at me. "I'm sorry, little one, but this is nothing new with Marc. The only difference between now and every other time he's toyed with your affection is that there is someone else in the picture this time. Someone you are wild about and who's obviously wild about you." He points to the pastry that Ryan left for me. "So, maybe this is the opportunity that you've always wanted but never had before. Tell Marc that you and your muffin have met someone else and moved on."

I sigh heavily, knowing that I've never had the strength to reject Marc before, so why should this time be any different. "True or not, I can't imagine having the strength to say that to him."

"It isn't going to be easy, darling," he says as he checks his phone. "I have to run, so blind c.c. me on the email reply to Marc," he says on his way out.

I roll my eyes.

The next email I have is from Julie. Thank God Adam has left my cube. I read it in solitude.

Tried to reach you all day yesterday! What gives? Call me at work.

-J

I respond immediately.

Sorry about that, Blackberry issues. I will call you when Brooke leaves. Just got an email from Marc. He wants to talk.

-Kat

That should divert her attention from my disappearing act yesterday. This charade can't go on for much longer. Never in my life have I lied to Julie, let alone avoided her like this. My temples begin to pulsate just thinking about it.

I spend the next ten minutes focusing on the email from Marc and formulating a reply. I shake my throbbing head at the fact that just when I meet someone new, and attempt to put my relationship with Marc behind me, he comes back all sweet and considerate like I wanted him to be months ago. I don't have it in me to send some rejection letter back to him. I will meet with him and discuss things in person. He deserves that. I reply:

Hey Marc,

Good to hear from you. I would love to get together and chat. Pretty much any day this week after work, besides Friday, is good for me. Does tomorrow work for you? If so, I can meet you at the Starbucks by my apartment around 6:00pm.

-K

I will see him tomorrow and take care of things. Now I begin to feel somewhat relieved that I had the chance to tell him about my date with Ryan weeks ago. Even though it seemed like a bad idea at the time, at least I won't have to break it to him tomorrow. Just then my phones rings and it's Megan.

"This is Kat," I answer.

"Well, hello, Kat," she mocks me. "Can you still do lunch today?"

"I believe I can, and I've got lots to fill you in on." I plant the gossip seed this time, so she'll be sure and keep her marital angst to herself.

"Do tell!" she demands.

"Not until lunch. You can't break me today, I have to go. Work, work, work."

"You suck. Fine, meet me at Panera at twelve thirty."

"Perfect, see you there."

I hang up the phone and fight the urge to walk over to Ryan's office and chat. The more intimate we get, the more I worry about office snoops, so I decide to text him instead.

Thx for the muffin!
I say.

My pleasure.
He replies.

Busy?
I ask.

A little, come see.
He says.

Will do.
Screw the snoops.

I walk over to Ryan's office and pass Adam's desk on the way. He's on the phone and gives me an animated wink as I breeze by him. Ryan is also on the phone when I arrive, so I take a seat in one of the chairs across from his desk. He smiles at me.

"Shut the door," he mouths as he finishes up his call.

I close the door behind me, and within seconds I have a text from Adam.

Niiiiiiice.
He texts, clearly enjoying himself.

Get to work.
I send back.

Any more love pastries in there?
He asks.

Ryan hangs up the phone and leans back in his chair. He looks typically spectacular this morning, wearing a navy dress shirt with a pair of khaki pants. His sleeves are pushed up past his elbows, and his skin looks freshly scrubbed and smooth. I can't help but blush as he's staring at me.

"I have to go to Vegas with Dave on Wednesday," he says and stretches his back.

"What for?" I ask.

"We're presenting the new Bellagio creative. Dave says they're putting each of us up in our own suite."

"Sweet," I say. "Yes, well Adam and I are going to Gurnee Mills Outlet Mall, so take that."

He laughs. "We get back on Friday night. Are you available?"

"I will be." I nod.

"Perfect, I'm looking forward to it."

"Me too, although the week isn't going to be much fun around here now. Try not to gamble away all the money you'll be spending on me Friday night."

"I'll do my best." He places his phone in his front pocket and then lets out a concerned sigh, "Okay, you, I really should get some of this copy done, and it's not going to happen with you in here."

"Gotcha. Come find me later if you get bored," I say and head back to my desk. Adam waves me over as I'm about to pass him.

"How can I help you?" I ask as I saunter toward him.

"What's going on behind closed doors?"

"None of your busy-bodyness."

"Well, I'd be more than happy to cover for you if you need me."

"Thanks, perv," I say and walk away.

When I get back to my desk there's another email from Marc:

See you tomorrow at 6.

Marc

So it's settled, Marc has confirmed our meeting at Starbucks and I will have to be a big girl and tell him about my relationship with Ryan.

The morning is going pretty quickly. Brooke seems preoccupied with berating two of the accounting interns, so I'm able to hibernate in my cube and make a dent in my workload before lunchtime. I always try to avoid Brooke at all costs when she's in a bad mood. When lunchtime rolls around, I send Ryan a quick email saying I'm meeting Megan at Panera Bread for lunch and sneak out without Brooke noticing.

Megan is waiting for me when I arrive, without Miles this time.

"Where's Milo?" I ask, slightly disappointed not to see my bald nephew.

"I have a sitter today."

"That's nice, good for you. Anything else fun planned besides lunch with me?"

"Oh yes, let's see…Target, Costco, and ooooh I also need to get gas and stop by the bank. Does any of that count as fun?" she questions me.

"Honestly, it sounds better than dealing with Brooke lately and being trapped in my gray cube all afternoon."

She takes a sip of her Diet Coke then waves her hand excitedly. "So what's going on with you? What's the scoop? It has to do with Marc, doesn't it?"

Where do I even begin? So much has happened since the last time she and I sat down to talk, I'm not even quite sure I can properly update her in forty minutes. I start with the wedding, since she knew how nervous I was to see Marc that night. I then proceed to tell her about how he came by my apartment afterward and I sent him packing. All the while she's cringing for him and giving me some great semi-supportive facial expressions. She never interrupts though, saving her commentary for later. Then I break the news about Ryan. I describe how irresistible he is, and how much better the office atmosphere has been with a little sexual tension around. She's smiling and applauding as I'm describing our first date and subsequent rendezvous. However, her mood shifts when I divulge that Ryan is, or was, formally referred to as The Chef, and that the night I met him he was with Julie…and

I was with his friend, Pete. Megan raises a hand, "I'll get to Marc in a minute, but how does Julie feel about all this?" she poses the obvious question.

"She's fine," I lie and pick at my salad.

"Really?" she asks. "Wow, that's impressive for her."

I shake my head. "I'm lying. She doesn't know. I haven't said anything to her about it yet."

"Why not?" she wonders with genuine concern.

I scratch my forehead. "Good question. I'm just being a massive wimp, I guess."

"Kat, you *have* to say something to her. What if she were to see the two of you out somewhere?"

"I know, I know. I figured you'd say something like that, and trust me, it's tearing me up. I just really like him and I'm nervous. I know I have to tell her," I say. "I initially thought they weren't dating anymore and then I find out that Julie might still be interested in him, even though Ryan isn't interested in her."

Megan gives me a familiar sisterly glare. "The sooner you say something the better you'll feel, Kat. And if you really like him, do it sooner than later," she reaches out and pats my hand. "So, what about Marc?"

"Well that's my second source of queasiness this fine Monday." I sigh. "I hadn't even heard from him since the wedding a few weeks ago, until this morning. He emailed me about two hours ago and wants to get together tomorrow and talk," I tell her.

"Uh oh."

"Yeah. So I agreed to meet him at Starbucks after work."

"And?" She stares at me.

"And what?"

"And what are you thinking? Are you prepared to let go of everything you have with Marc for this new guy? You've been praying that Marc would come to his senses, Kat, and maybe he has. Do you really want to start over with someone new before you give your relationship with Marc another chance?"

I unnecessarily check my phone in hopes of evading the bevy of disparaging questions she just coughed up. A moment of silence passes as I resist the urge to answer her with a defensive dissertation. "Well, I don't even know what he has to say." I shrug my shoulders, hoping to leave it at that.

"I'm sure he's going to want to get back together. Why else would he want to see you in person? Especially after you squashed his booty call the night of the wedding," she says.

I reach for my wallet, and try to think of any other visual cue that might end this meal. "Who knows what he wants. His email said he's been thinking about me a lot, and I think he feels badly about the way we left things between us after the wedding, but who knows with him."

"You're the one that should feel badly."

My body tenses. "Why should I feel bad?" I snap as my tolerance for her advice hits a new low.

"Because he put himself in a vulnerable position and you made him feel like a fool."

I place my purse in my lap, and rest my hands on it. "Megan, I know you're trying to help," I say with a dollop of sarcasm, "but what was I supposed to do? He came over in the middle of the night and caught me in a vulnerable position of my own. He clearly is not mortified by what happened that evening, so please stop trying to make me feel like shit about it."

She pauses to sip her drink. "Well, you're right about one thing, I'm just trying to help," she says flatly, taking offense to my defense. "Kat, you and Marc have a long history and possibly even a long future. I just don't want to see you throw it away for someone you just met. I have seen Marc grow over the years, and all I'm saying is that maybe the time apart from you has made him finally appreciate what he had."

"Well, maybe it's too late. Maybe I shouldn't have had to end our relationship in order for him to realize that. This has been hard on me too, but for the first time I decided to stop feeling sorry for myself, and step out of my comfort zone," I say and look to her for validation. "And you know what? There's something special about Ryan that I'm not willing to give up on, just because Marc decides he wants what he can't have."

Megan reaches over the table and conveys her support with a squeeze of my hand. "You better call me the *second* you walk out of Starbucks," she demands.

"Get in line." I sigh.

CHAPTER THIRTEEN:
Too Little Too Latte

The next morning, Ryan asks me if I want to grab dinner after work since he's leaving for Vegas tomorrow, but I have to turn him down because I'm meeting Marc for coffee. Not only did I have to say no to Ryan, but I had to lie to him too. I still couldn't bring myself to talk about Marc with him. At first, I didn't want my ex-boyfriend to seem like baggage, and now I don't want that baggage to seem like some sort of threat. I always thought that if Ryan ever did ask me about my past relationships, I would be honest about everything - but so far he hasn't asked.

At the end of the day I go looking for Adam and find him sitting in Dave's office. I poke my head in and greet both of them.

"Hello, short one," Adam says.

"Am I interrupting?" I ask Dave.

"Never, come on in," he says and gestures to the empty seat next to Adam.

Adam puts his feet up on my lap as soon as I sit down. "Why don't you tell Uncle Dave about all your love troubles, Kitty?" Adam says.

I shoot Adam a dirty look. I'm never quite as at ease around Dave as Adam is yet he never seems to take that into consideration.

"Oh, please, like he doesn't already know every uninteresting detail," Adam announces.

I turn to Dave and my cheeks go flush from embarrassment. Dave is always very professional, but he does his best to make me feel comfortable during most of Adam's tirades.

Dave smiles at me, his hands folded in his lap. "So, you and Ryan?" He feels obligated to comment.

"I hope we aren't sending H.R. into a panic," I say attempting to laugh it off.

"Not as far as I know," he says. "He's a good guy, Ryan. I've known him for many years."

"You have?" Adam and I both say in unison.

Dave lets out a small snicker. "Yes, I have."

"Spill it," Adam says to him.

"There's not much to spill. He used to work at an agency that I did freelance work for a few years ago, and I always thought he was a great writer and a real stand-up guy. I'm actually a bit surprised by all this because I remember him as being kind of shy and keeping to himself mostly. I will say he's always grabbed the ladies' attention, so to speak," Dave said with a nod.

A pang of jealousy rings in my head.

"How the hell old is this guy?" Adam questions Dave.

"Early thirties, I guess," Dave answers. "He was just starting out when I met him."

Adam looks astonished for no real reason. "Well, who knew?"

"Way to hold out, Dave," I say.

"Sorry, I didn't think it was my place," he says.

Adam removes his feet from my lap and reaches for his cell phone. "Well, Kat's off to meet with her ex-boyfriend right now anyway," he announces.

"Oh?" Dave questions me, feigning interest.

"It's nothing all that interesting." I stand and excuse myself. "You and Ryan have a great trip to Vegas tomorrow."

Dave gives me a consoling glance. "You want me to keep an eye on him for you?"

I shrug my shoulders. "Whatever you think is right, Dave."

"I don't think you have anything to worry about, Kat. If he's expressed any interest in you, I'm sure it's genuine."

I nod my head. "Thanks, Dave."

Adam smiles proudly at his man, and I marvel at their rapport.

By the time I reach Starbucks it's twenty minutes past six o'clock, and I figure Marc will be about ready to kill me. He hates when I'm late. Over the years it's been one of his biggest points of contention with me. I rush through the front doors of Starbucks, spot him immediately and greet him with a weary, apologetic look that he's seen a thousand times. Usually he shakes his head in disapproval and gives me the silent treatment for a good five minutes, but this time he stands up when he sees me and gives me a kiss on the cheek.

"Hey there," he says.

"Sorry," I apologize. "I couldn't decide whether to take the bus or not and then once I decided not to, I couldn't get a cab."

"Where's your car?" he asks.

"I loaned it to Adam. He needed to run some errands."

"Can I get you anything?" he offers before sitting back down.

I decline with a shake of my head.

I join him at the table and we both adjust our posture in our chairs for a few seconds before he continues.

"So how was your first date?" Marc can't resist asking.

I glance down at the table. "It was fine."

"Good, good, that's good," he says watching me intently. "Well, I didn't come here to talk about that," he says and clears his throat. "Like I mentioned, I've been thinking a lot during our time apart and I know it's been hard on both of us. I thought about how you said I was acting distant a few months ago, and you were right. I'm sorry. I've been going through a lot of crap at work, and I wasn't giving you the attention you deserve."

"It's okay, Marc," I say.

"Well it obviously wasn't okay, and you had every right to be frustrated with me. There were a hundred times I wanted to call you, but I thought I should get my head straight first - to be fair to you. I could tell you were suffering and I never meant to hurt you like that." He takes a sip of his coffee. "I only hope I haven't waited too long to get my shit together."

I shift my eyes away from him, not knowing how to respond. Seeing Marc is almost indescribable. It gives me an immediate sense of comfort. He represents almost everything that brings me peace and safety, and today is no different. Except that today is different - today I have moved on. Today I have already begun to find solace in someone else, but the thought of banking on Ryan is almost as terrifying as the thought of losing Marc forever.

My throat is parched and I regret not at least getting a glass of water. "I don't know if it's too late, but I just don't think I'm ready to jump back into things the way they were," I say.

"I don't want things to be like they were either, Kat. That's what I'm trying to say to you. We're both in a better place now, and we've had some time to see what we really want, and I want to take things to the next level. Let's get back on track, let's go away together. I think we need that," he says.

I look into his eyes this time. Marc's engaging personality and good looks are what initially drew me to him so many years ago, and his boyish charm hasn't faded one bit. The original Backward Baseball Cap frat boy. An irresistible flirt with a knack for breaking hearts and taking names. How could I let him slip away? I hear Megan's voice ringing in my head, saying *"Give him another chance, he deserves it."*

I sink lower into my chair. "Marc, believe me, I was desperate to have this conversation months ago," I say and do my best to convey my sincerity. "But things have changed."

He gives me a stern look and cocks his head to one side. "Are you still seeing that first date guy?" he asks in disbelief.

"Yes."

Just then, like a flash bulb, Julie appears at our table. "Well, hello!" she squeals, her voice purring with curiosity.

Surprised, Marc and I both turn to face her.

I jump to my feet and give her a hug. "Julie, what's up?"

"You kiddies tell me," she says and leans down to give Marc a kiss.

"How's it going, Julie?" he greets her.

She ponders and nods. "Things are good, thank you, nice to see you two spending a little caffeinated, quality time together."

I sit back down and muster a smile. "Are you headed home?" I ask, desperate for some air and a reason to get out of there.

"Nope, I'm headed to the grocery, just popped in for a mocha frap," she says. "I think I hear them calling my name, but I couldn't resist stopping by this little party," she turns to Marc. "Lovely to see you, Marc. Kat, call me when you get home."

She scurries away just as quickly as she'd arrived, and my lungs deflate. I dab my brow trying to make it look as though I'm brushing some loose hairs out of my face instead of wiping off the beads of sweat.

Marc glares at me as if Julie was never there. "Kat, what are you doing? How serious is it with this guy?" He doesn't miss a beat with his questions, and his tone is much less polite than two minutes ago.

"Well, he and I have been hanging out a lot. He works with me, at the agency."

Marc manages to stay calm and folds both hands around the bottom of his coffee cup. "I see. Well, I guess I did wait too long."

"It's only in the early stages," I backpedal.

"You don't have to make excuses," he says and backs his chair away from the table.

I've done it again. I've squashed his ego. "I know, it's just that I'm not sure what else to say. It's hard hearing all this from you right now."

"Sorry, I guess I wasn't aware of the time limit you'd imposed. I should've asked if you were with someone else before laying all this on you," he says as the regret starts to consume him, yet again.

"Marc, please," I say and place my hand on the table, reaching out to him. "I have waited so long for you to come around. It's just..."

"Bad timing," he cuts me off and stands.

"Marc," I utter his name in an attempt to lure him back into the chair.

He gives me an awkward salute with his right hand. "I understand. Thanks for coming to meet me."

"Of course," I say as he turns his back on me and walks away, leaving me dumbstruck in Starbucks.

As I grab my purse and make my way to the door, tears begin to well up in my eyes. I simply can't contain them and start to cry softly to myself as I step outside. I go to wipe my eyes with the back of my hand and when I look up I see Adam leaning against the side of the building with his arms extended.

"Come to Adam," he offers. "You didn't think I'd let you go it alone, did you?" He embraces me as I soak the front of his shirt. "Do you want to talk about it?" he asks my hair.

"I just hope I did the right thing," I mumble.

"I'm sure you did." We hug, dry my eyes and head to my car.

FLASH! Julie comes running up to us from across the street. "What the hell?!"

"Hello, darling," Adam welcomes her nonchalantly as if he expected to see her there.

I wipe off the runny makeup under my eyes. "Marc wanted to have a talk and discuss where things stand with us. He wants to get back together," I inform the two of them.

"Wow, what'd you say?" she asks.

"I said I wasn't ready, and that I had to think about it. And he wasn't all that pleased with my reply."

She crosses her arms. "Well, well, well, look at you playing hard to get. I'm very impressed," she says and looks at Adam in amazement. "I must say, I thought you would've caved for sure."

"Our little girl's all grown up." He feigns choking-up.

Julie turns back to me. "I can't believe you didn't fill me in on all this. Why didn't you tell me you'd heard from him?" She slaps my arm.

Just then it occurs to me that I hadn't even told Julie about what transpired with Marc after the wedding. Perhaps I've been more preoccupied than I've realized. "I don't know, I'm sorry, work's been busy and..."

Adam cuts in. "The maturation process has taken a lot of energy out of our little kitty cat here," he says and pats me on the head. "It's a shame you haven't gotten any taller with all this growing you're doing."

Julie ignores him. "Call me later, I want details." Kiss, kiss and she's gone.

Adam swings my arm humming "I Will Survive," as we walk to my car.

CHAPTER FOURTEEN:
Lying in Wait

I don't hear from Marc after our meeting at Starbucks, and I'm really not surprised. Once again I debate calling or emailing him but I just don't know what to say. There is still a small part of me that selfishly needs him in my life and I can't bring myself to do anything that will cut ties completely. There was a time, not long ago, when I assumed he was the one. I was invested in Marc - and as Megan reminded me earlier — I always assumed that my future was with him. The only reason I broke up with him was to get him to appreciate me and realize what was at stake. And now he has.

It's Friday morning, and the first chance I've had to call Megan all week. After talking with her, she, of course, feels badly for Marc and questions my intentions. Having never met Ryan she still has a soft spot for my relationship with Marc and, like everyone else, assumes he and I will end up getting married one day. So now that I've all but severed those ties and retreated back to square one at the age of twenty-six, she's noticeably concerned for me.

"I just hope you know what you're doing," she says over the phone. "I think you and Marc are past the game-playing stage and this may be his ultimatum for you."

"He didn't give me an ultimatum," I correct her.

"Not in so many words, Kat, but this is as open and defenseless as he's ever been, and I don't think you'll get another chance like this. He's not going to keep begging."

I'm not in the mood to listen to her lecture me this morning. "Megan, he wasn't begging, and it's over. I did what I felt was right, and I really don't feel like talking about it anymore."

"Just because someone disagrees with you doesn't mean you should end the conversation. You know I love you, and I just don't want you to regret anything. Look how upset you were only a few months ago when you thought you'd lost Marc completely." She's quick to remind me.

I close my eyes and prop my head up with my hand, elbow resting on the desk. "I have to go."

"I'm just trying to help, Kat."

"I know, thank you. I do have to go, though…I'll call you later."

"Bye," I hear her saying as I'm hanging up.

I rub my forehead with the heel of my hand and text Adam who's tied up in a scheduling meeting all morning, making him unable to properly coddle me right now.

I need a noose.
I text.

Top desk drawer on right.
He replies.

What time do our boys get in from Vegas?
I ask referring to Dave and Ryan's return.

2:00
Adam texts.

Are they coming to the office?
I ask.

I'm in a Goddamn meeting!
He reprimands me.

I log onto Facebook and work at beautifying my land on FarmVille. I'm pleased to see that prior to his scheduling meeting today, Adam found the time to gift me two goats, two tabby kittens and a golden chicken. Just before I can disable the sound feature, Brooke approaches my cube as one of my horses lets out a thunderous NEIGH!

"I'm going to pretend I didn't hear that," she begins. "When it's convenient for you, I need the Chase billings finished by two o'clock. I have to have them on Dave's desk before he returns."

"Sure thing," I say and spastically log off the Internet like a teenage boy who just got caught surfing porn sites. "Sorry, I was trying to..."

"Seriously, Kat, just get it done!" She erupts with a loud reprimanding howl that makes my heart skip a beat and then storms off.

"Whoa," I whisper to myself.

Besides Brooke's new bi-polar disorder, it's been pretty uneventful at work with Ryan being in Vegas for most of the week. I hadn't realized how much I would miss seeing him until he was gone. And because I had my talk with Marc on the night before Ryan left, I never got a chance to say goodbye. He called me on Thursday and sent a few texts in between, but now I want him home. When I spoke with him from Vegas he sensed something was wrong with me, but I played it off as being tired. I've yet to fill him in on anything that's happened with Marc, and the more I try to devise a way to bring it up, the more I decide it's a bad idea. I don't want to scare him off, or let him think I'm trying to make him jealous, or worse - think that I have this ex-boyfriend drama that I carry around with me. I just can't find any good reason to tell him about my relationship with Marc, especially now that I'm trying to move on and put the whole thing behind me.

Once Adam is through with his scheduling meeting he stops by my desk. "Are you busy?" he asks.

"Brooke busted me on Facebook again and now I have to finish all the Chase billings by two o'clock. So I'm trying to win back a few points with her and finish them by one."

Adam waves his hand in my face dismissing what I've just said. "Did you get the golden chicken?" he asks excitedly.

"Yes."

"And the goats?"

"Yes! Now leave me alone before harvesting livestock is the only job I can find." I push him away.

"Well, to answer your earlier question, the boys are coming straight to the office from the airport," he informs me.

I light up. "That's awesome, thank you for sharing."

"You're welcome." He turns to leave.

"Hey, Adam." I stop him. "Do you think I should tell Ryan about Marc?"

He matches my curiosity. "Tell him what exactly?"

"I don't know, any of it? I just feel like I'm lying to him by keeping all of this bottled up, but I don't want to burden him with it either."

Adam gets a kind, reassuring look on his face and sits down on my desktop. "I don't know, sweetie. It's a tough call, but I can't see why you need to say anything to him now. You're both obviously crazy about each other, and this beginning stage is the best part of any relationship. He's such a strong, confident guy, that I'm sure it wouldn't bother him one bit, but why go there unless you really need to. Let him think he's the only thing on your mind. He deserves that."

He's right; Ryan does deserve that, but dosesn't he also deserve the truth? Ryan has been so open and honest with me from the beginning: no games, no pretenses, nothing but putting himself out there one hundred percent, and a part of me feels obligated to honor his sincerity.

I reach for Adam's hand. "Thank you, seriously, for everything," I say. "You're right. Most importantly, I want him to know how much I care about him. It's just that he's been so unbelievably straightforward with me."

"I don't see any good reason to mention it," he says matter-of-factly, then gives me a look of apprehension. "I do, however, think you should break the news to Julie one of these minutes."

I bury my face in my hands. "I know, I know. We have plans this weekend and I am going to say something then."

"That's ma' girl, and remember who's got your back, okay?"

"Okay, thanks," I add and give him a little peck on the back of his hand.

He nods. "As it should be."

I finish my work by half past one and go put the Chase billings on top of Brooke's desk so she can review them. As I walk into her office expecting to find her, it looks like she's gone home for the day because she's not in there, and her tote bag and cell phone are missing from their usual spots. She never takes her tote bag with her anywhere until she leaves for the day, so I head over to the front desk to see if Carrie has any information on her whereabouts.

"Hey, Care, have you seen Brooke? Do you know if she's left for the day?" I ask mid-stride as I approach her desk.

"She left for the day," Carrie says without looking up from her magazine.

"Did she say if she was coming back?" I ask in a much cheerier tone, hoping for more details.

"Brooke said she was leaving for the day," she repeats, simultaneously turning a page in her magazine and answering a text on her cell phone.

My frustration builds and my tolerance fades. "Did she say anything else, like where she was going?"

Carrie shifts her head to the side and finally looks up at me. "No." She pauses. "If you give me her cell number I can call her for you."

Unbelievable. "I'm capable of that, thank you."

"Great," she says. "Do you need something else?"

"No, thank you," I say shaking my head, and just as I'm about to head back to my cube the elevator doors open and out walk Ryan and Dave.

My mood shifts into a giddy euphoria as Ryan and his expansive shoulders exit onto the floor. He has a leather duffel bag thrown over one arm, with his other hand tucked neatly into his front pocket. He looks at me with an unexpected tenderness and walks straight to where I'm standing in front of the reception desk.

"Have you been standing there all week waiting for me to return?" he asks.

"Welcome back, Ryan!" Carrie interjects, oddly not so interested in her magazine anymore.

"Thanks," he says to her, never taking his eyes off mine.

A childish grin appears on my face, and I'm frozen as he walks closer and places his hand on the small of my back. "Hey, you," he says.

I strain to suppress the urge to French kiss him right in front of Carrie. "Hey," I reply, relieved to see him.

"Come with me," he declares and leads me toward his office with his hand still touching my back.

"I thought you guys were getting in later," I say once we enter his office.

"We caught an earlier flight." He smiles and tosses his duffel on the floor. "It's great to see you." He spins around, leans against the desktop and pulls me toward him.

"You too. I missed having you around here." No lie there.

"So, what are the plans for tonight?" he asks and kisses my neck.

"Something with you I hope?" I say sheepishly, chills running down my spine.

"Great, let's grab dinner. I want to run home later and shower, but how about I come by your place around eight o'clock?"

"Sounds perfect," I say and lose myself in his eyes. His face is so peaceful and self-assured.

He leans down, kisses me on the lips, and releases my hand. I take two steps back and he walks around to the other side of his desk. "Great, I'll see you then," he says, then turns his attention to his computer.

I float out of his office and practically skip back to my desk. When I arrive, I see that Brooke has not in fact left for the day and is walking past reception to her office. No surprise that Carrie was either completely oblivious or purposefully screwing with me. Within seconds my office phone is ringing and it's Brooke.

I answer it and immediately start talking. "Hey, Brooke, Carrie had said you left for the day."

"Why are the *Chase* billings on my desk? Where are the ones for Bellagio I asked you for?!" She's clearly back at the office.

"You asked for the Chase billings," I say, mildly panicking from her tone, but damn well sure she asked me to work on the Chase ones, not Bellagio.

"Jesus, Kat, I said Bellagio, and Dave is waiting for them!"

I'm sensing she's not in the mood for me to stand my ground right now so I take the high road and suck up her mistake. "I can have them in thirty minutes, sorry."

She slams the phone, and I'm left holding the receiver in astonishment. I realize that I may be a little distracted at the office lately, but this was her mistake; I'm sure of it.

Care to join us for a macchiato?
Adam texts me.

Can't. Brooke f'd me up.
I reply disgruntled.

WTF?
He asks.

She said I did the wrong billings, now I'm scrambling.
I answer.

You probably did.
He concludes.

I didn't!

I toss my cell phone into the desk drawer and begin frantically working on the paperwork for the Bellagio account instead of the stupid Chase ones. Which, by the way, are now done ahead of schedule - but who pays any attention to the positive things around here. Just then my office line rings again, startling me because I'm now scared to hear Brooke's voice, but it turns out to be Megan.

"This is Kat," I answer quickly.

"It's me. I'm just bored and wanted to see if you could meet for lunch tomorrow," she asks.

"Tomorrow is Saturday," I say.

"So what? You can't meet your sister for lunch on a Saturday?" She sounds offended.

"No, it's just that we normally meet during the week, Miss Sassy Tone," I say. "And I have plans tonight that I'm hoping will spill over into tomorrow." I smile to myself.

"Oh, fine, be that way. That fun, carefree, single, no worries way that you are."

"Someone a little bitter?"

She sighs. "It's just that our sitter canceled, leaving me with no Saturday night plans, and basically wanting to hang myself. I begged Henry to watch Miles for me during the day and told him that you and I were having lunch and running some errands."

"So stick with your story, and he'll never know," I suggest.

"It's not worth it. I don't even have any errands to run. I just wanted some time alone is all. I'll see, maybe I'll keep our fake plans." She laughs. "So how are things with you and Shakespeare?"

"Very cute. He's good. He just got back from Vegas and we're going out to dinner tonight."

"Don't get pissy with me for asking, but have you said anything to Julie yet?"

"I plan on telling her tomorrow, actually," I say as a lump forms in my throat.

"Well good, at least you have a plan. I don't think it's going to be easy for you but I know you'll feel better once it's off your chest," Megan says. "Have fun tonight with Ryan - I'm jealous."

"Don't be. I love you. But I do have to go, because Brooke is on a rampage this week, and if she catches me on a personal call, I'm a goner."

"Got it, love you," she tells me and hangs up.

CHAPTER FIFTEEN:

No Regrets

I manage to get the Bellagio work done in a couple of hours, but when I go to bring them to Brooke I see she is officially gone for the day this time. I figure there's no reason to confirm that with Carrie, and take it upon myself to make sure the billings get to Dave, personally. Now all I have to do is go home and get dressed for my date with Ryan.

Ryan arrives right on time and meets me in the lobby of my building, so we decide to grab dinner somewhere we can walk to from my apartment. There is a little pub down the street called Smitty's that serves beer and wine and the kinds of foods one would expect from a place called Smitty's. Things like mozzarella sticks, chicken wings, mini burgers and jalapeño poppers. It's located in the garden level of a building on Clark Street so we take a small stairwell down in order to enter the place, and Ryan has to duck his head slightly to get through the entrance. We grab a bar table near the window which gives us a lovely view of people's shoes as they walk by.

I want to tell him how much I missed him and how much I'd been aching to spend more time alone with him. But from day one, even though he's been nothing but open with me, he's still a little hard to read. I'm constantly nervous about putting myself in a vulnerable position with him, and I certainly wouldn't want him to pull away because I wasn't hard to get anymore. I've been to that party and it's nothing but a bad time.

Ryan settles onto his stool and leans his body against the wall behind him. "So how did you busy yourself this week?" he asks.

"Same old, same old," I say.

"I was wondering if you've talked to Julie? I've been meaning to ask you about that whole thing."

That "whole thing" is such an odd way of referring to it. Does he mean my friendship with her or his relationship with her? "What do you mean by that?" I attempt to clarify.

"I was just wondering if she knew that you and I have been hanging out," he explains. "Would you like me to talk to her?"

I fumble with the laminated drink menu sitting atop our table. "No," I answer. "I have plans with her during the day tomorrow, in fact. I'm going to break the news to her then." I scan his face for a reaction.

"That's good. What are you planning to say?"

"I'm not really sure. I want to be honest, but I'm nervous — I just don't know whether she can handle the entire story all at once."

Ryan grabs a handful of complimentary peanuts and ponders my plan of action. "Well, you know her better than I do. If you think that's the best approach then that's what you should do," he tells me. "Are you worried about her reaction?"

I let out an uncomfortable laugh. "Yes," I say. I'm dreading that moment like no other. I have always thought one of my best qualities is my true and loyal friendship. Undying servitude to those I hold dear. If one of my friends cheats on her boyfriend, I am the one she will confide in and trust with her darkest secrets. If someone wrongs her, I am the friend who will talk smack about that person who hurt her. You will never see me giving the time of day to someone who insults a friend of mine. No, I am the one you can count on to be there for you no matter what. The friend who will never do anything to weaken such an important bond. So breaking the news to Julie that I'm falling in love with a guy that she's interested in is not a moment I'm looking forward to.

"Look, Kat," he continues. "I think you know how I feel about you, but the last thing I ever wanted to do was get in the middle of your friendship with Julie."

His reply is not exactly what I was expecting. "I know that," I say.

"And I would completely understand if you weren't comfortable moving forward with this," he tells me.

I freeze. "Well, I'm not comfortable with it. But what exactly are you saying?"

The waitress brings us our two beers, giving him a moment to formulate his answer.

"I'm just saying that I hate putting you in this position," he says.

I am now desperate for some clarification on where he is going with this. "Well it's not exactly a *situation* yet, but don't you think I should say something to her?" I question him and begin to realize that he can sense my panic.

"Here's the thing, Kat. I care about you a lot, you know that."

"You said that," I reply stone-faced.

"Okay." He smiles and reaches for my hand. "I just don't want to cause any trouble between you and Julie, that's all."

"Well I don't know what she's going to say, but what if it did cause trouble between us?" I ask on the brink of suffocation.

He lets go of my hand. "That would be terrible, don't you think?" he asks.

"Yes, of course, but I just want you to know that I realize what is at stake here and what I'm willing to risk to be with you." My statement carries a deeper meaning than just my friendship with Julie, only Ryan doesn't know it. He doesn't know that I have also destroyed any future relationship with the man I thought I was going to marry. All because I've chosen to gamble and bet all my chips on my feelings for Ryan. I take a breath and remind myself that he is unaware of what's truly at stake here for me. I continue with a much more encouraging demeanor. "I don't want to sound like I'm making some pathetic, pressure-filled declaration, but as much as Julie means to me I feel that you might mean more. I would never jeopardize a friendship over someone I didn't truly care about. And my hope is that she will see that."

He leans forward and kisses me on the lips almost knocking both beers over. "Okay, okay. I understand. I just felt like I should say something before you go through with it. I don't want you to resent me for anything."

We hold hands on the walk back to my place but don't say much else on the subject of Julie. My heart and mind are racing and I want him to know that I meant what I said. What began as a crush and a distraction from my relationship with Marc has turned into so much more. Maybe Ryan and I are meant to be together. Maybe there is hope for me to forge a new future for myself. I haven't let myself believe it until now, and I feel the need to show him.

Seeing him walk into my apartment makes the whole place look even smaller than it already is. His height combined with his wide shoulders makes my doorway seem like it belongs in a dollhouse. As soon as he squeezes through, he starts to head for the couch, but I grab his hand and lead him to the bed instead.

"Where are we going?" he asks.

"Shhh."

I begin to unbutton his shirt and he doesn't flinch. I can see goose bumps materialize all over his smooth, enormous chest as I brush his shirt to the floor. His arms are so broad and toned that I have to pause for a moment.

"Are you sure you want to do this?" he whispers, without moving a glorious muscle, as he knows exactly what I have in mind.

"Shhh," I repeat.

"Kat," he whispers my name quietly and tightly grabs the back of my neck.

I decide to relinquish control at this point. I sit on the edge of the bed and he kneels down on the floor in front of me. As he begins to kiss my face, my skin shivers as I fall backward. We spend the rest of the night making sure I have nothing to resent him for.

CHAPTER SIXTEEN:
Friendly Fire

It's the morning after my first truly intimate evening with Ryan, and I'm feeling great despite the fact that I'm supposed to have my dreaded talk with Julie. Today is Saturday, and also the highly anticipated Old Town Art Fair—a fabulous annual booze fest, mildly camouflaged by various artisans trying to sell their wares. I'm scheduled to meet Julie at her apartment at eleven o'clock for Bloody Marys and then Beth will meet up with us at the square outside St. Michael's Church. Ryan snuck out of my apartment around seven thirty to go for a run. I don't have any definite plans to meet up with him later, but a day of drinking in the sun with hundreds of people is sure to elicit a text from me at some point.

As I walk to Julie's place, all I really want to do is replay the fabulous, heart-pounding events of the previous evening over and over in my head. It's been years since I've lusted after anyone like this. Years since my skin has literally trembled from someone's touch. Ryan has become like a drug to me, and this morning I can barely tolerate the withdrawal. Unfortunately, I have other things to concentrate on, so I let my nerves take over instead and focus on my conversation with Julie. I've decided to tell her first thing and get it out of the way in the hopes of moving past it and getting on with our day. For some reason, I have convinced myself that she will understand that my behavior is entirely out of character for me, and that I must only be acting this way because I care about Ryan and am ultimately meant to be with him. Surely she'll understand and think twice about it before arguing with fate. Right?

Julie lives on the top floor of a three-story walk-up and her door is open as I reach the landing. "Hello?" I call from the entryway.

"In here," she yells from her bathroom. "Should I do a ponytail or hair down?"

"You're asking the wrong person. You know I'm Team Ponytail," I respond and take a seat on one of the stools at her kitchen island.

She saunters out of the bathroom and joins me. "You're right, but if the Old Town Art Fair is known for one thing it's gorgeous, single men and my hair looks much better down, dont'cha think?" she asks, not really needing my answer. "Grab a Bloody. I left a pitcher on the counter."

I go to pour myself a drink and she meets me in her kitchen.

"What time is Beth meeting us?" she asks.

"I think she said noon, right?"

"Okay good, I should be able to finish two of these by then. So what's going on? Did you and Adam end up grabbing dinner after work last night?"

"No, actually, I went home and hit the couch. I have close to six hours of shows recorded on my DVR I'm trying to get through," I lie.

"Well, you'll be happy to know I've joined your True Blood bandwagon," Julie says. "I'm halfway through season one and I'm obsessed," she declares and walks around to the sink.

Nothing would make me happier than to discuss True Blood right now. To sit and debate the varying degrees of blood-sucking testosterone brought to the screen by Bill and Eric each week. The latter being my favorite. But I have more pressing issues at hand.

"I need to talk to you about something," I stammer.

"What's up?" Julie asks and leans back against her kitchen sink.

"Well, it's about Ryan."

She scans her brain to confirm whom I'm referencing. "The Chef?" Her nose crinkles. "What about him?"

I sit up a little straighter hoping better posture will give me the added strength I need to get through this conversation. "Well, the thing is…he asked me out," I inform her and wait for her expression to change, but it doesn't, so I continue. "Anyway, I said yes, and we went out on a date."

She tilts her head slightly and responds immediately. "You're telling me that you went out with Ryan?" Her disbelief forces her to pause. "And you didn't ask me first?"

I nod and release the breath I'd been holding onto. "Yes, and it's been killing me."

"You look okay to me," she says.

Julie stares at me for a moment trying to gauge, not only my level of betrayal, but also my level of interest in him, I guess. I'm certain she didn't suspect that we'd already gone out. She'd never imagine that I would deceive her in that way. I watch her take a drink of her cocktail and bob her head very slowly. I can't tell if she's waiting for me to interrupt her thought process or not, so I decide to wait for her response.

"I don't know what to say. I'm shocked he asked you out," she says.

I ignore the insult and move on. "Julie, if you don't want me to continue to see him, then I won't. But I have to tell you that I honestly feel like there is something special between us." I pause, hoping my words will make an impression. "I can tell you're uncomfortable with it."

"Do you *want* to continue to see him?" she poses the obvious question.

"Well, yes, but I don't want to make you upset. I thought you two were over, and I don't want things to be weird."

She's taken aback. "Oh, you thought we were over?" She raises her eyebrows slightly then turns to rinse something in the sink.

"Aren't you?"

"Apparently we are!" She laughs, not really humored though, and then spins back around to face me.

My hand is resting on her island and I raise my fingers involuntarily in some sort of defensive move. "You are clearly uncomfortable with this, so forget it, seriously," I blurt out because I don't know what else to say. I'm not sure what reaction I'd been expecting but this wasn't it. I've just become much more stressed than relieved at having confessed.

"No," she lifts a hand to me. "What I am *uncomfortable* with is you coming in here all...dumping this on me and saying that you're going out with Ryan."

"I didn't say that I'm going out with him exactly," I correct her incorrect assessment of what she doesn't realize she's correct about.

"What do you want me to say? Do whatever you want, Kat, that's what you always do anyway!" She walks back around to the other side of the kitchen island and goes to grab her purse from the couch.

I turn to face her. "Julie, look...wait, what does that mean?" I ask flustered and confused by her side comment.

"It means you do what *you* want, and I'll do what *I* want, okay?"

"I don't want to fight about this—forget I said anything." I make a weak attempt at saving face and get up off my stool.

"And what about Marc?" she fumes.

"Marc and I broke up."

Julie throws her arms in the air. "Please, Kat, you break up all the time! And you were just with him, crying over how he wants to get back together, and how you need to think about it. You know you're going to get back with Marc, but in the meantime you're willing to piss me off over some fling with one of my boyfriends? That's what I *mean*. You just do what you want, Kat, and don't worry about anyone else."

My lungs tighten, making it hard for me to speak. "That's not true at all. I do worry and I've been sick about having to tell you about this. I guess I thought for some strange reason that you might understand." I shake my head. "You're right, I was devastated by Marc, but as you also know, I am trying to move on."

"With Ryan?" she asks smugly.

"Yes."

We stand in silence for a minute. She begins to text someone in the middle of our conversation, intending to make me feel insignificant, I assume. It works.

"I don't really feel up to the art fair anymore," Julie says, still texting.

"Seriously?"

"Seriously, Kat!" she yells without looking up from her phone.

I don't know what else to do besides leave at this point. The entire conversation has gone up in flames faster than polyester pajamas. I stand in defeat watching her text and fumble around in her purse.

"I'll go catch up with Beth," I say to her. "I really hope you'll reconsider coming with us," I say, but she doesn't even look at me as I grab my bag and head for the door.

Once outside, I begin to walk in a daze. Carefree people line the streets everywhere, spilling out of bars, hanging out on porches and crowding roof decks while I roam the sidewalk on the verge of an emotional breakdown. I head toward the church's courtyard to meet Beth as my fight with Julie weighs heavily on me. Not only have I potentially alienated one of my best friends, but what will Ryan say now that his fears have been realized? If I lose both Julie and Ryan over this, I'm not sure I'll be able to recover. I text Adam.

I need to talk asap.
I type furiously with my thumbs.

What's up?
He texts back.

It old Julie.
I text.

Whats old Julie?
He asks.

I TOLD JULIE!
I go with All Caps.

About a second later my phone rings and it's him.

"Spill it," he says.

"Weeeeell, let's just say I'm wandering the streets alone and she's back at her apartment throwing darts at my picture."

"What happened?"

"I went over to her place this morning and told her that Ryan asked me out. I didn't give her any details, simply that he and I had gone out. Anyway, she basically told me that all I ever do is think about myself and I'm a cold, selfish whore who is willing to ruin my friendship with her and sleep with Ryan to get back at Marc."

"What'd she really say?"

"Honestly, it wasn't much different than that," I assure him.

"Look, she's insane. Are you trying to tell me that if the tables were turned Julie wouldn't do the *exact* same thing to you?" He tells me what I want to hear in an effort to calm my nerves.

"Apparently not," I respond.

He clears his throat. "She will recover, I have no doubt. And I can guarantee the thing she's most upset about is that Ryan chose you over her. She could probably care less that you're interested in him," he says. "It's the blow to her ego that's made her so upset."

"I don't know. I've never seen her like this," I mutter as I step gingerly over a smashed pile of dog poop.

"Julie will be fine."

My call waiting beeps, so I look down at my phone. "I'm getting a call from Beth on my other line. Julie must have updated her by now; let me call you back," I say and quickly click over to answer her call.

"Hello," I answer.

"What's going on?" Beth asks politely.

"I assume you talked to Julie?"

"Listened is more like it," she says.

"I'm on my way to the church now. I'll fill you in when I get there."

"Okay, Kat, I'm here waiting."

I weave my way through as many alleys and side streets as I can find in hopes of avoiding running into anyone I might know. I'm not in the mood for small talk. The church is just a block away and I can see Beth sitting on a concrete bench in front of it. She notices me walking toward her, stands and heads my way. Beth is, and has always been, a peacemaker. Not that our group of friends ever has much turmoil to deal with, but she's consistently trying to see the good in any situation, and there's no one else I'd rather see approaching me at this moment.

"Are you crying?" she asks surprised.

"Not yet," I say with a forced smile.

"Oh, honey, don't get upset."

"She's so pissed at me," I say.

Beth reaches out and grabs my hand to guide me over to the bench where she'd been sitting. "Tell me what's going on. The Chef asked you out?" She tries to make sense of the few details Julie has just given her.

"Yes."

"And from the looks of it you want to go out with him," she confirms.

I nod and tell Beth the truth. "I already have," I say.

She looks surprised, so I fill her in on how Ryan and I have become close at work, and subsequently close outside the office as well. Granted she's not invested like Julie is, but she senses my sincerity and knows immediately that I'm not being frivolous. Something I was clearly unable to convey to Julie.

"Then you should continue to see him," Beth says. "I think Julie will be just fine," she says to pacify me.

"You don't know that."

"Kat, she's moved on from him and she knows it. And if she could see you now I think she'd see that this is important to you."

"I think I'm falling in love with him," I say as the tears that were temporarily restrained during my walk start to spill out onto my cheeks.

"Oh my," Beth whispers.

CHAPTER SEVENTEEN:
When One Door Opens, Another One Slams Shut

Ryan and I had talked a couple times over the weekend but we never had the chance to get together, so I was really looking forward to seeing his face today at the office. I managed to tell him what went down between Julie and me over the phone, and his reaction was comforting and perfect. He was really encouraging and did whatever he could to assure me that everything would work out beautifully in the end. I want to believe him, but I haven't talked to Julie since I left her apartment on Saturday. I tried texting her a couple times but I didn't want to annoy her any more than I already have. She needs time to get past it on her own and I want to give that to her.

As I enter my cubicle I notice a Post-it on my computer screen that reads *come see me when you get in. Ryan.* I kiss the pale yellow piece of paper then gently tuck it away in my top drawer. There's nothing I want more than to go see him right now. I put my purse away and turn my computer on first before heading over there, and just as I'm about to exit my cube, Brooke appears.

"Can I talk to you?" she asks solemnly.

Terrific, all I need now is to lose my job, too.

"Of course, uh, right this minute?" I ask.

"Just meet me in my office when you can," she answers and walks away.

I send Ryan a quick email before heading to her office.

Brooke needs me, probably getting fired, office romance no longer an obstacle. I'll come by as soon as I can.

I don't have time to wait for a response, but I know he's in his office so I assume he'll be reading it within seconds. I decide to also text Adam before heading in to see Brooke.

On my way to get sacked.
I text.

Man he's good.
Adam replies.

Not the good kind.
I tell him.

Then please don't bother me. Luv u.
He texts.

Why I continually look to Adam for comfort is beyond me. Brooke's office is located across the floor near Dave's. Pretty much all of the senior people are clustered together. Clueless and Cubeless, as we underlings like to joke. I don't seriously think I'm going to get fired, but with the way things have been going for me these days it wouldn't surprise me, and Brooke's mood swings coupled with my personal distractions make for a bad combination. Her door is shut so I knock before entering.

"It's me," I call out.

"Come in," Brooke says. "Close the door behind you, please."

I do as she asks and then stand in front of her desk and rest my hands on the back of one of the guest chairs. She is typing on her computer and has yet to make eye contact.

"Should I be nervous?" I blurt out.

"Why?" She looks up from her keyboard with a sad, confused look on her face.

"Am I getting fired?"

"Good Lord, Kat, do you really think you're getting fired?" Now she's just looking at me like I'm an idiot.

I take a seat and collapse into the chair. "Well, it's been a rough week," I say.

"Tell me about it," she responds then takes a deep breath and closes her eyes. "Drew is cheating on me."

I rewind my brain to make sure I just heard her correctly. My eyes widen and my lips part. I'm not shocked that he would do such a thing, but hearing her say it has definitely caught me off guard.

"What?! Oh my God. How do you know?" I question her.

"I just know," she says quietly and glances up at the ceiling before turning her gaze back to her computer screen.

"Brooke, I am so sorry. Did he tell you?" I ask and lean forward to the edge of my seat.

"No, he did not. I've been checking his phone for the last couple weeks and figured it out."

That ungrateful, fat piece of shit, I think to myself. "I am so sorry, Brooke, did you confront him?"

"Yes, and he told me it's someone from work and it's nothing, and I'm being paranoid, *and* I should mind my own fucking business."

"Is there a chance he's telling the truth?" I ask even though I know the answer.

"No."

I wait a moment before continuing. "What are you going to do?"

She folds her hands on her desk and faces me but doesn't look me in the eyes. "I don't know. I asked him if he wants a divorce and he said no. And I asked him if he'd go to counseling and he said no. Then I asked him to stop communicating with this tramp and he said no. He said they work together and he can't," she says blankly.

I can tell she's been crying and I'm equally certain that admitting all of this to me is extremely painful for her. However, Brooke knows I've never held Drew in the highest regard, so that must be of some comfort to her now.

"What an ass," I say.

"Yeah, it's pretty mortifying," she adds, nodding.

"Brooke, he is the one that should be mortified! You have nothing to be ashamed of, he does," I try and convey to her.

"For him to look me in the eye and lie to my face after I've spent two weeks listening to voicemails from this woman and reading the texts that he's sent her. It's…it's…I just can't even put into words what I'm feeling right now."

"Did you kick him out?" I ask with hope.

"No, not yet. I don't know what to do," she says, defeated.

I place my palms on her desk. "You need to kick him out."

"I want to burn that whore's house down is what I want. I want to call their boss and tell him about all the afternoons she's been out screwing my husband when she should be working. I have to find out who it is. I don't know if she works with him or if she's a client or what," she says with a wild look in her eye. "I need to find her name. She has messed with the wrong person."

There is a fire in Brooke's eyes, and I can tell I'm going to need to find the right words to talk her off the edge. Her focus has shifted from Drew to this other woman, when clearly she needs to concentrate on extricating him from her life. "Brooke, I know she's a filthy piece of shit too, whoever she is, but don't waste your time on her. She didn't cheat on you - Drew did," I state, trying to keep her thoughts on track. "Who knows what he's been saying to her, what lies he's been telling her. Drew is the one who is at fault here."

Her eyebrows elevate as she continues to concentrate on revenge, and instead stays intent on ruining Drew's mistress. "She's going to pay for this. I'm sure she's been saying she's out on sales calls when she's with Drew. She messed with the wrong person," she repeats.

I pause before speaking again to determine the best way to keep her from getting off track. I can see how she could easily overlook what Drew has done to her and focus solely on making life miserable for this - obviously blind - other woman. Because that's where Brooke's comfort zone lies, in ignoring and accepting Drew's faults. "I understand you want this woman to suffer, but she did not break any vows with you, Drew did," I remind her.

She shakes her head. "I know that, and he's a piece of shit too," she says. "Look, I just wanted you to know what's going on because I'm evidently not myself lately and thought you might want to know why." She musters a smile and continues. "So since you thought you were getting canned when you walked in, this must be great news for you." Enter self-deprecation.

"Please, Brooke."

"I'm kidding," she says and rubs her temples.

"What can I do for you?" I ask.

"Nothing, just let me apologize in advance for making your life hell around here. I can't be expected to handle this misery alone."

"No apologies necessary. Run me over the coals as many times as you need until you feel better. And I wish I could say that I'm surprised, Brooke, but I'm not. He's an asshole and you deserve so much better." That felt great to say to her face.

"Thank you."

I walk around the desk and give her a hug. "Please let me know if there is anything I can do," I repeat.

She gives me a nod. "Just promise not to look at me that way. I don't want anyone's pity."

"I promise."

When I walk out of Brooke's office, I suddenly feel the need to reach out to Julie again. I guess Drew's infidelity has left me feeling guilty about my own indiscretions. Thankful for the crutch that is email, I sit down and compose a more heartfelt apology than my earlier one.

Julie,

Please forgive my cowardly attempt at reaching you through email, but I'm really not sure if you would take my call or not. First of all, I should have been more sensitive to your feelings and shouldn't have dumped things on you before we were headed out to the Old Town Art Fair. I apologize for my poor timing. Secondly, I apologize for doing anything that would ever hurt you or make you look at me the way you did last weekend. I treasure your friendship and would NEVER want to lose it or do something that I thought would jeopardize it. I hope you truly understand that. Please let me know when we can get together. Don't hate me.

-Kat

Just as I'm about to begin doing actual work, I get another email on my personal account, this time from Marc. He's building a reputation for ambushing me and I need to work on being better prepared for these things. The subject line reads "us."

I shouldn't have walked out on you the other day. The thought of you with someone else is not easy for me to digest. I can't tell if you're doing this to make me appreciate you or what, but I can't promise I'll still be here when you make up your mind. Come o,n Kat, let's patch things up and move forward.

Instant stomachache.

I understand that it would never occur to Marc that I might seriously decide to break away from him and forge a new life for myself. I understand this because I've never given him reason to believe it or to doubt my loyalty to him. As much as I have counted on him to be there for me in the past, he's relied on me even more. And his use of the word "appreciate" is too perfect for him to have come up with on his own. Which only means that he must have gotten some advice from one of his friends or sisters or something. Once again I have no idea how to respond to his passive aggressive approach. Is this the subtle ultimatum Megan had warned me about?

Marc,

You know me well enough to know that I would never do anything to hurt you intentionally, or bring someone else into the picture for the sake of making a point. I had a very difficult time when we broke up, but I have been working on healing myself. I promise you that none of this is about hurting you. It's about me trying to move forward like you mentioned. I have never stopped caring about you, and I hope you understand how difficult this is for me too.

-K

I wait all day for a response, but never get one from either Marc or Julie. I decide that I need some fun back in my routine. Less drama, more fun. I've let myself get sucked into such an indecisive state lately that I've lost the pleasure of my friends' company. I set out to arrange a girls' night out and decide to invite Brooke along to cheer her up and get her mind off things. I'm going to plan everything and quit waiting for people to make decisions for me. I'm also going to include Megan because she keeps complaining to me about being confined to the house. I feel good about my plan and send emails out to Megan, Brooke and Beth. The decision not to include Julie is a hard one.

CHAPTER EIGHTEEN:
Girls Gone Mild

Although my attempts at hosting an evening of fun are met with gratitude, Beth declines due to work-related commitments. So I beg Adam to join Brooke, Megan, and me on our girls' night, but he says he has no interest in listening to Brooke complain about losing her useless husband or Megan complain about having to sleep with hers.

I stop by Megan's house first to pick her up at seven o'clock and find that she's not ready to go as I had expected. When I walk in she has Miles under one arm and a bowl of oatmeal in the other.

"Can you hand me that bib on the counter?" she asks.

"Sure," I say and grab the bib. "Are you almost ready?"

"I'm dressed, I just have to feed him quickly and then we should be good to go."

"Where's Henry?" I ask.

She rolls her eyes and gestures to the stairwell. "He's upstairs on the computer."

"I see."

"Just...here you feed him and I'll go find my shoes." She plops Miles in his high chair and he immediately starts banging on his tray.

"Will bang for food!" I say to him and he gives me a disgruntled look. Megan hands me the bowl.

I start to feed Miles and can hardly keep up as he's inhaling every rubber tipped spoonful like a vacuum. I can't imagine how pissed he's going to be when he gets a full set of teeth and is forced to chew before swallowing. As I'm feeding Miles I notice Megan running back and forth like a squirrel behind me.

"What are you doing?" I shout over my shoulder, careful not to miss Miles's tiny mouth.

"Every damn pair of shoes I have is an uglier version of the next! It's like a clog factory blew up in here," she panics. "I have no shoes to wear."

"What about those Stuart Weitzman slides I used to borrow from you? The red ones with the wedge heel."

"They don't fit anymore."

"How about the camel suede platforms?"

"They don't fit, Kat. My feet grew when I had Miles and never recovered. I can't go," she says wryly and puts her hands on her hips. "Unless we're headed to the beach, where I can either go barefoot or in rubber flip-flops, I can't go."

"You're being ridiculous. We're going for dinner and cocktails and your fat feet will be tucked away under the table where no one will even notice. Just find a pair of black anything," I tell her as Miles lunges at me for what little bit of food is left in the rabbit-shaped bowl.

"This is ruining my night," she whines.

"Do you think you're possibly overreacting?" I ask calmly. "Would you rather slap on those nurse shoes or stay home tonight?"

"I'll be down in one second." She smartly gives in.

We leave Megan's house by seven thirty and head over to pick up Brooke. Of course, when we arrive she's waiting out front looking annoyed. She is wearing cute shoes, however.

"Hi, Brooke!" Megan yells out the window. "Sorry we're late, my fault. I was having shoe drama."

Brooke gets in the car. "No worries."

Brooke and Megan have met a few times, yet the three of us have never hung out socially before. But since Drew is wreaking havoc on Brooke's life — and in turn making mine miserable at the office, Megan and I have agreed this will be a nice thing for her. Brooke has asked Drew to move out, but he's refused. So the poor girl is basically living at the office and doing whatever she can to avoid spending any time at home.

We head over to Scoozi for dinner before hitting the bars. The plan is to have a nice meal and then lift everyone's spirits with some cocktails and cute bartenders at P.J. Clarke's afterward. As we enter the revolving door to the restaurant, we walk into an expansive, open dining hall that is packed with hungry patrons and buzzing with energy. There's an enormous papier-mâché tomato hanging from the ceiling, and hundreds of bottles of wine lining each wall. We're given a booth in the center of the room, and as I'm conditioned to do, I become unbearably famished as soon as I am handed the menu.

"The prosciutto-wrapped mozzarella appetizer is beyond amazing. We have to start with one of those," I announce.

"Sounds good, and I'm definitely getting pasta for my entrée. I've been craving a vodka cream sauce," Megan chimes in.

We order a bottle of wine and continue to have a combination of great conversation and great food. Brooke had asked me not to tell Megan about her problems with Drew, so of course, I told Megan—but made her promise to act like she didn't know anything about it. It's not like Megan would've asked Brooke about him anyway. Asshole.

Bored?
Adam interrupts my meal with a text.

Nope, go bother someone else. You had your chance.
I reply.

I don't believe you.
Adam says.

Swear, having a blast.
Okay, that's a stretch but he'll never know.

Just as I'm texting Adam I realize that Megan is angrily texting Henry, who's been pestering her throughout the meal with child-rearing questions that, according to Megan, he should have the answers to. Meanwhile, neither of us is talking to Brooke so I place my phone down and convince the ladies it's time for dessert.

When we finish our profiteroles and fried doughnuts, a symphony of yawns escape both Brooke and Megan's mouths at the same time.

"Oh, no you don't! We're just getting started," I point at them.

"Sorry, Kat. You picked the wrong gal for dinner, desserts, *and* drinks," Megan says. "I told you not to bring me here first if you wanted a late night."

Brooke laughs. "I agree. Pasta, wine, profiteroles. I think I'm done too," she states and gives Megan a knowing smile.

I shake my head in dismay. "Are you two kidding me? First of all, these are *starter* cocktails and the carbs are for energy."

"Don't be mad, Kat, but I'm exhausted," Megan says. "I'm really tired, and Henry's having a tough time getting Miles down." Her voice trails off as she checks her phone again.

"Oh my God, if you leave me now I do not want to hear *one word* about how jealous you are of my single status," I say to Megan. "Ever."

"Fine." She yawns and then her eyes immediately go wide with a look of astonishment as she forcibly squeezes my leg under the table.

"Ow, what the…?" I look at her, and her eyes are transfixed on the entrance to the restaurant.

"Marc is here," she whispers, as if he might hear.

My neck freezes. "What?"

"Marc just walked in with a group of people," Megan says urgently as she retracts her hand from my leg.

"Did he see us?" I ask, panicked. "Is this the only place to get a bowl of pasta in this city?" I stay firmly planted with my body facing Megan and my back to the front door.

"I don't think he saw us, but don't stress out. We're about to leave anyway, so we'll pop by his table and say hello and then goodbye. Okay?"

"When's the last time you've seen him?" Brooke asks.

"Last week. We met for coffee one night after work," I answer.

"Well then, it shouldn't be too awkward," Brooke offers.

Megan interjects. "Except for the fact that he wants to get back together with her."

"Ahhh," Brooke nods.

"Which reminds me, Brooke, you'll have to give me the scoop on this Ryan guy before we leave," she says.

"Would you two just stop for a second," I call out.

I never seem to be at ease where Marc is concerned lately, and seeing him always makes me question everything else in my life. I gather a drop of confidence, turn my head and glance toward the entrance. He has moved from the front and is now standing in the large bar area with three other men and one woman. He doesn't know I'm here. But there are no walls in this place, so sneaking out like a thief in the night is not an option. We'll definitely have to walk past them as we leave. Megan is right. I should just go say hello and be done with it.

"Kat, I can tell you're nervous," Megan says to me. "And there's nothing to worry about. Let's just go over there, I'll lead the way."

I tug on my napkin. "I just wasn't expecting him to be here, that's all."

"Well he is, and it's no big thing, just try and be chill," she reassures me. "This is a small city, and you're bound to run into him from time to time."

"I'm fine," I say. Marc looks great, and warm, and comfortable, and it's killing me. He's leaning against a bar table with one hand in his pocket, wearing dark pants and a striped dress shirt, no tie. All eyes in the group are on him, and he's clearly leading the conversation as usual.

Brooke and Megan gather their purses while I gather my strength, and the three of us head over to where he's standing. As soon as we're about ten feet away, he spots me. I see him lift a finger to his group and excuse himself before walking toward us.

"Hey there, Meg, long time," he greets her first with a strong embrace.

She pulls back with her hands still on his shoulders. "Nice to see you Marc," she says. "How have you been?"

"I've been good, thanks. Hi, Brooke, how's it going?" they shake hands.

"Just fine." She smiles at him and then at me.

"Hey, you," he says and gives me a hug similar to the one he just gave Megan. And as expected, he smells delicious. Freshly showered and gelled.

"Hi, Marc," I say.

"Looks like girls' night out."

"It was, until these two began yawn-a-palooza about ten minutes ago," I tell him.

"Bummer, you all heading home already?" he asks.

"I'm afraid so," Megan says.

"Well, why don't you stay and hang out for a little while?" Marc turns to me and offers. "I'm here with some guys from work, and I'm sure these two big girls can find their way home." He looks to them for support.

Megan answers before I have a chance to respond. "Yes, of course we can. That's totally fine; Brooke and I can jump in a cab."

Brooke nods.

I interject. "Oh, no, I don't want you two to have to do that."

Megan brushes me off with a wave of her hand. "It's no big thing. We were feeling terrible about ending your night early, so why don't you stay with Marc and have fun," Megan says and grabs Brooke's purse strap.

They walk away leaving Marc and me standing there.

He gently touches my elbow. "Will you come join us for a drink?"

Despite my mess of nerves, being close to him still brings me a sense of contentment.

"I probably shouldn't," I say. My feet feel like I'm wearing cement boots. I want to take a step, in either direction quite frankly, but my stance is frozen with uncertainty. Marc and I aren't casual friends—we never have been, and it would be ridiculous to pretend otherwise.

In fact, I can't think of one instance where the two of us have spent time together in a bar that wasn't immediately followed by a sleepover.

He senses my hesitation. "Have one drink with me. I promise to behave," he says and smiles.

I follow him over to where his friends are standing and he does a round of introductions. He orders me a glass of wine, and I position myself next to him as I've done so many times before and listen to him engage everyone in story after story. Marc has a knack for conversation and does an exceptional job of making any topic sound interesting. I can't help but marvel at him completely at ease in his element. Periodically he makes eye contact with me when someone else is doing the talking.

After about an hour, it's time for me to leave. I've now had two more glasses of wine since finishing dinner, and Marc is looking more and more attractive with every one of them.

I place my glass on the highboy table in front of us. "Thanks for the wine, Marc."

"You heading out?" He looks surprised.

"Yeah, I've got an early morning tomorrow."

"Well, thanks for staying and hanging out with me."

"Sure, it was really nice," I say.

Marc leans down and gives me a quick kiss on the cheek close enough to my lips that the corners of our mouths gently graze each other. "See you around," he says, then turns back to his friends, leaving me to walk away from him this time.

CHAPTER NINETEEN

So Good You Can Taste It

Ryan has suggested we try an Italian restaurant in Lincoln Park called Rose Angelis. And after a week filled with confronting Julie, consoling Brooke, and bumping into Marc - I'm eager to be alone with Ryan again. Rose Angelis is a tiny little hole in the wall that has built a reputation for great food and large portions. We walk in and get a table near the front window. Once we're seated I have a better opportunity to admire his face. It's then that I notice he's clean-shaven and looks about five years younger than he does when he sports his usual stubble. I had inhaled his cologne when I got into the cab earlier, and even now with all the garlic and olive oil in the air, I can still taste his scent in my throat.

He's staring back at me. "You look beautiful."

"Thank you, so do you," I say.

"I mean it Kat. You look really beautiful tonight."

"Thanks." I blush. "Candlelight is my best accessory."

He cocks his head and looks puzzled. "Why can't you take the compliment?"

"What do you mean? I said thank you."

"But you made a joke. You're uncomfortable with me telling you how beautiful you are?"

I twist the ends of my hair. "No, it's just, I don't know how to answer."

"It's not a question," he says and lowers his chin.

"I guess I'm uncomfortable with hearing it from someone like you."

He furrows his brow. "What on earth does that mean?"

"It's just that you personify the word with little or no effort on a daily basis. I see you walk in a room and heads turn. Everything about you is beautiful. Your face, your shoulders, the back of your hands." I pause. "And so much effort goes into me looking the way I do right now, you have no idea."

"Okay, okay." He throws his hands up. "I should've known you'd turn it around somehow."

He seems content to change the subject and move on. Obviously I'm elated that he feels that way about me. The mere fact that he's sitting across from me, focusing on my face alone is enough of a treat.

"Shall we get some wine?" he asks.

"I'd love some."

He waves our waitress over and orders a bottle of Chianti from the wine list. My neck relaxes, my shoulders loosen, and I'd be perfectly happy sitting here drinking wine and cologne for the next four hours.

He glances down at his menu for the first time. "So what do you feel like eating?"

"I feel like pasta," I say.

"Sounds good. Dave told me the veal is fantastic, though, so I may have to go with that."

"Dave is typically right about everything, so that sounds like a smart call," I note.

"How is Brooke doing?" he asks and places his menu down on the table.

I had confided in him about what had transpired on Monday after my little meeting in Brooke's office. I trust Ryan to keep her secret, and I'm glad to see him so concerned for her.

"She hasn't mentioned much in the past few days, and I'm afraid to ask. I'm guessing things aren't good. I know she asked him to leave, but he refused."

Ryan shakes his head. "That's a real shame. I don't know her that well, but I'm sure she deserves better."

"That's what I'm always telling her," I say. "Do you think Dave knows what's going on?" I wonder.

"Not unless you've told Adam."

I snicker. "I haven't," I say proudly. "I have some sense of decorum."

We order our food and settle into our bottle of wine. He's leaning all the way back into his chair with his mile-long legs stretched out, and even in this position he easily reaches for my hand across the table. I take a slow sip of wine and then tell him about my email to Julie.

"I wanted to let you know that I reached out to Julie again."

"Oh?"

"I sent her an email the other day, but haven't heard back from her."

"She'll come around," he says with certainty.

"I hope so."

I purposely neglect to tell him about Marc's email, however. I can't think of any reason he'd be eager to learn about that subject. And despite this wonderful dinner at Rose Angelis with an unbelievable man who has just said I'm beautiful, Marc is still weighing heavily on my mind.

We finish our dinner and take a cab back to Ryan's place. He stops me in the poorly lit foyer and gives me a garlic-infused kiss outside the elevators. My eyelids are heavy from the wine, so I lie down on his couch as soon as we enter his apartment. Ryan parks himself next to me and lifts my feet so that he can sit down under my legs before grabbing the remote. I curl up slightly and close my eyes for a minute.

"Good night, beautiful," is the last thing I remember hearing.

CHAPTER TWENTY:
The Mother Load

I know I drank my fair share of two bottles of wine last night, but I'm still surprised by the horrible ringing that's going on in my head. It takes me a second to realize that it's Ryan's phone and not my hangover that's jarring me awake this morning. He becomes equally startled as I yank the covers over my face and makes his best effort to answer it quickly without disturbing me.

"Hello," he whispers. "Hi...no...because I can't...no. Some other time." He sighs then rubs his eyes. "Because I said so...yes...yes...no. Fine, what time? Goodbye."

As a result of only hearing his side of the conversation, I'm now wide-awake and extremely curious, so I roll over and give him an inquisitive look.

A silly grin forms beneath his tired eyes. "My mom wants us to meet her for breakfast."

My body jolts into an upright position. "Shut up!"

"She doesn't like to take no for an answer, as I'm sure you just heard."

"Did you tell her I was here?" I ask in horror.

"She sort of figured it out. She doesn't care, she wants to meet you," he says and then releases a huge yawn.

"I cannot meet your mother this way! First of all, I only have last night's outfit with me," I say and point to the back of his desk chair. "Not to mention last night's makeup, hair, and breath—and now she thinks I'm Raggedy Tramp."

He stretches and laughs simultaneously. "You look perfect and she doesn't care. And more importantly neither do I," he says as he leans over and kisses me. "I'll call her back and say no then." He reaches for the phone. "It makes no difference to me."

"No!" I swat his arm. "Then she'll think I'm the horrible woman she imagined when you were six years old. The unappreciative floozy who stole your heart and won't let you visit your mother," I yell in a panic.

Ryan remains perfectly content through all my ranting and even attempts to close his eyes again while trying to repress his amusement. "Kat, we can do whatever you want. I really don't care. Just don't worry about any of it, okay?"

I scrape the sleep sand out of my eyes. "We should go," I say, focusing.

"You sure?"

"Yes," I tell him and jump out of bed. I grab my clothes off his chair, scoop my purse up under my arm and head for the bathroom. "You don't have any concealer, do you?"

We both get ready and I beg Ryan to wear something a little dressier than usual to offset my eveningwear. His parents live five blocks from his apartment in a gorgeous high-rise overlooking Navy Pier. When we reach the thirty-second floor, his mother immediately bursts through their front door and greets us at the elevator.

"Good morning!" she says and gives both Ryan and me a hug.

"Mom, this is Kat," Ryan says.

"Hi, Mrs. Sullivan."

She wags her hands at me. "Please call me Judy. Come in, come in."

We follow her into the condo and take a seat on her white leather couch. In front of us, on the white marble coffee table, is a white laminate tray filled with bagels and cream cheese. Next to the tray is a white ceramic plate with lox, cucumber slices, red onion and chives.

"What can I get you to drink, Kat?" Judy asks me.

"Coffee would be great."

"Me too, Mom," Ryan adds.

"Sorry to force this delicious breakfast on you both this morning," she says. "But you see, Kat, my son has not called me in over a week and I've just about had it with hearing how busy he is at work."

Ryan looks at me.

"Don't be silly. Thank you for having me. It's not often I get to enjoy a bagel that doesn't require defrosting first," I tell her.

"Well, then it's a treat for all of us…HARVEY!" she yells over her shoulder. "THE KIDS ARE HERE!" She turns back to face us. "He'll be out in a second. So Kat, what do you do?"

I squirm as she begins her interrogation. "I work at Lambert & Miller, with Ryan."

"Really? Well isn't that lovely. I apologize. Had Ryan called me recently I might have known that already." She smiles at him. "And how are you, my darling boy?"

"Good, Mom." His smile is forced, yet endearing.

"Good, good, I bought the salmon spread you like. You'll take it home with you," she says to Ryan. "HARVEY!"

Ryan's father finally emerges from the bedroom buttoning the sleeves on his dress shirt. "For Pete's sake, Judy, the fire escape is in the hall so you know I couldn't have gone anywhere without you noticing. Hi, kids."

I stand to shake his hand. "Hi, I'm Kat."

"Nice to meet you, Kat."

"So, honey," Judy addresses Ryan, "your grandmother and I are going to be in Las Vegas next week when you're there. Can we all meet up for dinner one night?"

"I don't meet you out for dinner here in Chicago, Mom, why would I meet you for dinner in Las Vegas?" he taunts her.

"You're a little shit. You'll meet us for dinner when we're all there," she says, attempting to seal the deal with her tone.

"Mom, it's a work trip; have your own dinner, please."

"How about breakfast one morning then?" she asks.

Ryan acts as though he's considering it. "It would be interesting to see you order pancakes and then send them back. I'll think about it."

Judy shoots him a dirty look, and Harvey cracks up.

I turn to Ryan. "I didn't know you had to go back to Vegas."

"Yeah, next week for Bellagio again."

I take the bagel that Judy is waving in front of me and place it on my plate. "You creatives get to have all the fun," I say.

"Try the cream cheese, dear. It's from Kaufman's," she says, assuming I should know that makes it better than regular cream cheese. "Do you get to travel much, Kat?" Judy asks me. "Do your parents live around here?"

"My parents are divorced," I alert the media. "My mom lives in Gurnee, and my dad moved to Grand Rapids about ten years ago."

"I see," Judy says. "How about for vacations? Where do you like to go?" she asks, thankfully glossing over my family drama.

"I have a cousin who lives in Miami, and I've gone there a couple times to stay with her. Although it's been a while."

"Oh, we love Florida! My mother has a condo in Aventura, and Ryan spent most of his school breaks down there. We also love to visit the Bahamas. Have you been to the Bahamas, Kat?"

Ryan quickly changes the subject before I can respond and maybe before his mom can invite me to the Bahamas for the holidays or something. "What's new with you, Mom?" he asks.

"Nothing much. Your father and I are taking Grandma to Vegas like I said and then we're going to California to visit his cousin Margaret in Palm Desert. You remember daddy's cousin Margaret, right? Her son Michael is your age and you used to go fishing together when we'd visit there."

Ryan nods. Judy then proceeds to tell me story after story about old family vacations and various places she used to take Ryan when he was younger. Most of them seem to involve some sort of gambling, everything from casinos to Jai Lai to horses. I like her more and more with every tale.

After an hour and a half of reminiscing, Ryan gets to his feet and announces our departure. I can sense he has a great deal of love and respect for his parents, but that he can only take them in small doses. Judy gives me a big hug as we head out the door and I tell her how much I enjoyed the breakfast.

"It's been wonderful to meet you, Kat; come by anytime and I'll feed you whatever you like, with or without this one," she adds, poking Ryan in the ribs.

"Thank you so much. It really was a treat and your home is beautiful," I say.

"Thank you, darling."

"Bye, Mom," Ryan kisses her on the cheek.

"Goodbye, my angel," she says with a wave of her hand.

As we get in the elevator, Ryan apologizes for the unannounced change in plans this morning. "Thanks for being a good sport. I know she enjoyed meeting you."

"She's terrific and you guys have a great relationship. Have you ever cooked for her?" I ask.

"No," he says.

"Why not?"

"I could never cook for her," he chuckles. "It's always too much oil, something on the side, too salty, undercooked…you get the idea."

I smile at him and he grabs my hand as we exit the building.

Ryan walks me back to my car around one o'clock, and I have a moment of weakness. "Would I be entirely pathetic if I ask what you're doing later?"

He takes a step closer to me and puts both hands around my waist. "I would love to see you later," he says. "But I need to get a couple things done first. How about I come by around six o'clock and we can order dinner?"

"I would love that," I say and elevate my body onto my tiptoes.

"Okay, see ya later." He bends to give me a kiss and heads home.

I plop down on my couch and take a deep breath. I am fully enamored to the point of not wanting to be without him. Never did I imagine feeling this way so soon into the relationship. I decide to take a nap, a shower, and clean my apartment for my evening dinner guest.

My household chores take longer than expected, but by late afternoon I'm ready to get in the shower. After a good long scrubbing, I grab my robe from the back of my bathroom door and hear the phone ringing in the other room. I run to grab it, water dripping down my back, and check the caller ID before answering. It's the lobby line, and someone is calling from downstairs. I glace at the clock on the microwave. Five o'clock. Ryan must have finished his errands early.

I grin with excitement. "Hello?" I answer.

"It's Marc. Can I come up?"

CHAPTER TWENTY-ONE:

Katastrophe

This can't be happening! I'm in my robe, expecting Ryan, and Marc is once again deploying his sneak attack from the lobby. I close my robe and break into a cold sweat.

"What are you doing here?" I ask into the receiver.

"I need to see you," he says. "Is someone there?"

"No, no one is here, but I just got out of the shower."

"Can I come up?"

I shake my head in disbelief. Seconds turn into years as I search my brain for an answer other than "sure, come on up." "Why don't I get dressed and come meet you down there," I suggest. "Give me five minutes." I hang up the phone and rush into my bedroom where I drop my robe and put on a pair of navy sweats and a white Polo shirt. Both have been on my closet floor for over a week. I give my hair a couple quick shakes with the blow dryer then grab my keys and run downstairs.

Once I reach the lobby, I find Marc sitting on the edge of one of the couches in the waiting area. I walk over and stand in front of him, knees shaking.

He seems tense.

"Hi," I say.

He takes a deep breath and looks up at me. "Kat, I'm sorry to bust in on you like this, but I've come here to ask for your forgiveness once again. I got sidetracked when we met at Starbucks, and I never meant for that to happen. Then, running into you the other night made me realize that I gave up too easily."

I tentatively sit next to him. "You have nothing to apologize for, Marc," I say.

"Please let me finish." He pauses, turns his body to me, then takes my hand in his. "You know I love you and that I would do anything for you." I nod and he continues. "You can count on me for anything you ever need, Kat, and I never thought we'd be apart for long. In fact, I welcomed the break at first because it gave me the time I needed to re-evaluate what's really important to me - and that is you." He releases my hand and squares his shoulders before continuing. "When you told me that you had started seeing someone else, it was like a blow to the gut. I was so stunned by the mere possibility of it that I didn't know what else to do besides walk away. But the more I thought about it, the more I realized that I have never walked away from anything that was important to me, and I'm not going to start now."

"Marc," I try to speak, and shift my posture.

He lifts a finger to silence me. "So I realize that I'm coming here again unannounced - and uninvited for that matter, but I have to know if there's still a chance for us."

His words hang there, waiting for me to lob them back over the net and keep this volley going, but I don't know what to say. I clear my throat.

Then he does something I would never have been prepared for under these circumstances. He gets off the couch and down on one knee in front of me.

"Will you marry me, Kat?" Marc asks.

At that moment the blood starts to drain from my skull. I quickly lose control of my senses and can feel my jaw open wider than I thought possible.

"Marc, oh my God. What are you doing?" I manage to ask, given all the confusion in my brain.

"I don't have a ring yet, but I mean it," he says, his eyes fixated on mine. "I cannot lose you, Kat. I know marriage is what you want and I'm willing to do whatever it takes."

Then, like a scene from a Wes Craven movie, I get an eerie sense that we're not alone. I turn, in slow motion, to look away from Marc's eager face, and there standing near the lobby entrance is Ryan. I catch his curious expression as he gives me a strained wave with his right hand. The heat under my skin reaches boiling and engulfs every limb in my body as my eyes roll back into my head and I hit the floor.

CHAPTER TWENTY-TWO:
Make Nice

As I slowly come to, I discover that I'm lying horizontally on the couch, and Marc is sitting next to me with a bottle of water in his hands. I try to sit up, but manage to only prop myself onto my elbows. It isn't until the events of the past five minutes slap me in the face that I can elevate my torso entirely.

Marc gently puts his hand on my leg. "Are you okay?"

"Oh my God," I whisper and close my eyes.

"Was that him?" he asks and lowers his head to get a better look at my expression.

"Yes," I glance at my keys lying on the floor. "Is he gone?" I ask.

"He's gone."

"Oh my God," I repeat.

I understand that as much as Marc is concerned for my well-being, he's obviously waiting for an answer to his question that I tried so tactfully to avoid by losing consciousness. However, I hesitate to tell him that having just been faced with his marriage proposal, all I can think about is Ryan. My nerves begin to unravel like a ball of yarn and I'm struggling to maintain my sanity as Marc places his arm around my slumped shoulders.

"That didn't go as planned," he says.

I look into his eyes, and I can feel his pain too. Neither of us could have imagined what just happened nor wished it upon each other. Once again as a result of being with Marc, I begin to cry. I bury my head into his chest and switch to sobbing hysterically. And it's ugly. Snot is pouring out of my nose like tea from a kettle, and no portion of my short sleeve is equipped to absorb any of it.

"Kat, please stop crying," he says and rubs the back of my shoulders. "This is not how I wanted to see you after proposing."

I had a vision while I was unconscious. A snapshot of my wedding flashed before my eyes. Moments before walking down the aisle I stood, red roses in hand, and paused to observe the many people who had gathered around me. I could see their faces clearly, but I was having difficulty focusing on my groom at the end of the aisle. At first he was a blurry silhouette, then after a few seconds passed, I saw Ryan wave at me with curiosity.

Marc and I sit in the lobby of my building as I calm down and catch my breath. I feel obligated to speak.

"Marc, I don't know what to say," I muster, figuring honesty is the best policy from here on out.

"How about starting with an answer," he says sternly and releases his embrace.

I sit straight and wipe my face. This has gone on long enough.

"Marc, the answer is no," I say. "And it kills me to say this to you, but I think I have moved on." I weep again at both the thought of hurting him and losing him all in the same moment. He does not reach to comfort me this time. "Trust me, I was stunned by the mere possibility of it as well, and even more shocked at how fast things have progressed with Ryan. But to be fair to him and most importantly, fair to you at this moment, I have to be honest with you and stop being selfish. Whether Ryan and I are in this for the long term, I don't know. But you deserve the truth. I have never, not one day, stopped caring about you and I hope you can see that. But I'm with Ryan now." I pause and give him a troubled look. "Or at least I was as of this morning," I mumble to myself.

Marc stands, his fingers curled into fists. I swear I can see steam coming out of his ears.

"Are you kidding me? You're going to throw away everything we have for someone you just met at work." He goes to take a step, then turns back to me. "You are unbelievable, Kat. You're making a huge mistake, one that you will sorely regret," he says and kicks my keys before storming off.

A wave of fear washes over me as I watch him leave. As usual, I have to fight off the urge to run after him and soothe him, not wanting him to be sorry about what he's done. It takes only a second before my mind shifts back to Ryan. I can only imagine what he must be thinking.

Since I cannot even fathom what to say to him at this moment, I decide to call Adam.

"Hello, hello," he answers his phone.

"It's Kat," I say through sniffles.

"Just because I don't answer, 'Hi, Kat!' doesn't mean I can't read the caller I.D. What's up?" he asks. "Are you crying?"

"Yes, are you busy?"

"Dave and I are just fighting over what to delete on the DVR. Do you want to come over? We're ordering Thai for dinner."

"Marc just proposed."

There is a brief silence. The only thing I can hear is a low jingling of keys and whispering in the background before he speaks. "I'll be there in ten minutes."

"Thank you," I say and head back up to my apartment like a zombie.

It takes Adam closer to thirty minutes to arrive, but I'm too stupefied to care and simply relieved to see him when he walks in. The look on his face is almost worth the drama I've just endured.

He gives me a hug and places his index finger over my lips before I can say anything. "Before we begin, I'm going to need to know every detail, do not leave one thing out, and a Diet Coke with a glass. No ice."

I fetch his beverage as he makes himself comfortable on the couch. Despite my shower, I look like an absolute mess. My hair, left to dry on its own, is now haggy and straw-like, and the swelling in my eyes is just starting to inflate. I grab a glass of wine for myself and sit with my favorite friend.

"Start talking," he says.

Once I finish the story, Adam's face takes on a peculiar shape wherein his mouth is wide open but he's also smiling. I'd say he's speechless, but that's impossible.

He slowly closes his jaw. "I'm sorry, what was that last bit?"

"I fainted."

He bursts into hysterics. "You fainted! Oh my God, just like Keira Knightley in the *Pirates of the Caribbean*. Thank God you weren't standing on a turret!"

"I'm so glad you find this amusing," I growl at him.

"I'm sorry, this is just too much. You should write a book," he suggests. "So, who played Johnny Depp when you came to?"

"Marc did," I lament. "Ryan was long gone."

Adam takes a breath with his eyes closed, as if he's in the middle of a yoga class, in order to maintain his composure. "Oh, honey, what did you say to him?"

"I told Marc I didn't want to marry him, and now I'm left with neither of them." I throw my arms in the air.

"Ryan is going to forgive you," he says and points a finger at me. "Let me rephrase that. Ryan will understand. Kat, you haven't done anything wrong."

I lift my head sharply and shake off the numbness that has consumed me. "Except lie to him for months!"

Adam's tone gets very frank. "You never lied, you just never told him about Marc. Poor Marc," he shakes his head at the side note. "And Ryan is an honest, reasonable guy who is crazy about you and will understand once you explain everything to him."

"I don't know that. I mean, what the *hell* was Marc thinking? We're not even dating anymore! I'm just in shock over the whole thing. My brain is incapable of calculating it all. I have no idea what to do now."

"What would you say if Ryan proposed?" Adam questions me.

"Why are you asking me that?" I wonder. "Do you think I'd say yes?"

"Don't answer my question with a question," he responds.

I'm beginning to get annoyed with where this is going, so I speak slowly as to convey said annoyance. "Much like Marc, Ryan has no reason to propose to me on this day, which would force me to, yes... say *no*." I'm treading lightly because like me, Adam has always wanted to get married, and since he and Dave started living together over a year ago, he brings it up more than ever. He and I have our agreements and disagreements about this subject, and he tends to chastise me for taking it for granted, since I'm legally allowed to marry whomever, whenever...and he is not. I look up at him with my best girl-in-distress eyes. "Please don't get off track," I plead. "I really need your help here because I have to call Ryan now, and I can't even imagine what he must be thinking."

"Look, love, you have two really great guys vying for your affection and sometimes you have to take a step back and make sure you're thinking with your heart *and* your head. Marc loves you and you love Marc, so make sure that letting him go is what you want and for the right reasons." He lowers his chin but keeps his eyes on mine. "And Ryan, ooooh that Ryan. Well that gorgeous love pastry has had eyes only for you since the day you met him, and I know he'd be crushed like a bug if you left him now, especially for some old-news, clandestine lover he was unaware of." He grabs my hand. "So if Ryan is what you want, and you know it is, then just tell him the truth. He'd be a fool to let you go over this. It won't happen," he assures me and gives my hand a squeeze.

"I do want Ryan," I say.

"I know you do."

"Do you promise he won't dump me?" I ask Adam.

"No," he says.

I stand up and grab my cell phone from atop the coffee table. "Should I call, text, go over to his apartment...what?"

"You should call him this minute and see if you can come over and talk to him in person," Adam instructs me with authority.

"Can I text that to him?"

"If you're a pussy," he says.

"I am."

"Just call him."

"I'd rather text, I'm a complete coward."

"Give me the fucking phone," Adam says then grabs my cell phone and starts looking for Ryan's number. Once it's ringing he hands it back to me.

"Hello," Ryan answers, which surprises both Adam and me.

"Hey, it's me." I swallow after I get the words out, but there is very little moisture in my throat.

"Hey."

I decide to leave any trace of an explanation for our face-to-face encounter if he is willing to see me again. "Can I come over?"

"Sure," he says.

"Okay, thanks." I shrug my shoulders at Adam while still on the phone. "I'll be there in half an hour."

"See ya then." Click.

I hand my phone to Adam and he tosses it over his shoulder.

"Well, he's agreed to see me," I say.

"It's not the mob for God's sake; just relax, everything is going to be fine."

"What should I wear?" I ask.

"Now there's ma' girl."

CHAPTER TWENTY-THREE:

Save It

In hopes of helping my plight, I arrive at Ryan's apartment five minutes early. If nothing else, my punctuality should show him how sorry I am. When I reach his building I sit in my car for a moment trying to decide where to begin. Adam had suggested I go for the lighthearted, humor-laden approach, but somehow I'm not convinced that's going to cut it this time. I have to put myself in Ryan's position. If I'd just found out that Ryan had been hiding a serious relationship from me all this time, then I accidentally discovered the truth as this mystery woman was on her knees begging him to marry her, I can't say I'd be all that forgiving.

Instead, it's me that is in the awful position of groveling and asking for forgiveness, a task that I loathe almost as much as Ryan's new pretend lover. Up until now I have tried to lead an honest life, one where friends can count on me not to steal their boyfriends, one where I am honest with the person I'm dating, and one where I never have to be in a position to apologize for being a complete sorry ass.

The thought of the static sounding, evil door buzzer being our first means of communication is also making my nerves go ape-shit. I approach the buzzer with trepidation like a dog that is about to get zapped by an electric fence.

"Hello," Ryan says through the intercom.

"It's me," I respond.

Bzzzzzzt!

Once I exit onto his floor, my fear reaches a new height as I creep down the hall like a scene from *The Shining*. I'm preparing myself for an axe to come crashing through his door as soon as I knock. I gently tap on the door, half-hoping that he's come to his senses and escaped out his back window, running far away and never looking back. Instead the door opens slowly and he is standing there holding it with one hand while the other is tucked away in the back pocket of his jeans. His magnificent face catches me off guard, as it almost always does, and I can see that his lips are pursed, but smiling. Very, very slightly. As soon as our eyes meet he gestures for me to come in. I brush past him and catch a whiff of his scent that fills my lungs with regret. All I want to do is crawl into his huge arms and inhale every part of him. But I can't. That is absolutely not on this evening's agenda anymore.

I take a seat on the edge of his couch and he sits on the coffee table facing me with his hands folded, elbows on his knees. Frightened and pathetic, I force myself to take evenly paced breaths like I do when my physician has a stethoscope on my chest. I must keep my tears at bay because I did not come here for the sympathy vote.

Ryan makes no attempt to speak, so I endeavor to break the dangerously thin ice by starting the conversation. "So, I'm guessing you're wondering what happened earlier?"

Although his posture is serene, his eyes are like laser beams, fixated on me, weakening my strength. "You could say that," he says.

I lower my head just a touch in an effort to circumvent the lasers and then roll them back up to meet his face before I begin. "I was in a relationship with a guy named Marc for four years after college. You saw him today," I add the unnecessary reminder. "We broke up a few months ago but haven't cut ties completely. And until recently—and today, of course—the first time I'd even spoken to him in months was at my friend's wedding, the night before my first date with you."

"Okay," he says.

"And last week I met him for coffee, when you were in Vegas," I say, cowering, "and he asked me if we could get back together, if there was still a chance for us." I pause for a second. "I told him that there wasn't a future for him and me, and that I was dating you," I say, trying not to sound defensive.

"Okay," he repeats.

I clear my lungs and let out a profound breath. "Then today he stopped by and said he wanted to talk, so I met him downstairs because I knew you were coming, and like an idiot, I thought that was the best plan. He then made one last petition for our relationship, and for some godforsaken reason, he proposed to me. And that's when you walked in."

My eyes begin to well up so I look away. I'm determined not to release one drop. All the while, Ryan is sitting across from me perfectly still until he runs his right hand through his hair. A small sigh escapes his nose.

Before he has a chance to speak, I continue. "Ryan, I can't imagine how I would feel if you were saying these things to me right now, nor can I imagine what you must have thought when you walked in on us. All I honestly care about is that you know how unbelievably sorry I am to have kept all of this from you. If I could change how I've handled things…I would do anything," I say.

He unfolds his hands and leans backward on them. "Well," he starts. "It's nice to have an explanation, I guess." He nods once; and then his mood shifts as he stands up and steps away from the table, and from me. "Kat, I can tell you're getting upset, and that's the last thing I want to happen. I'm not angry; I'm just not sure what to say."

I heed Adam's advice and make a meager attempt at lighthearted humor. "Want to write it down?"

"No," he says in a distant voice before continuing. "I want you to know that I believe you…what you just told me."

His statement leaves me only partially relieved. "But?" I ask.

"But I also have to believe that there must be more to your relationship with Marc for him to come to you like that and propose." He looks at me questionably while his words sink in. "And since I've already come between you and Julie, maybe it's just too much. Maybe it's not meant to be with us, you know? Sometimes when there are too many hurdles, there's a reason for it." He stops talking and looks over at me.

I manage to stand, despite my weak knees. "It's no surprise to me that there are hurdles standing in our way, because that's how it is, nothing good ever comes easy," I say, pleading. "Especially for me."

He sits down on one of the stools at his kitchen island and I can see by the scrunched skin on his forehead that he's truly conflicted. We'd had such a fantastic time together this weekend and I just met his parents this morning; he can't possibly pull the plug on us now!

"Look, Kat, I want this to work out, you know I do. But my gut tells me that maybe you need some time to take care of the situation with Marc." He looks down at the floor. "I've been in a similar position before, and it didn't bode well for me in the end." He finally makes eye contact again. "I'm not saying that history will repeat itself, I'm just saying that I've been here before and if I could've changed anything it would've been to let *her* figure things out before being with me."

So that's it, I'm not the only one keeping secrets. Ryan Sullivan has baggage of his own. "Ryan," I begin softly. "Obviously I don't know the specifics of the situation you're describing and I don't need to. Because what I do know is that I have nothing left to figure out. I've made my decision, and have no regrets." I walk closer to him. "I promise you I have no agenda here other than being with you. It's what I want, you know that."

He's still looking at me, but with the same conflicted face. "I know, Kat, but a man just proposed to you today and it wasn't me," he states. "I think you have a few loose ends to tie up."

Having already fainted once today, I have faith that my brain will keep me on my feet for the remainder of this conversation. That being said, I can't fend off the dizziness for much longer. I concentrate on breathing again, and choose not to look him in the eyes anymore because that will surely exacerbate my lightheadedness. He and I have never had so much as a disagreement over what channel to watch, let alone one of this magnitude. I know deep within my bones that he's not someone who is easily swayed once he's made up his mind, and I sense the agony of defeat start to come over me like a dark shadow.

"Okay," I whisper.

"Sorry, I think it's for the best. If we're going to be together, I want it to be under the right circumstances."

Breathe in. Breathe out. Breathe in. Breathe out. "Just to be clear, are we breaking up?"

"Let's just take a break, so you can..."

"Work things out, right, right," I say to myself in dismay.

"Kat, I've been here thinking about what happened at your apartment today, and where to go next," he says." I don't think there is any other answer."

"Right."

I make my way to his front door without looking back. He follows close behind and sees me out. I have nothing else to say to him at this point and have lost the will to fight.

"I'm going to Vegas on Wednesday, but let's talk when I get back, okay?" he says.

"Okay."

"Goodbye, Kat."

"Bye."

It looks as though Adam was wrong; Ryan was not willing to consider my explanation. I leave his building and walk over to a park bench before heading to my car. I sit and cry my eyes out for the second time today. I place my head in my hands and release every ounce of sadness and frustration that I've been holding onto for the last half of this wretched day. After I compose myself, I retrieve my purse from the sidewalk. A girl needs her best friends at a time like this, so I reach for my phone and dial Julie's number.

CHAPTER TWENTY-FOUR

A Friend in Need

There's no way to mask my sobs when Julie answers the phone, so after assuring her that I'm in no physical danger she generously agrees to meet me back at my apartment. I tell her I'll fill her in when she gets there. I'm able to comfort myself long enough to get home and splash some water on my face before she arrives. I buzz her up and wait in the hall for her. Just seeing her face brings tears to my eyes. Yet again.

"You better be dying," she says as she approaches my door. "I'm sick with worry."

"No such luck," I say as she enters the apartment. We go to take a seat and carry a half-empty bottle of wine to the couch.

"What on earth is going on?" she asks.

"Before I begin, I want to say I'm sorry again, for our fight."

"If the tears are meant to make me feel badly for you, they're working." She smiles. "Is that what this is about?"

"No, it's not. But before I get to that…"

"Hold on," she interrupts me. "I know I was hard on you, and even though you attempted to tread lightly and explain the situation, all I heard was betrayal. Ryan and I weren't that serious, and I shouldn't have attacked you like I did," she takes a breath. "And I did get your email, and I appreciated what you said. I wasn't planning on ignoring you forever, you must know that."

"Thank you."

"So, what the hell is going on?" she asks.

I proceed to tell her how everything has progressed with Ryan and me. I then profess my feelings for him and confide how terribly insecure I feel about everything. Next comes the update on Marc and his recurring attempts to patch things up. And then comes the story about the proposal. The real zinger. That jaw-dropping moment where Marc pulls an ace on the river, wins the game and leaves me royally flushed. Lastly, I describe what has taken place over the last hour between Ryan and me. Somehow when you're either dumped or dissed by the person you love, you're desperate to talk to someone - anyone - who knows them and might have some insight into the pain you're going through. This wasn't the only reason I called Julie, but it was one of them. She shakes her head and sips her wine during my entire narrative, and when I'm through she settles back into the couch and circles the rim of her glass with her index finger.

"Wow."

"Yeah," I say, bleary-eyed and exhausted.

"First of all, I wish I had some idea what Ryan was thinking, or some way of reassuring you where he is concerned, but I clearly don't know him nearly as well as you do," she says. "Secondly, I'm mortified by the fact that you felt unable to share any of this with me earlier. I should've been there for you through all of this and I'm so sorry that you weren't comfortable talking to me. I understand why, and I completely blame myself."

"I'm the one who should be, and is, apologizing to everyone," I clarify.

Julie sits up and leans over to give me a hug and it's exactly what I need. "Alright, let's try and put this behind us, you and me. It's done, okay?" She sits back into a more relaxed position. "Now let's figure things out here I mean, what in the hell was Marc thinking?!"

"I know!"

"Did Ryan see you faint?" she wonders.

I nod.

"And he just left?" she asks.

"What else was he going to do? I'm lying there unconscious with a man who just asked for my hand in marriage." I shake my head at the memory. "I'm sure he couldn't get out of there fast enough."

"So what exactly did he say when you went over there tonight?" Julie leans forward off the back couch pillow, her body language indicating she needs more of the play-by-play. Unfortunately, it's all a blur to me at the moment. My head aches as I try and run through the details with her.

I'm rubbing my temples to alleviate the guilt and the tension. "I honestly can't think of his exact words, because as soon as I realized where he was going with it, I tuned out the details."

"Just try," she demands.

"He basically said, 'someone just proposed to you…it wasn't me…I've been hurt before…and you need to clean house before bothering me again…if ever.'"

Julie gets inquisitive, "He said he wanted to propose to you?"

"No." I shook my head.

"Well you just said something like, 'it wasn't me' and 'I've been hurt before?' He obviously has some issues of his own here. Number one, he is way into you, because he's scared of you hurting him, and we all know you can't be hurt by someone you don't truly care about. And number two, he's actually considered marrying you I bet, or he wouldn't have even mentioned something like that. And both of those things are two huge points in your favor," Julie says, very proud of her ability to decipher his man code.

"I don't know."

"Well I do know. If there's one thing that I know for sure, it's men." She crosses her arms. "Had you told me about all these Marc invasions over the past few months I could've predicted his indecent proposal as well," she claims with confidence.

"So now what do I do? I can't just keep bothering Ryan and try to present my case over and over. He told me to take some time. Doesn't that clearly translate to 'leave me alone, freak?'"

"He's scared. He just took you to meet his mother this morning for Christ's sake! I absolutely think you should do whatever it takes to let him know how you feel. If Marc had done that with you, like he realizes now that he should've, we probably wouldn't be having this conversation. Because you would've taken him back," she concludes. "But you know what, when the two of you broke up, you were the one who was scared. Terrified, in fact. You were scared of being alone, of not having him in your life, of him not changing...of a lot of things. He knew what you were going through and what did he do about it? Nothing." She stops to make certain I take a moment to remember. "Now you are in a similar position, only you're the one that's going to have to do what Marc didn't do. You're going to have to put an end to Ryan's fears, and fight for what you want."

She makes perfect sense. She's eloquently put into words precisely what I need to do; only I know I'm not going to be able to do it. Like that time when my uncle was teaching me how to water-ski. I was bobbing up and down like an apple floating in the lake, holding on to the little bar while a boat idled in front of me. "Just keep your arms straight, stand up when you feel tension and let the boat do all the work," he said as I looked up at him, my face and hair dripping from the first six failed attempts. Sure, I understood what he was saying; I just didn't have the confidence to make it happen.

"Can you do it for me?" I ask Julie.

"I wish I could, sister."

"Me too."

"Hey," she wonders. "Did he ever cook for you?"

"Yeah," I say with a not-so-innocent grin.

"And?"

"It was hot."

"Damn," Julie shakes her head and takes a sip of her wine.

CHAPTER TWENTY-FIVE:
Misery Loves Company

Much to my displeasure I have to be at work early on Monday and it's certainly not going to be as fun as the past few have been. As expected, no Post-its or pastries from Ryan to welcome me into my cube of doom either. This is going to be a rough day. I wish I had some other distraction from my work besides Scrabble and Facebook. I do my best speed walking to get from the elevator to my desk without seeing anyone; however, my efforts do not get past Adam.

"I'm assuming everything went fine considering I didn't hear from you?" He questions me and plops down in my desk chair as I'm putting my purse away.

"Quite the opposite." I remove my sunglasses and expose a set of swollen eyes.

"Holy Evander Holyfield, what happened?" he gasps.

I put my glasses back on and could care less that Maureen from H.R. is giving me looks from her smelly cube. "He broke up with me."

"He didn't," Adam responds instantly. "You're lying."

I wave for Adam to get out of my chair, but he doesn't. "Do I look like I'm lying?"

"Did you tell him everything?" he inquires with an accusatory tone like I *must* have done something wrong.

"Yes."

"Did you tell him you have no intention of marrying Marc?"

"Yes."

"Well what gives then?" he asks me.

"Apparently I'm not the only Brutus to his Caesar, and he's all 'been there done that, didn't work out before, sorry.'"

"He's wild about you and you know it," Adam tries to reassure me.

"I don't know anything anymore. I know that my ex-boyfriend comes back into my life after I've vowed to get over him and move on. And I know that he decided to propose to me months after I'd stopped wishing he would. I sigh heavily and lean against my desk. "Oh, and I know that Ryan has no time for someone as useless and deceitful as me. That spot on his dance card has apparently been filled already."

Adam gets to his feet. "Let's take a walk."

"I am not leaving this cube until five o'clock. So if you care about me at all you will bring me a bowl of mushroom barley and a demi-baguette around twelve thirty."

He places his hand on the back of my jeans and yanks upwards. "Get up," he says as I stand up with my glasses on and my shoulders slumped.

"Adam, I don't want to see him. Please, I love you. Leave me alone today."

"He's not here, little kitty. He and Dave and the design team are out all day," he informs me.

"What? Really?" I squeal with disappointment.

As much as I dreaded seeing Ryan today, I really need to see him. The fact that we work together gives me an advantage I wouldn't otherwise have in a typical breakup. The opportunity of chance encounters. However, it looks like that isn't going to be the case today. How can I begin fighting for what I want with no opponent?

"Really," Adam confirms as I follow him to the elevators and then outside for some fresh air. "So exactly what happened?" He wants to know and he deserves to know, but I do not have the energy to relive the story right now.

"Honestly, I don't have it in me at the moment."

"Excuse me?" He places his hands on his hips. "Muster it up."

"I'm emotionally exhausted and I just can't drudge it all up again right now," I tell him. "I can't afford to get all emotional at the office."

"Well you look like shit, so I believe you, but could you at least give me the Post-it note version? I'm dying over here."

I spy a bench in front of our building and walk toward it as Adam follows. If I'm going to host yet another pity party in my honor I may as well be seated.

"He's had his heart broken before," I begin, "and he doesn't feel like having it done twice. He thinks we should take some time so that I can 'work things out' and join Two-Faced Tramps Anonymous in the meantime," I say methodically.

"Wow."

"Yeah, that's pretty much the response I'm getting."

"Getting from who?"

"Julie came over last night and I spewed out every detail of my recent, indecent past and we had a love fest."

"Good for you," he commends me with a silent handclap.

"Thank you."

"So what's Julie's take on it?" Adam asks and leans back on his hands.

"Gloves on, pride off."

"Not a bad plan," he says.

"You think?"

"Yes," he says. "Aren't I the one who sent you over there last night in the first place? You should absolutely wipe this pus off your Noxzema-moisturized face and let him know how weepy and pathetic you are without him."

I grab Adam in a huge embrace and thank him before heading back to work.

"As much as I was avoiding Ryan this morning, I was sort of hoping to run into him and just see what would happen," I tell Adam as he's tapping the button for the elevator.

"I hardly think he'd be anything but kind, Kat. He's not like Marc."

"That's for sure," I add. "When will the design team be back?"

"Not until late afternoon, if at all," he says, still tapping away. "I could get crow's feet waiting for this thing."

We finally exit onto our floor, and I can see Brooke leaving a note for me on my desk as I round the corner. "Hey, Brooke," I say.

She crumples the note. "Can you take a conference call with Chase at one o'clock? I have to leave early today," she says as more of an order than a question.

"Sure, what's up?" I ask her and she looks at Adam before speaking.

He looks at me, then back at her, and takes an uncomfortably long time to get the hint that he should leave. Finally, he waves his hand in front of her. "I don't need the face, just say go away." And with that he disappears.

Brooke waits until he's out of sight before explaining. "I think Drew is planning to meet *her* at our house today of all places, so I'm planning on being there as well," she tells me with little emotion.

"What?" I gasp.

She tosses the crumpled note into my garbage can. "You heard me, Kat. So I need you to take the conference call for me."

"Brooke, do you really think that's a good idea? What are you going to do if you walk in on them?"

"That's my plan," she says, annoyed by my unsupportive response and starts walking toward her office.

I follow behind her. "Brooke, let me go with you, something like this shouldn't be done alone," I offer.

"Thanks, that's generous of you, but I'm fine."

"Brooke…STOP!" I yell, eliciting stares from at least three nearby cubes.

She halts her stride and turns to face me in front of her office door.

I swallow and begin talking much quieter. "Look, I can't say I know exactly what you're going through but I do know that you could use a friend right now," I say. "If you insist on doing this, please let me come with you."

She checks the time on her phone. "Fine," she says exasperated. "Meet me in the lobby at noon," she states and walks into her office.

I scurry back to my desk, dial Carrie's extension and ask her to tear herself away from YouTube long enough to reschedule the Chase conference call. A moment later Adam texts me.

WTF?
He inquires.

What?
I play innocent.

Spill it.
He demands.

Just work stuff, u freak.
I text.

Really, or Drews affair?
He replies.

You suck.
I say.

Why didn't u tell me??
He has the nerve to ask me.

It's a secret!!
I say.

My interoffice phone line rings and I see it's Adam tired of texting. "How do you know?" I ask him immediately when I answer my phone.

"I know everything."

"She confided in Dave obviously?" I assume.

"And Dave in me. Aren't you proud I didn't tell you?"

"You just did, fool," I remind him. "You didn't know I knew about it when you just texted me."

"Whatever. So what's the big secret meeting today for?" he asks excitedly.

Since I despise Drew, and Adam already knows that, I make the simple decision to fill him in on our *Cheaters* style entrapment this afternoon.

"I'm coming with," he declares.

"Are you out of your freaking skull?!" I whisper-shout into the phone. "She will *kill* me if she finds out you know, regardless of whether it was Dave who told you or not. Keep your trap shut," I threaten him.

"Dammit! Fine, but don't pull your little 'I'm too sad and rejected to call Adam' routine like you did last night. I want details on this one. Train wrecks like this don't happen every day, you know."

"Good Lord, you need a hobby," I say and hang up on him.

At five minutes to twelve I head down to the lobby and see that Brooke is already there waiting for me, showing no appreciation for my promptness. We walk to her car without speaking a word, both because I have no clue what to say in a situation like this, and because she's probably trying to forget that I'm with her. As a matter of fact, she barely even acknowledges me. When we reach her car I can see that the front passenger seat is littered with boxes, paperwork, empty fast food bags and DVDs. She doesn't even make the slightest gesture to move any of it out of the way for me, so I awkwardly force myself into the back seat.

Brooke lives in an area called River West, which is just west of the Chicago River but still close to downtown. She and Drew bought a townhouse in a development there about a year ago. As we approach the complex she starts to talk in a low, barely recognizable voice.

"He's not here yet."

I peek around from the back seat. "How do you know?"

"I don't see his car."

"What if they took a cab?"

"He's too cheap," she quickly replies.

We sit in silence for about ten minutes during which I applaud being shunned to the back seat because it allows me to text Adam without appearing insensitive.

Sitting outside her house in car.
I type.

Crouching Brooke, hidden Drew.
He says.

Exactly.
I reply.

What now?
He asks, dying to be crouching next to me.

In backseat, texting u, feeling more ridiculous than I have in long time.
I confess.

That says a lot.
He adds.

Just then Brooke sinks down into her seat and remains very still like a preying animal. I'm not sure why we're hiding because if he sees her car he'll obviously know she's either in it or in the house. I start to regret my decision to be the supportive friend and prepare for my approaching nausea.

"It's him," she whispers as though he might hear, but at least she's acknowledged my involvement. "And someone else is in the car."

"Can you tell who it is?" I whisper back.

"Not yet."

I grab the headrest of the front passenger seat and scootch myself forward a little. "What is the plan by the way?" I wonder, hoping she'll say something like "drive away" or "confront him via email" from back at the office.

"I'm going to bust them as soon as they get out of the car."

Crap.

She tilts her head backward while keeping her eyes on his approaching car. "As soon as they're in the house I'm going in after them," she informs me.

"Do you want me to go with you or wait in the car?" I ask, and pray she tells me to wait in the car.

"Wait here."

Yes!

WTF??

Adam interrupts my panic mode with a text.

He's driving up, someone's with him.

I reply.

As Brooke and I see Drew's car get closer, we also notice that our embarrassing excuse for a cover has been blown. I watch in horror as Drew and his passenger, whom I recognize immediately from Brooke's unfortunate bowling alley bridal shower, make direct eye contact with us as they drive by.

OMG it's the slut from her bridal shower!!

I frantically text Adam.

Whoretencia???

He spells out.

YES!

I answer.

What r u doing??
Adam asks.

Freaking out!
I type.

Just as I look up from my phone Drew peels away in his car, causing Brooke to accelerate, hot on his trail. Their residential development is in a round formation and has a main drive that circles the entire group of townhomes with only one exit. I'm literally holding on to the little handle bar above the window, the one I hang my dry-cleaning on, because she is driving so fast and seriously testing the turning radius on her car.

"Are you sure we should be doing this?" I ask, frightened.

"I'm not letting him get away." She continues to drive her car like an arcade game, while I hang onto my seat belt likes it's a fireman's pole.

"He knows you saw him, and so does she," I shout, but Brooke is not listening to me.

"Can you believe that little slut?" she asks. "Always pretending to be my friend. Unbelievable! I should have known," she says as she punishes the wheel with a good whack then reaches for her phone. I prop myself up and text Adam.

Literally driving in circles chasing them.
I say.

OMG, can't stand it!
He texts.

Life flashing before eyes.
I reply.

Just then Brooke makes one last desperate move and does a tire screeching u-turn as she's dialing her phone. She tears around the corner and brings her car to a dead stop causing my phone and purse to hit the floor.

"You have some fucking nerve, you fat ass!" she screams into her phone and exits the car leaving the driver-side door open behind her.

Brooke is now standing in the middle of the street as Drew's car comes hurling toward her, then stops a questionably safe distance away. It's a stand-off. If only Clint Eastwood were here.

"Where are you and your piece of shit, lying slut-bag going to go now?" she wails into the phone with Drew on the other end. I seriously cannot believe he answered her call, and has stayed on the line.

On the floor of the car listening to her scream.
I update Adam.

Where is she?
He asks.

Outside yelling at them.
I type.

I hope ur packing heat.
He says.

This is going to get ugly.
I text.

What are pimp and ho doing?
Adam wonders.

I can't see, on floor of car!
I remind him.

"Get out of the Goddamn car!" I hear Brooke shout to Drew.

I inch my way back onto the seat and peer over at the drama. Brooke is screaming into the phone, which means this moron has yet to hang up on her, and she's waving her arm for him to dare approach her without his vehicle. Hortencia is crouched down, much like me, yet still visible with her right hand covering most of her face and her elbow resting on the door. Neither of them looks as though they're going to budge.

Brooke takes a step forward and repeats her request, "Get out of the car, you cowardly piece of shit!"

Rather than oblige her, Drew puts his car in gear and lunges forward just enough to catch Brooke off guard and instinctively make her jump to the side. Then he hits the pedal and speeds past her. Not one to be outdone, Brooke hurls her cell phone at his back windshield, hits her mark, and leaves a web of crackling glass in its wake.

"Yes!" I scream aloud from inside her car. I'm so proud of her right now I could cry.

I pry myself from the back seat and make my exit. Brooke's attention is fixated on Drew's car, which has now spun back around and is heading toward her. He comes to a stop and erupts from his vehicle screaming obscenities at her and pointing at his shattered windshield. My eyes go to Brooke, and her demeanor is unrecognizable to me. She is standing tall, arms crossed, with a fire in her eyes I never dreamed she'd be capable of lighting.

They continue arguing and screaming at each other while Hortencia sits in the battered car and I stand off to the side wishing I'd stayed in the back seat. Just then Hortencia leans over and lays on the horn of Drew's car, causing all of us to jump and look in her direction. Drew decides to answer the page and storms back to his car, leaving Brooke standing there alone.

She and I watch Drew and Hortencia burn rubber onto the main road and out of sight. I take a few cautionary steps toward her.

"Brooke," I start softly. "Are you okay? I don't know what to say."

"Me neither," she says, staring in the direction where Drew just drove off.

"Both of them are disgusting," I add.

"I know," she says breathing heavily. "Aside from the obvious betrayal, it's just, so humiliating."

"I know it is." I decide to agree. I want to tell her that she shouldn't be embarrassed, but I realize that she must be mortified to have had this done to her. Not only by him, but with the same pathetic woman who threw her an equally pathetic bridal shower.

"Why don't you stay here and I'll jump in a cab back to the office?" I suggest.

She nods. "Okay, thanks."

"I really wish there was something I could do to help," I tell her.

She nods again and I give her a hug.

I walk away remembering I'd been hoping for a distraction from my own pitiful set of circumstances. Note to self: Be careful what you wish for.

CHAPTER TWENTY-SIX:
Withdrawal

I stopped by the bookstore after work last night to pick up some self-help books for Brooke. I really want to do something nice for her and I know she would never purchase something like this on her own. I found three that looked helpful: one on divorce, one on building self-esteem after a tragedy, and one on powerful women. Taking the time to focus on Brooke, and her problems with Drew, has proven to be a wonderful way to avoid my own. As I was perusing the book titles all I could think about was how she managed to reach deep within herself yesterday and face Drew head on without backing down. She should be really proud of herself, and I'm going to make sure I tell her that.

When I got home from the store last night, I realized I didn't have any wrapping paper so I stacked all three books together in a nice pile and covered them in tin foil. The packaged trio actually looked all retro and shiny then, but this morning it's a little more crinkled and stupid looking than I had hoped. Regardless of my lack of gift-wrapping skills, I'm certain she will appreciate the gesture.

Just as I'm waiting in my office lobby for the elevator, I bump into Adam and he starts telling me a story about how he and Dave went out to dinner last night and ran into Dave's ex-boyfriend, Brian. He then proceeds to tell me that they got into a huge fight afterward because Adam was drunk and found out that the real reason Dave and Brian broke up is because Brian wanted to have a commitment ceremony and Dave wouldn't. And even though Dave insisted it was because he didn't love Brian, Adam decided it was because Dave was afraid of commitment. So apparently, poor Dave had been committed to the sofa.

"You're a real shit. Dave is absolutely in love with you, and you know it. You can't just get all pissy with him because you bump into his ex, that's not fair to Dave. He would never treat you like that," I say and squint to get a closer look at his face. "Are you wearing rouge?"

Adam rubs his cheeks and turns his back to me. "Oh, I'll be looking to you for relationship advice," he spews.

"And I'll be looking for you to help get me from the elevator to my cube in record time before anyone sees me," I say as the doors open on our floor.

"You can go public with your shame again today; Ryan's not coming in."

"What?!" I stomp my foot. "Where the hell is he today?"

"I'm sorry." Adam pauses. "But didn't you just ask me to assist you in avoiding him?" he questions me.

I stop walking, forcing him to do the same. "Yes, but just so I could get focused before I start patrolling the floor...Where the hell are they?!"

"Out in Oak Brook pitching McDonald's."

I exhale with a snort-like noise and walk slowly to my desk. Adam follows me, and watches as I remove Brooke's present from the grocery bag I transported it in.

"What's with the Easy-Bake Oven?" he asks with a look of disdain and points to my foil-wrapped gift for Brooke.

"Just leave me alone," I say.

"Look, sad kitty, why don't you try giving him a call or sending him a pathetic text or something? Let him know you're thinking about those hunky biceps."

"I did," I confess. "Last night I broke down and texted him, but he didn't text me back."

"Maybe he didn't get it," Adam offers, knowing it's not likely.

I shoot him a dirty look. "He got it."

"Well what moronic sentiment did you text him?"

"Just, 'hi…thinking about you…would love to talk…miss you.' I think that was all. It was short and feeble."

"Like you," he jokes. "Well, I know he and Dave have been busy with today's meeting and the trip tomorrow. Ryan's a very focused guy and he's probably just trying to concentrate on work right now." Adam does his best to reassure me. "Maybe he's waiting for you to submit a status report on your *working things out* progress," he says with a smile.

I grab my calendar. "You have to find out if they're coming in tomorrow," I command of him. "This is crazy. I need to see him before they go to Vegas. Because if I don't, it's going to be another week before he gets back and I really don't think you want to deal with me and my bruised ego under those circumstances."

"I'll find out." He nods and then heads toward the reception area.

"Thank you!" I call after him and grab my pile of aluminum to bring to Brooke's office. It's about nine forty-five when I check the clock, but she's nowhere to be found. I leave the books on her desk with a note and check with Carrie to see if Brooke has called in this morning.

"Good morning, Carrie," I chirp with my best forced smile.

She nods.

"Have you heard from Brooke?" I ask.

She shakes her head.

"Can you let me know if she calls in for any reason? Or better yet, please put her through to me and let her know I need to speak with her."

Carrie finally looks up and removes an ear bud from one side of her head. "What?" she asks.

My eyes widen. "Did you hear my first question?"

"No, sorry," she mutters.

"But you nodded," I tell her, amazed at her lack of consideration.

"Sorry, what's up?"

"Please let me know if Brooke calls in."

"Brooke's not coming in today," Carrie says and rolls her thumb over her iPod.

I have just about had it with Carrie. What is it with this girl? Why is everyone so careful with how they speak to her? No one ever wants to upset Carrie, like she's going to order you the wrong size binder clips - God forbid! Sadly for her, this is not the week to mess with me.

"Carrie," I say sternly, and mime pulling the plug out of her other ear so she has a visual aid of what I'm asking of her. "Get Brooke on the phone and put her through to my desk."

She rolls her eyes. "If you want to give me her cell number I can..."

"Now!" I shout, cutting her off, and then march away trying to imagine the look on her face.

My phone is ringing when I reach my desk. "Brooke?" I answer.

"Hi, Kat," she says.

"Hey, how are you?"

"I'm just really tired and I'm not coming in today. I talked to Dave, so if you need me for anything just call my house phone," she says. "My cell phone took a beating yesterday."

"Have you talked to Drew?" I ask.

"I had a locksmith come after you left, and put a suitcase of clothes on the front patio for him. It was gone by this morning, so it looks like my marriage is over. I have no intention of trying to work things out with him."

"Wow," I whisper. "I just wanted to let you know that I'm so proud of you. You did the right thing, Brooke, and don't think for one second you didn't," I say.

"Thank you, I know. Like I said, I'm not looking back and I'm definitely not going to forgive him - not that he's asking me to," she comments. "I'm sorry you had to partake in the drama, but I do appreciate you being there. If I'd had to face him alone, I'm not sure I would have had the same strength."

"Don't mention it," I say. "Are you sure you're okay being alone today?"

"I'll be fine, I just need a day or two to clean up my pride." She lets out a small laugh. "When I called my mom last night she actually sounded happy for me - which made me all the more embarrassed for myself. But I'll get through this."

"I know you will. And I realize I'm no relationship guru, but if it's any consolation…I have a feeling this may be the best thing that ever happened to you." After the words came out of my mouth I wonder if I've said the wrong thing. Her pain is still pretty fresh and she might not be ready to view her husband's infidelities as some sort of blessing quite yet. "I just mean that you deserve so much better and I'm sure that's what your mom was thinking as well," I quickly add.

"I know. Thanks, Kat."

"All is well here at the office; don't worry about a thing. In fact I haven't even logged on to Facebook once this morning," I assure her.

"And for that I am proud of *you*," she plays along. "Okay, Kat, talk to you later."

"Bye." I hang up the phone and try to imagine what she's going through. Even though Drew is a diseased ogre and completely awful for her, I know that the blow to her ego is probably harder. Losing her husband is one thing, but for someone like Brooke, the drain on her already low self-esteem can be devastating.

In hopes of helping her find someone who will give her the praise and appreciation that she deserves, I decide to spend the remainder of the day registering her on various dating websites under my email.

They're not coming in today or tomorrow.
Adam texts me around four thirty.

Why??
I ask.

Dave is leaving tonight, Ryan in the morning.
He says.

UGH!!!!!!
I text back.

Call him then.
He replies.

He won't even return my text.
I remind him.

Btw did you like the rouge?
He asks.

Enough with Adam, I pick up the phone and call Julie. There is no way I'm letting Ryan get on a plane and spend a week in Las Vegas without talking to him first. This is not like him to avoid me, even if he is horribly upset with me, which I don't think is the case. He told me to take some time, but he didn't say "lose my number" or anything. It just doesn't seem like him. And besides, he knows that we're bound to see each other on a daily basis. He can't avoid me for too much longer.

"Hey there," Julie answers my call. "I am so sorry, I meant to call you yesterday and see how things were going."

"Ryan's been out all week and I haven't even been able to orchestrate a chance encounter," I tell her.

"When's he due back?"

"That's the problem; he's not. He's going to Vegas with Dave tomorrow through Sunday. I'm a mess."

"Then call him," she says.

"And say what? I already sent him a text, and he didn't respond."

"Maybe he didn't get it?"

"Why does everyone keep saying that? I'm sure he got it. Since when don't people get their texts?"

"Then pick up the phone and call him like a big girl," she says. "If he doesn't answer, leave a message so he can hear the sincerity in your voice."

"I'm nervous," I confess. The truth is that I hate confrontation. One time in the third grade, one of my classmates was making fun of me on the playground. She said my jeans were too short and that I'd probably had the same pair since kindergarten, eliciting laughs from two other girls standing with her. Then she hiked her pants up and started dancing around me, which drew an even larger crowd. I burst into tears and ran inside. Later that day, my mother got a call from the girl's mom saying that she would be bringing her daughter to our house so that she could apologize to me. I screamed with dread. That girl was the last person I wanted to see. I begged my mom to make the whole thing go away, but she said it was the right thing to do. I was nearly doubled over with nervous tension as I waited for them to arrive, and when they did, the girl wasn't remotely remorseful. She was only apologizing because she had to. It was the right thing to do, and her mom was making her do it. She knew that, and I knew that. I remember staring at the floor through the entire twenty-second apology praying for it to end, and I don't want Ryan to sees me as that girl—apologizing only because she got caught.

"Kat, please, there's nothing to be nervous about," Julie says.

"It's not the call that makes me nervous; it's hearing him say something that I don't want to hear. I hate groveling."

"Well you'll never know until you try," she says, throwing a cliché my way. "Not that I support this, but you could just leave a message on his home phone since you know he's out."

"He doesn't own a land line, but thank you for that. I know you've got my best interests at heart."

"Always my darling. Now run along and patch things up; I gotta go," she says and hangs up.

I grab my cell phone and head over to Adam's desk for some moral support. If nothing else, he'll be excited to be included on any level. I plop down in a chair across from him.

"I'm going to call Ryan now, or hopefully leave a heartwarming message-slash-plea asking him to see me tonight before he leaves," I tell him. "And I came over here for your support, so you better produce."

"Like an underwire bra, I am here for you," he says and folds his hands in his lap giving my Blackberry and me his full attention.

"Here goes," I announce and dial Ryan's phone. "It's ringing," I whisper.

Adam gives me a thumbs-up.

"Hello?" A voice answers.

"Ryan?"

"No, it's Dave."

I give Adam a "what-the-hell" look and cover the phone so I can whisper-shout, "IT'S DAVE!?"

"Hey, Dave, it's Kat," I say. "Sorry, I thought I dialed Ryan's number."

"You did," Dave informs me. "He left his phone in my car but I won't see him until tomorrow in Vegas. I saw your name so I thought I'd pick up."

"Oh, I see."

"What's going on?" Adam raises both hands looking for an explanation.

I take the phone away from my mouth. "Dave has Ryan's phone and I have no way of reaching him."

CHAPTER TWENTY-SEVEN:
Buzz Off

I sit immobilized as my own words start to sink in. There is no way for me to talk to Ryan now and I'm beginning to have visions of myself curled up in bed, chewing the ends of my hair for the remainder of the week. Adam grabs the cell phone out of my hand and talks with Dave. All I can hear is his one-sided version of their conversation.

"Hi, honey, yes." Adam looks over at me. "She is...okay... okay...*Biggest Loser*...love you." Click.

I'm shaking my head in dismay, looking for him to quickly relay any information that will put me at ease.

"Dave wanted me to record something for him," he says and hands me my phone.

"Adam!"

"Sorry! Well, your sour love muffin clearly doesn't have his head on straight given all that you've put him through, and he left his phone in Dave's car, as you know," he says.

I close my eyes and breathe deeply through my nose. "What now? He has no home phone either."

Adam folds his hands on his lap again. "He'll have his phone back tomorrow afternoon and you'll talk to him then. Why don't you just shoot him an email?"

"I don't want to. I need to speak with him."

Panic sets in as I'm internally fuming and cursing everything and everyone that has led me to this point in my life. First and foremost Marc, who should be punished for behaving so irrationally. Ryan is no game player; he did nothing to deserve these feelings of betrayal and uncertainty…all on the day he introduced me to his mother! I clutch my stomach and Adam comes around the desk to comfort me.

"Kat, I think you're overreacting. I can see it in your beady, little, short person eyes that you're about to turn this into a disastrous event for yourself. So let's just gather our things, head back to my house and order sushi," he states. "We can have a sleepover if you'd like," he suggests. "I'll even let you use Dave's La Mer."

"I think I should go over to Ryan's apartment," I blurt out. "I have no other way of reaching him and I can't let him leave town like this."

Adam looks at me with pity for a moment while he ponders what I've said. "Okay, if that will make you feel better, then you should," he says.

"Will you come with me?" I ask.

"Wouldn't miss it for the world," he says smiling. "Can we still get sushi after?"

"Yes."

It's almost five thirty as Adam and I leave the office and head over to Ryan's place. Earlier in the day I could barely get up the nerve to text him again, let alone stand before him, begging forgiveness. But I have convinced myself that if he gets on that plane with our last conversation being the one we had on Sunday, I am guaranteed to make this a disastrous event as Adam has predicted.

Adam decides to drive, leaving me to obsess in the passenger seat about what I can say today that didn't come across on Sunday. Will I have the strength now that I didn't have when I made my initial plea?

Adam's voice is a welcome distraction. "Alright," he starts. "Just go in there and be clear and sincere. But no water-works, please, Kat. It makes you look like a spineless, defensive woman with something to hide."

I glare at him as he continues.

"I'm serious, tears are not your friend—I am. And I'm telling you that sobbing is not going to work with him."

"Thanks, but I don't exactly have the control over my emotions that you would like me to. I don't like being a blubbering fool any more than the next person," I sigh. "I promise to do my best, though."

"That's ma' girl."

"Are you just going to wait down here for me?" I ask.

"Not all night," he says. "So if you think you're going to be more than five minutes, text me."

"Five minutes?" I shake my head. "I'm not delivering a pizza."

"Just text me if you're *staying*," he reiterates.

"Fine, pull over up here on the right." I indicate with my finger.

Adam pulls the car to the curb and leans over to give me a kiss on the cheek. "Go get him." He claps.

"Thank you, I love you," I say.

"Go," he says and shoves me out of the car.

I walk into the lobby and head toward the door buzzer. I feel the buzzer judging me as I stand there, so I push it extra hard.

No answer.

Don't toy with me, buzzer. I press harder.

Nothing.

I press the hang-up button nearly forty times and try again.

Still nothing.

Much to my own surprise, I start banging on the buzzer demanding to be let in.

"Jesus, Mary, and Josephina!" Adam shouts from behind me as he barrels through the glass lobby doors. "What are you doing?"

I turn to him with a fury in my eyes that would make Glenn Close quiver. "It's not letting me in!"

Adam puts his hands up slowly like he's about to talk someone off the ledge of a building. "Step away from the buzzer," he whispers strictly, then walks up to it himself and tries to ring Ryan's apartment.

No answer.

"He's not home," Adam concludes.

"Try again," I say and attempt to press the buttons.

"Away from the buzzer!" Adam yells.

He tries the buzzer one last time and there is still no answer.

"He's obviously not home. Either that, or he has a closed circuit camera allowing him to witness your lobby tantrum - wherein, he's made the correct decision not to let you up." Adam grabs my hand. "Now let's go before you chain yourself to that hideous couchette from Ikea in the corner over there."

"Where could he be? He's leaving in the morning." I follow behind like a kid being dragged out of the mall.

"The boy has a life, my dear, and he's politely asked you not to screw with it for a few days and you can't even give him that. So, I let you come here - it didn't work out - now it's my duty to get you home and keep you under surveillance before you do something to ruin things for good."

I rub my forehead with my free hand. "I'm going crazy. This is not like me. You know that, right?" I look to him for reassurance.

"Yes, little darling," he says, more appeasing than convincing.

"Seriously," I continue. "I am desperate for him. I can feel it. And everything was fine until Marc ruined it."

Adam stops me when we reach the car. "Kat," he begins, and places his hands on my slumped shoulders, "yes, it's beyond unfortunate what went down on Sunday. But I think maybe Ryan wants you to take ownership of your fault in this debacle, and not just Marc's."

"But I did. I explained everything to him, and said above all that I was most sorry for having lied to him."

"I know, but maybe...and I'm just guessing here...maybe he sees himself in Marc's shoes somehow? Maybe he feels sorry for Marc and thinks you were too hard on him."

"What are you saying?" I ask for clarification.

"I'm just saying that sometimes people pay attention to how you treat other people. Maybe he's bothered by how you ditched a guy who proposed to you and ran to him instead? I honestly have nothing to back it up." He shrugs. "Just a theory."

What Adam is saying isn't entirely off base. But why wouldn't Ryan have just told me if that was the case? He simply said I should take some time and figure things out. He'd said that he spent the evening thinking about it, but what does that mean? Crap! Where is he? How could he not be home at a time like this? Doesn't he need to pack?

I wrap my arms around my mid-section and rest my head on the glove box as Adam drives off to pick up the sushi. I'm doing everything I can to convince myself that I have no other choice but to wait for Ryan to get his phone back.

Just as we pass the corner of Clark and Division, I spot Ryan's parents walking into Walgreens. "Stop the car!" I scream.

"Why?!" Adam yells back, startled.

"I just saw Ryan's mom and dad walk into Walgreens, turn around!"

Adam pulls over and nearly gets rear-ended as he abruptly stops the car. "What in God's name do you think you're going to do with his parents?"

"Maybe they know where he is? Maybe he's meeting them for dinner? I remember his mom saying something about getting together for dinner with him before he left," I say. "Please turn around."

"And then what?"

"And then I'm going to nonchalantly walk into Walgreens and bump into them," I tell him.

"Don't you think you've done enough damage for the night? It's not like Ryan couldn't get in touch with you if he wanted to." Adam goes for the jugular.

"Thanks," I growl. "I realize that, but please allow me this one last psychotic scheme and I promise to behave from here on out."

He shakes his head. "The things I do for you," he mumbles and turns the car around. Adam parks the car obnoxiously right in front of the entrance to Walgreens with two of the tires up on the curb. "Hurry," he says.

"I'll be right back," I assure him and hop out of the car.

After a quick spin through the revolving doors I begin my search for Ryan's parents. I thoughtfully grab a basket so it looks as though I have a legitimate purpose for being there; however, the absence of my purse, which I left in the car, may prove detrimental to my plan if I'm forced to confront them at the checkout counter. I start to head toward the pharmacy, believing that's where they might be, but there's no sign of them there. I slowly make my way through the back of the store peering down every aisle. Just as I pass the deodorants, I spot Ryan's mom and dad one aisle over in greeting cards. I take a quick step backward, out of their view, and think up a contrived greeting of my own.

"What a pleasant surprise," I squeal and round the corner.

Both their heads spin to face me. "Well, hello, Kat, how nice to see you," Judy says. "Do you live nearby here?"

"No, actually my friend is in the car and I just ran in to get some...uh...paper towels...and cheese," I say with determination.

"I see. Well, we're just grabbing a thank you card and heading over to some friends for dinner," she says and then gasps. "Oh no! Harvey, we forgot the bottle of wine. It's on the table in the front hall."

"How about I stick a check for eight dollars in the card then?" Harvey jokes.

"Well wouldn't you know it," Judy shakes her head, ignoring him.

"There's a liquor store two doors down," I advise.

"Yes, yes, but I hate to buy another one. Oh, well, it's no big thing." She shrugs. "What is my son up to tonight?" she poses the question of the hour.

I don't want to let on that I have no idea what her son is doing, so I stall by dropping my empty basket. "Whoops! Sorry about that." I go to retrieve it from the floor. "Ryan is packing, I think, for Vegas."

"Ah, yes." She smiles proudly. "I'm sure he told you that I bullied him into coming to Palm Desert afterward?"

Whenever you've just broken up with someone, the last thing you want to hear are sentences that begin with "I'm sure he told you." I do my best to wipe the dumbstruck look from my face and recover nicely from this new information.

"Palm Desert? Oh, yeah, he did say something about that. For some reason I thought that was next month?"

"No, no, he's meeting us there after his work in Vegas, for Harvey's cousin's birthday. I wish you could join us," Judy offers up.

She wishes I could join them? Was I invited? Had Ryan declined for me, or was she simply tossing out a conversational gesture. More concerning is that Ryan is now going to California after Las Vegas. My skin is getting warm and Harvey is getting impatient.

"Well, have a great time on your trip," I say to both of them. "How long will you all be out there?" I inquire, hoping to get a few more details before Harvey pulls the plug on our conversation.

"We'll be there for two weeks; Ryan can only stay for one, as you know."

I nod with great certainty. "Well, it's wonderful to see you both. Hopefully we can run into each other when you get back."

"You too, darling," Judy says and follows Harvey toward the front of the store.

I can only imagine that the horn I'm hearing outside is Adam. I drop my basket again and head to the exit, making sure Ryan's parents are nowhere in sight. Adam is just about to honk again as he sees me spinning through the revolving doors.

"Didn't you get my texts?" he questions me.

"I left my phone in my purse...in the car with you, moron," I say as I get in and slam the door.

"Dammit, I wanted a Vitamin Water," he says. "So what happened?"

"Ryan's not coming home on Sunday. He's meeting his parents in California after his Vegas trip," I say and toss my head back.

"He is?"

"Yes, his mom just told me. She actually assumed I knew, which was highly embarrassing, but then she told me that he's spending a week there with them."

"So big deal, he's coming back eventually and he'll have his phone tomorrow," Adam says.

"It is a big deal! I can't get a hold of him, he won't contact me on his own, and he's planned a vacation and didn't even bother to let me know. He's so over it," I moan.

"He's not over it, Kat, and you will talk to him tomorrow night."

I drop my head back again as Adam maneuvers the car off the curb. "I hate talking over the phone about things like this and I *really* hate hoping that he'll answer my calls even more," I say. "I can see it now, a simple text from him saying, *let's talk when I get back*, two weeks from now!"

"You're overreacting and you need nourishment. Let's just pick up the food and head back to my place. You can start your pity party as soon as we get home. I'll even break out the streamers."

"Oh please, my party has been in full swing since I hit the buzzer."

"Let's never mention the buzzer," he says.

CHAPTER TWENTY-EIGHT:
Raw Fish and Fresh Meat

Adam and I hit his favorite sushi spot in Old Town called Kamehachi. It's a family business that's been around for years, and the woman who owns it, Julia, is an old friend of Dave's. He and I particularly love the bagel roll. Adam makes me come inside with him to pick up the food because he doesn't trust leaving me alone.

We walk up to the hostess and Adam asks for his order. I take a seat on one of the padded vinyl benches near the entrance as Adam waves down Julia from the back of the restaurant. She immediately runs over to greet him while we wait for our food. As I sit, perched near the front door, I'm constantly distracted by an annoying sleigh bell that's attached to the door handle and jingles every time someone enters or leaves the place. I begin devising a plan to unhinge it while Julia is detained.

In a very Pavlovian way I can't stop from looking up each time I hear the bell, and it's starting to anger me. I hear it again and again, and do everything in my power not to look at the door each time. I will not be defeated by two doors in one hour. The eighth time it rings, I triumph over the bells and keep my eyes focused on the floor in front of me. This time, however, a pair of shoes stops awkwardly close to me. I raise my head slowly and see Marc standing in them when I look up.

"Hey, Kat."

And there he is again. Dressed, pressed, and obsessed with catching me off guard at my weakest moments. I look into his eyes like a puppy that has lost her bone, begging for comfort and compassion from anyone who can help.

I jump to my feet and Adam rushes to my side before I can speak.

"Marky Marc," Adam exclaims. "Of all the gin joints!" he says and pats Marc on the shoulder.

"What's up, Adam?" Marc greets him.

"Nada mucho. Kat and I are having a little slumber party at my house. Care to join?" he asks.

Marc smiles and politely declines with a shake of his head.

"Suit yourself," Adam says. "And who do we have here?"

Until Adam posed the question, I hadn't even noticed the girl standing next to Marc. Upon further study, she's very blond, very attractive, and very tall. She smiles at Adam and me, and exposes teeth white enough for Adam to envy. I quickly envision her, ten years from now, with a wide headband in her hair and a North Face fleece pullover on her way to play paddle tennis. Also in my vision are two little blond girls trailing after her with colossal grosgrain bows in their hair. Either that, or she for sure has some sort of pageant title in her future.

"Uh, this is..." Marc begins to say.

"Awkward?" Adam blurts out with a small laugh and I give him the death grip with my eyes.

"Kiki, actually," Marc finishes his sentence and turns toward her.

How the name didn't come to me with the pageantry vision I will never know.

"Well, hello, Kiki! I'm Adam, and this little chatterbox is Kat."

She extends her hand as I wave, leaving her hand dangling alone. Then I go to shake her hand as she retracts it, and all the while Adam's head is going back and forth like he's watching a tennis match.

Adam claps his palms together. "Well this has been fun, seeing you two, together like this. But we really need to be going. *Biggest Loser* isn't going to record itself now, is it?" he questions Kiki.

She shakes her head.

"And Marc, you're looking dapper as always. Might I *propose* you try the Dragon roll? It's a Kamehachi classic," Adam whispers to him.

I shrug my shoulders, mortified, left with absolutely nothing of any possible merit to say, and follow Adam out the door.

But before I can berate him and get in the car, someone grabs my arm from behind - and this time I'm pretty freakin' sure I know who it is.

"Kat," Marc says as I turn around.

"I'll be in the car," Adam informs us and then taps his wrist impatiently where a watch would be if he owned one.

"Hey, Marc, sorry about that," I say and point to Adam.

"Some guys never change."

"Or gays." I smile.

"Kiki is a client," he says and gestures awkwardly toward the restaurant. "It's a work thing."

I nod and decline from commenting on how lovely his client is. Either way, he owes me no explanation, and did not need to follow me outside to clarify anything. It's then that I look up at him and wish that things had been different. Not that Marc and I were still together, but that I had been honest with both he and Ryan from the very beginning. Had that been the case and I'd looked Marc in the eyes and told him about my feelings for Ryan early on - when I was sure of them myself - it would have set him free months ago. He would never have had to muster up the courage it took to ambush me all those times and try to get back together. A moment of clarity is shining as bright as the full moon poised over Marc's head. Suddenly I see what it is that Ryan must be thinking, because he's right on the money. He knows that Marc would've *never* proposed to me out of the clear blue sky with absolutely no encouragement from me. Guys just don't do that! And while he was at his apartment—prior to me coming over all weepy-eyed and sorry-assed—he must have been thinking to himself that I'd been lying to two people. And if I was lying enough to make one poor bastard ask for my hand in marriage, then I clearly have issues to work out!

I shake my head vigorously and then gaze into Marc's eyes. "Marc, I owe you an apology. If I had not been so cowardly, selfish, and insecure, none of this would've happened. I wasn't honest with you and I wasn't honest with Ryan. And quite frankly, the fact that you're even still talking to me proves you're a much bigger person than I am." I pause for a second. "You deserved to know the whole story a long time ago, and I am so, so sorry I didn't give it to you."

Marc manages a smile. "I do wish we were able to work things out, but most of the blame falls on me, and I realize that," he says. "Whether I was incapable of showing you or not, I truly do want what's best for you."

"Thanks, Marc."

"I'll see you around," he says then leans around me and shouts to Adam, "Always a pleasure!"

Adam blows him a kiss.

I jump in the car with a sense of peace and understanding, because I get it now. Ryan was able to determine precisely what had been going on behind his back by witnessing Marc down on one knee. He could see my betrayal, my deceit, and worst of all - my indifference to it. When he said he'd "been there before," I'd assumed he meant that some girl he'd dated dumped him for her ex-boyfriend. But now I think—no, I know—that where Ryan has been before is in Marc's position. I want to scream out the window at the clarity this has given me, but instead I bang out a drum roll on the dashboard.

Adam gives me a curious look. "You're just lucky sushi doesn't get cold," he says. "How many ruffies did he just slip you?"

"Get a move on it," I roar. "You better get a good night's sleep because you're driving me to the airport first thing in the morning."

CHAPTER TWENTY-NINE:
Check Your Baggage

Adam spent a large part of last night trying to convince me to think rationally and not humiliate myself. He told me to wait until I had a more civilized opportunity to confront Ryan. He reminded me of Ryan's laid-back demeanor and suggested that a surprise attack at the airport might be a little too much for him, especially considering the theatrics he'd witnessed between Marc and me. However, I have no intention of listening to Adam.

He may be right about his character assessment of Ryan, but there is nothing that's going to convince me to sit around and hope that Ryan will answer my texts at some point over the course of the week. My eyes will bleed from furiously checking my phone. I'm done letting everyone else take control. It's my turn to take a stand for what I want. No matter how many times Adam tells me otherwise. My whole life people have made decisions with no regard for how they will affect me. Did my parents ask me whether I wanted them to get divorced? No. Did my father ask me if it was okay for him to cancel plans with me at the last minute? No. Did anyone ever ask me if I was comfortable being left alone in the house at eight-years-old so my mom could get her hair done? No. I've been programmed to accept what's handed to me. To be weak. To feel sorry for myself. But I'm a big girl now, and I have no one to blame but myself anymore.

So instead of waltzing in to work with our bellies descended from all the white rice we consumed last night, Adam and I are racing to O'Hare in the middle of rush hour traffic.

"I can't believe you've turned me into a bit player from a bad Jennifer Aniston movie," he says, then curses at the car in front of us.

"I know you think I'm being absolutely ridiculous, and I don't disagree. But I just have to try," I say.

Why had I waited so long? Why had I thought I was above common decency? If I had only been straight with Ryan and Marc from the beginning, I wouldn't be in this embarrassing situation. Instead, I'd be sitting at my desk with a cinnamon scone and a Post-it note that read: *To my little showgirl, see you when I get back from Vegas.*

So, with no way of reaching Ryan, it's now imperative that I get to the airport before he boards his plane. And since he moronically left his phone in Dave's car, he is going to have to endure a face-to-face confrontation at the airport, assuming Adam and I can make it there in time. We park the car in hourly parking and sprint toward the terminals.

"I really wish you'd given me a little heads-up on the flight time," Adam yells breathlessly as we're running.

"All I can say is how much I love you for doing this. Mostly because I don't have the lung capacity to say anything else," I gasp, and lead the way.

We stall at the bank of elevators until Adam spots a nearby escalator and yanks my arm like the starter cord on a lawnmower. Once we reach the next level he and I two-step it up to Departures where we find the nearest American Airlines check-in desk. Adam stops me abruptly before I approach the counter and places his hands on my shoulders.

"Lucky for you, I have Dave's Amex card," he tells me with a wink. "However, as much of a romantic as he is, I'm not sure I can get away with charging two tickets."

I pause to catch my breath before responding. "I completely understand, and I will of course pay Dave back," I assure him.

As I'm saying this I imagine myself running toward Ryan's gate by myself. Then I imagine myself standing there as his flight inevitably pulls away from the gate before I can reach him, leaving me standing there alone. I nod, indicating to Adam that I understand and I would never ask him to buy a second useless ticket simply to get us both past security - but the tears begin to well up at the thought of missing my opportunity. Adam sighs then turns to the woman behind the counter and purchases two tickets on the next flight to Las Vegas.

"Thank you," I mouth.

He rolls his eyes.

Not that airport security is brief and painless at any airport, but when you're dealing with the country's busiest airport, you'd better not be in a hurry. Our pace has been brought to a screeching halt as we're forced to wait in line amongst the masses: business travelers, young couples, and moms with multiple children trying to brave the trip with strollers, car seats, sippy cups and lots of whining, all gathered with the common goal of getting to their destination safely and on time. And then there's me, simply desperate to reach the gate. No more, no less. No fancy umbrella drinks waiting for me on the other side. No germ-infested hotel pillow on which to rest my weary head. I simply need to get to the gate. My heart is pumping so fast that I can hardly believe my feet are at a standstill.

Adam looks at me. "It's okay, you need to calm down, you're going to pass out if you don't get it together," he whispers in my ear. "Worst case scenario is that he gets on the plane and you talk to him when he gets his phone back, in less than four hours."

"Yes, it is the worst case scenario," I remind him. "Because if he gets on the plane, it's over. I have made my bed - my stupid lonely, eighth grade, Laura Ashley-sheeted, piece-of-shit twin bed that I will have to lie in alone!"

He smiles at the two people in front of us who overheard my rant and are now staring at me.

"Okay, doll," he responds and crosses his arms.

"I really cannot even talk right now. I'm sorry, I just don't think I can say one more word until I see him."

Adam kisses my forehead, puts his arm around my shoulders, and I'm eternally grateful to have him here with me.

We march painfully slow through the security line, weaving in and out of the mind-numbing maze like cattle, until we finally make our way to the other side with our shiny new boarding passes. We glance up at the flight monitors, shove our feet back into our shoes and confirm the gate number, B22. Then, like we're being chased by schoolyard bullies, we run for it!

Our frantic sprint down the long spacious halls of O'Hare Airport doesn't draw too much attention because people do run to catch planes, after all. On our way we pass two McDonald's, three Starbucks, one Dunkin' Donuts and four newsstands before we reach gates B19-B22, and the end of our marathon. We stop at a circular cul-de-sac of gates with nowhere else to go. I begin nervously searching for both Ryan and B22, jerking my head back and forth as the whole terminal spins around me. I feel Adam's hand come up abruptly under my armpit as I start to lose my balance. And then I see him.

He's looking right at me, perfectly still, and clearly shocked. It takes me a second to focus, but when I do, I can see that he's leaning against a post and holding a magazine in one hand. Adam removes his hand from under my arm and gives me a slight tap on the rear. As I begin to walk toward Ryan I burst into tears. Weepy, blubbering tears dripping with regret and embarrassment. As I get closer, I glance quickly at Ryan's face to see if he's smiling, but I look away before I can confirm his exact expression. He doesn't move except to cross his arms. Is he glad to see me? Does he think I'm even crazier than I was two days ago? Have I ruined everything by coming here like this?

I stand before him, unable to look him in the eyes and begin to speak. "Ryan, I don't know where to start other than to say that I love you, and I am so sorry." I pause to wipe my nose and catch my breath. "I came here to ask for your forgiveness and to ask you to reconsider. I think I understand why you were so upset with what happened last Sunday - besides the obvious - and I just need you to know that I have made amends and apologized to Marc for being selfish and insensitive. I don't know what happened in your past relationship but please don't punish me for someone else's mistake," I say. "There is not a shred of doubt in my mind when it comes to my feelings for you. Please stay here and let's work this out together. I will do anything to keep you from getting on that plane." Being that I'm overly emotional at the moment, I have completely forgotten the calm, intelligent speech that I had planned. But that doesn't stop me from continuing. "Quite honestly, I really didn't think you'd still be here. Adam and I were so late, the traffic coming in was terrible, and we had to purchase two tickets to get through security." I fumble through some details and finally lift my head to meet his gaze. His eyes have narrowed slightly and I can see the silhouette of his tender grin.

Ryan loosely grabs my right hand. "Well, you really are full of surprises," he says. "I cannot believe you came all the way out here."

"Dave has your phone and I didn't know how else to reach you," I tell him.

"I will have my phone in a few hours," he says rationally.

I nod. "Look, I'm sure I must seem like a huge buffoon right now, but I was so upset with how we left things on Sunday and then I became even more panicked when I couldn't get a hold of you," I explain. "I really thought that if you left town without us speaking that things between us would be over for good," I say, and scan his face for any feedback. "Did you propose to someone before?" I blurt out the burning question in my head.

He takes a moment before answering. "Yes," he says. "I did, it was a few years ago, and we were engaged for three months before she decided she was still in love with her ex-boyfriend."

I shake my head. "I'm sorry, Ryan," I say, riddled with guilt for putting him through the same pain again.

"It's okay; I'm over it, really," he says with confidence, "and like I said before, I believe you, Kat. I believe that you love me." He bends down and positions his face directly in front of mine so that our eyes are at the same level. He pauses there for a moment and kisses me. Then he takes the back of one hand and wipes the tears from my face before pulling away. "I love you, too," he confirms, "and I want this to work." He pulls me closer to him and wraps both arms around me with such strength and deliberation that I become invisible within his huge frame, until I feel a tap on my shoulder.

Adam is now standing next to us hunched over with his hands on his knees breathing heavily. I pull back from Ryan's embrace and thank Adam.

I turn back to Ryan. "Do you have to go?" I ask, knowing his answer, but hoping he'll stay.

He nods and then grabs the boarding pass that I've been holding on to this entire time. "Why don't you join me?" Ryan suggests with a devilish grin. "You do have a ticket."

My eyes widen and I look to Adam for permission.

"What do I care?" Adam says and then waves us off.

CHAPTER THIRTY:
Two Years and Two Futures

No one in his or her right mind would plan a wedding outside in Chicago, which is precisely why I did it. Julie jokes that it's one last nail in her coffin. Today is a gorgeous Saturday in September and it's my wedding day.

As it turned out, Skankipedia.com did pay more than advertising, because once the company went public it paid Ryan's friend, Pete, more than he'd ever imagined. So it was on behalf of his generosity that we chose his amazing lakefront mansion as the setting for our nuptials today.

Megan has helped me plan the entire wedding; in fact, she's done so much of the planning that I'm actually somewhat surprised as I walk around admiring her choices in flowers and linens. Even though she complains about her husband at times, she has a wonderful little family and is beyond thrilled at the thought of me tying the knot and producing cousins for Miles one day.

For the most part, preparing for the wedding has been relatively painless. We easily picked our date, our wedding party, and our location. And once my parents were assured they'd be seated far away from each other, peace was restored. There is really only one thing in particular that I care most about. One detail that's an absolute in order for this to truly be my day, and I had only needed my father's blessing to make it happen. Since my family is not one to stand on ceremony, my dad agreed to let Adam walk me down the aisle. This is an important day for both of us, and because Adam has been right beside me at so many critical moments in my relationship with Ryan, it's essential that he be at my side on this day as well.

There's a flurry of activity in the bridal quarters that Pete has arranged for us in his master bedroom. He and his wife, Michelle, have dozens of pink roses and peonies in crystal vases all over the house. It's truly spectacular. Megan, Julie, Beth, and Brooke are all with me as I wait to put my dress on, and there's a really wonderful, relaxed energy in the room. Julie has been dating the same guy for over a year and has surprised us all with her monogamy. Beth is newly engaged to a guy she's known since she was five years old and happened to reconnect with once she got a Facebook page. As for Brooke, after countless inquiries from the various online profiles I set up for her, she finally found a nice half-Jewish guy of her own on JDate. His best quality is the fact that he compliments her almost to the point of repulsion.

About ten minutes before the wedding ceremony Adam joins us for a champagne toast. "Ladies and me," he begins. "I would like to propose a toast to my little kitty Kat on her wedding day," he says as we all raise our glasses. "We've come a long way since I was chasing her ass through airports, shipping thongs to Las Vegas, and spreading rumors about her around the office." He smiles proudly. "But in all seriousness, there is no one I would rather do it for, and absolutely nowhere I would rather be than right here, right now. Thank you for sharing your day with me and making me the second happiest man at this wedding," Adam chokes out the last couple words and there isn't a dry eye in the room.

I run over and embrace him without spilling a drop of his bubbly. Megan pats her eyes with a tissue and instructs us to line up. Brooke gives us a thumbs-up when all of the guests are seated. Most surprising to me is how tranquil my nerves are as I grab my bouquet of dark red roses with a steady hand, eager to see my future husband.

As we make our way downstairs I can see the French doors of Pete's foyer open onto the back patio as everyone begins to walk out. The guests are seated, the music has begun, and it's show time. Miles is almost three years old now and has perfected his best drunken-sailor march. Henry is at the end of the aisle with an enormous lollipop to bribe and guide little Miles toward his destination.

As Adam and I approach the edge of the doorway I crane my neck to get a glimpse of Ryan. And just as I hoped, his eyes are locked on me. He is standing tall with his arms straight, hands clasped in front of him, and looking as stunning as I've ever seen him. His face leaves me breathless and I notice his jaw clench as I float through the French doors, feeling blissful and resplendent. I'm completely unaware of the other people around me, just simply committed to keeping my eyes on Ryan and honoring his passionate focus with my own. As Adam and I reach the end of the aisle, Ryan grabs my left arm and pulls me toward him for a kiss. I am still arm-in-arm with Adam on my other side and I can hear people gently laughing behind us. Ryan then stands straight and gives my elbow a squeeze before folding his hands in front of him again.

I look at Ryan and ask him to give me a moment. I then turn around to face Adam. His eyes are filled with tears desperate to take the plunge but holding on for dear life. I hope he can see clearly, because Ryan and I aren't the only two people getting married today - it's Adam and Dave's wedding as well.

Adam and I turn together to our right sides and greet Dave, who has also been standing at the altar waiting for the love of his life. I lean up to give Dave a kiss and then give him Adam's hand.

Ryan takes one step closer to me, reaches for my hand and squeezes. I close my eyes for a second and take one last breath. When I open them, Ryan smiles at me, and our future begins.

The End.

Ten Fun Facts about *Kat Fight*

1. The first time I met my future husband was on a blind double date. He was dating my friend Susie, and I was set up with a guy who reviewed nude film scenes for a living. My date from that night has turned his obsession with nude celebrities into a million dollar enterprise. He was a great first date, and remains a great friend to this day. Check him out at Mr.Skin.com.

2. I fell in love with my husband the second time I saw him. He approached me at the health club and asked me for a ride home. After he exited my car I knew we would be married one day. I wish I could explain how I knew - but I can't.

3. Once I confessed my affection for my husband to my friend Susie - who had dated him - her reaction was nothing like Julie's was in the book. She was extremely understanding when I told her...and she wants to make sure everyone knows that. She remains one of my closest friends to this day.

4. I went to a gay bar called the Manhole one Halloween night with three gay co-workers of mine. My experience was identical to Kat's, and I have never had so much fun in my life.

5. Brooke's relationship with Drew is based on that of a very close friend of mine. She's an accomplished, witty, energetic and truly amazing woman. I disliked her husband since their wedding day, and watched her spend 15 years with him and his indiscretions. Brooke's car chase scene in the book was based on an actual event that my friend's husband put her

through as he drove circles around her with his mistress in the car. It gives me great pleasure to report that as of January 2010, she is finally divorced.

6. I met my future mother-in-law under the same circumstances that Kat meets Ryan's mom.

7. I dated a guy named Rob when I lived in L.A. for a year. He was a lifeguard, and we met exactly the same way Kat meets Rob at the beach. I woke up with a man being arrested for pleasuring himself next to me - also thankfully unbeknownst to me - and the lifeguard on duty that day became my boyfriend.

8. When my husband was six years old, my mother-in-law used to grill him about what he should say to his future wife if she didn't want to go to her house for dinner.

9. I don't have a gay best friend, but I would really like one.

10. I do have a gay babysitter, however, and his name is Adam. He has been sitting for my son since he was three years old. Adam hopes to have kids of his own one day and marry the man of his dreams. Nothing would make me happier.

Kat Fight

For more books and information visit
www.dinasilver.com

And now, enjoy an excerpt from Dina's debut novel, *One Pink Line*.

CHAPTER ONE

Sydney

Finals week hit me like a gust of wind, and before I knew it, I was cramming for my last round of college exams and trying to convince my mother to let me move back home after graduation. It was 1991, and she'd just started taking Prozac that year, so there was hope. A couple months earlier, after attending Purdue's spring career day, I sent my resume to five hotels in the Chicago area and was offered an entry-level job at the InterContinental on Michigan Avenue. I was due to start August 1st of that year, but had to get through finals, graduation, and potentially another summer living at home with that woman.

I knew my Spanish exam would be the hardest, because I barely paid any attention in that class, so I dedicated the most studying hours to that particular subject. Thursday night, as the intricacies of foreign grammar loomed heavily on *mi cerebro*, it occurred to me that I hadn't had my period in a while. How that uncertainty popped into my head at that particular moment, I have no idea. My conscience had snuck up behind me, tapped me on the shoulder, and derailed my train of thought.

I remembered the last time I'd had it though, because I was trapped in an English Lit lecture hall with no panty liner, no tampon, and no break for an hour. As soon as the bell rang I sprinted to the bathroom, only to discover the tampon dispenser hadn't been refilled since the turn of the century. It was a long, slow walk home with a wad of parchment-like toilet paper shifting around in my panties.

I grabbed my day planner and started flipping back through the pages to check the date of that lecture. The topic was Wicked

Women, and it was exactly eight weeks before finals. A small cloud of wicked panic moved in overhead as I realized I might be pregnant.

I grabbed the phone book and dialed the number for Wal-Mart. The woman who answered told me they were open until ten o'clock every evening, which meant I had exactly twenty-five minutes to get there. Unlike my mother's support, my menstrual cycle was always something I could count on, which is why I quickly abandoned my books that night and drove to the nearest, yet not-so-near-someone-might-see-me, super store. I convinced myself during the fifteen-minute ride that I was not pregnant. It had to be the stress of finals, the end-of-college anticipation, and starting my big girl job that was causing my ovaries to rebel. However, there was not a chance I would get through exam week without confirmation either way.

The Wal-Mart was just off State Road 52 and noticeably cleaner than the one back home. When I arrived ten minutes before closing, it was nearly empty, with the exception of a few weary people in the checkout lanes. I raced past them toward the sobering and well-lit pharmacy aisles, and managed to find the pregnancy tests ironically right next to the contraceptives. It took me all of four minutes to grab one, pay for it, and make my way out of there with nary a judgmental glance from the sales clerk. I tossed the bag in the front passenger seat next to me, and sped home. My phone was ringing as I put the key in the door, but I ignored it and let the answering machine pick up. My instinct was to grab it, because I hadn't heard from Ethan in three days, but I needed to stay focused on clearing my mind and getting back to my studies. The caller did not leave a message.

Once the bag was in my hands, I seized the box, dropped the receipt on the floor and began to read the instructions. Since I hadn't paid any attention to what brand I snatched off the shelf, I needed to know exactly what type of signal would inform me that I wasn't pregnant. It was a First Response test, and after unfolding the origami-like instruction booklet, I learned that my ultimate goal was to see one pink line upon completion. One pink line, one pink line, one pink line...

First: Remove the stick from the foil wrapper and remove the Overcap.
Easy enough.
Second: Hold the test stick by the Thumb-Grip with the Result Window facing away from you.
Done.
Third: Place the Absorbent Tip in your urine stream for exactly 5 seconds.
Damn.

I sat the test stick down on the edge of my pedestal sink and went to grab a Diet Coke and a No Doz. I drank half the can as fast as I could without inflicting brain freeze, and then waited. I wasn't sure which waiting episode would be more stressful, waiting to pee or waiting for the results. My phone rang again, and again, but I continued to let the machine answer it. The third time it was Jenna, but I couldn't take her call either. Instead, I threw a scrunchie in my hair, took the small white stick in my hand, and sat on the toilet with my sweat pants balled up around my ankles. The box said five seconds exactly, so I began to count as soon as I felt my bladder relax and release.

One-one thousand, two-one thousand, three-one thousand, four-one thousand, five-one thousand.

Fourth: Replace the Overcap, and lay the stick on a flat surface with the Result Window facing up.
Mission complete.
Fifth: Wait three minutes before reading results.
Wait on the toilet? Wait in the kitchen? Where was step six explaining how to maintain composure and process said results?

Five seconds passed.

I stood, pulled my sweat pants up, rolled the top to keep them from slipping, and checked the stick. Nothing.

Common sense whispered to me, "Move away from the stick."

Fifteen seconds passed.

A flash of warm nausea came and went, so I walked to the kitchen for some cold water. Two ice cubes that were fused together slipped out of my hands onto the floor, and I just stood and watched them begin their transformation into a small puddle. I had only one concern.

One minute down.

I walked back to the bathroom and sat on the floor opposite the sink with my toes pushed up against the white porcelain base. The air felt heavy and absent of oxygen. I closed my eyes and breathed slowly through my nose.

Two minutes passed.

By that point I'd convinced myself that looking at the stick prematurely would no doubt be misleading and uninformative. I pictured it like a slot machine, with various pink lines spinning around the tiny results window.

Two and a half minutes passed.

My lungs were contracting so I walked back to the kitchen, but sadly the air in there wasn't any better, and my socks were wet. I glanced at the clock on the microwave. Three minutes had passed.

I don't recall ever walking back into the bathroom...only sitting on the toilet staring at the stick on the edge of my sink. My shoulders slumped and heavy, keeping me from lifting my neck and properly viewing the window. I leaned forward, grabbed the stick tentatively like a shard of glass, and just as I brought it toward me, two bright pink lines appeared in the results window.

"Holy shit," I said aloud.

I held the little test stick, which now seemed so technologically un-advanced, that I could hardly believe something so disposable was capable of delivering such life-altering information. But there they were, two gleaming, fuchsia lines, and neither one were remotely pale in color or incomplete. I placed it back on the sink and buried my head in my hands, because as if seeing those neon stripes staring back at me wasn't bad enough, next came the realization of who the father was.

The slowest three minutes of my life were then followed by the passing of two hours in the blink of an eye. I sat on the floor, catatonic in front of my books until after midnight when I took my phone off the hook and went to bed.

Two Tylenol PM's and a Bud Light were all it took to get me to sleep.

Made in the USA
Charleston, SC
01 April 2014